Maggie Matheson: The Senior S

Meet Maggie Matheson

A potential reunion with the son she parted with at birth tempts 81 year old retired spy, Maggie Matheson, back into the Secret Service to tackle a criminal ring threatening multiple cyber attacks.

Computer guru she is not... but technophobia, government wide conspiracies and a touch of arthritis won't stop her doing exactly as she pleases.

To my sister, Jacqui,
... with lots of love.

Ian Hornett

Maggie Matheson
The Senior Spy

ISBN: **9798533165945**

* * * *

Chapter 1

Maggie pushed hard at the door to the restaurant, dragging her shopping trolley awkwardly behind her. It caught as the door pulled to, forcing her to lift and turn it to get both of them inside at the same time. This was the fifth place she had had to struggle into that day – was it really worth all the effort? Groceries could be bought and delivered online, people kept telling her, no need to even leave the flat. *Yes, Maggs,* she told herself. *It definitely was worth it!* She quite liked her magnolia lounge walls, but not so much that she wanted to spend the entire day staring at them.

Another minor battle won, she took a deep breath to compose herself, before pushing her glasses back firmly onto the bridge of her nose and surveying her surroundings. *'The scan'* was a routine engrained in her from another time, and one that had kept her safe on many occasions. These days, there was considerably less at stake in the places she frequented, with checks for booby traps being replaced by checks for trip hazards, and signs of an escape route out with signs for the toilets.

Scanning from left to right, her movements were slow, deliberate, and confident, like a conductor at the Albert Hall, acknowledging the musicians section by section. *Like a conductor at the Albert hall with cataracts, more like.* She was resigned to all aspects of getting old, except the decreasing functioning of her vision, hearing, hips and knees, and memory. And the boredom. And the loneliness. And the fact that most people she knew spent all day obsessing with these things.

Still, she clocked the customers one by one, starting with Betty who was seated at her usual table in the alcove on the right of the restaurant. As always, the window nearby was open. Betty did not much like it there.

'It's a bit on the chilly side,' she had complained to Maggie only last week, 'but they insist I sit here. I don't know why.'

'It's because they think so much of you, Betty love. No one else has their own table, you know. It's even got its own air-conditioning,' she added, pointing to the window. 'You're lucky!'

'I s'pose so. They must think I'm special then?'

'You certainly are, Betty. One in a million.'

Maggie did not mention the real reason. Obnoxious gas was a regular by-product of Betty's eating, and the owners had acted in response to customer complaints.

'That cake looks tasty, Betty,' Maggie said now as she worked her way past her table. Even without her hearing aid fully turned up, Maggie could hear the delicate parp that followed Betty's cheery wave.

Her eyes settled on someone she had not seen before – a middle-aged, balding man sitting in the opposite corner, wearing a dark blue business suit and large brown spectacles. He was cutting a sausage one-handed with his fork, while scrolling through pages on his phone with the thumb of his other hand. There was a loud clunk against the plate on each cut, his eyes never diverting from the screen as he prodded around haphazardly for a section, before snaring it and lifting it in the direction of his mouth. Eventually – and messily – it found its target and disappeared from view. Maggie noticed ketchup on the corner of his lips. She was sorely tempted to wet her handkerchief with her own spittle, and dab it on his face to clean it off. She stopped herself, deciding that tolerance towards the eccentricities of elderly ladies was unlikely to extend that far.

The young woman with short dark hair sitting on her own at one of the central aisle tables was not a regular visitor either. During her fight with the door, Maggie had noticed her briefly glance up over her red clutch bag, before hurriedly looking away. She seemed distracted and fidgety, her eyes flicking up from the menu every now and then towards the entrance

Her boyfriend's late, Maggie decided, *and she's worried about being stood up.*

There were two other people sharing a table close to the serving hatch. These two she did know, having struck up a close friendship with them since they all became regulars at the restaurant. Delighted they were in, she made a point of going over to talk to them.

'Morning, Bill. Morning, Ben.' Both men looked up and returned her greeting with huge smiles.

These were their assigned nicknames, based on the Flowerpot Men from the seventies children's show. Maggie had renamed them over a bottle of Chianti at the restaurant, after Bill had admitted that they both were partial to 'a little weed'. Their real names were Nigel and Darren.

'Morning, Maggie. How's it hanging?'

Bill was older than his companion by a good twenty years or so. Maggie reckoned he was in his late fifties or early sixties, although it was hard to tell as he wore quite trendy clothes and seemed always full of youthful energy. His blond hair was cropped very short, mitigation against the effects of balding, and he had a crooked nose with distinctively angular cheek bones, both features which might have made him unattractive to some. Not to Maggie. He had the most beautiful green eyes she had ever seen with a chiselled jaw that reminded her of her late husband, Frankie. He had that edge to him, too – something about him that made him stand out from the crowd – which she particularly liked.

Ben was not quite as handsome in her opinion. She always thought he could do a lot more with his thick dark hair, which tended to err on the tatty side. His features, partly hidden under a straggly beard, were much more rounded and less defined than Bill's. Of the two, he was always much more respectful and polite, not a bad trait in her book.

'How are you today, Mrs. Matheson?' Ben asked. 'Well, I hope?'

'Doing nicely, thank you, Ben, considering everything.' She smiled at both men. 'In answer to your question, Bill, last time I checked, everything was hanging more or less exactly where it's supposed to be at my age, notwithstanding one or two new droopy bits I had not spotted before. Goodness knows where they've appeared from!'

She was reluctant to elaborate further about her health, acutely aware of the glazed look that must come over her own face when she made the mistake of enquiring after friends of a similar age. It was not that she did not care about others – she did, very much. It was more that life expectancy was short enough already, without having to waste any of it using up whatever time they all did have left, speculating how short it might actually turn out to be.

'How are you both?' she added. 'Have you set a date for the wedding yet?'

'Next July, Maggie,' Bill replied. 'The Ivy Hotel on the seafront does the whole package, and it's a reasonable price. We'll send you an invite. It's going to be just like those good old East End knees-ups you used to host in that pub of yours before the war.' He flashed her a grin.

'Cheeky! I'm not that old, Bill.'

'You're right, Maggie. I'm sorry. You don't look a day over ninety-nine.' She punched him affectionately on the shoulder. 'Seriously though, we'd love you to come.'

'That's very kind. Though, I'd leave it till the last minute before you send an invitation, if I was you. I might die before then, and stamps are expensive.' Ben looked a little uncomfortable, but Bill laughed an infectious giggle that only made him more endearing. 'You boys enjoy your morning tea,' she said. 'Thanks for thinking of me.'

She slowly made her way over to a free table on the same side as the man with the phone who seemed frozen now, his mouth wide open, sausage poised in mid-air, obsessed with an item on his screen. Maggie wondered if he would actually notice if she did give him the onceover with her hankie. His mother would thank her for it, she was sure of that.

She squeezed onto the yellow plastic seat, and pulled her trolley over to stand guard next to her. The table cloth ruffled up, and she grunted uncomfortably as the table's hard edges made a straight fold through her cardigan underneath her open coat. Opening the menu as nonchalantly as her hunger would allow, she honed in on the sweet options. Her struggle to take her place had been a reminder from her stomach that she really ought to do something about the size of it. These prods only seemed to happen at a time when she was sitting in a place where everything was geared to do the precise opposite. However, this time, aware of the advice to have *Five a day*, her stomach held some sway. Pleased with her self-control, she opted for a slab of carrot cake.

The breakfast run was over and she could see the restaurant staff preparing the place for the lunchtime rush. There were clanging sounds from the kitchen at the back as pots and pans were readied. Every now and then a muffled, 'Shit' or 'Bugger' followed by a 'Sorry' would waft through the hatch that joined the eating and cooking areas.

Regulars were used to hearing from the cook, Dave. It was all part of the eating experience. His nickname, 'Gordon Blue' (so-called because of his use of colourful language when things were not going his way) was totally lost on him, and he would often be heard to mutter, 'Gordon? I don't even know anyone called Gordon, apart from that T.V. chef, I suppose. Bastard stupid colour too… Sorry… Bugger, I swore again.'

Maggie certainly had no problems with the choice of words. In her old line of work she had heard a lot worse. Besides, life was a tad monotonous nowadays; anything that livened things up a bit was welcomed. She sighed, realising the chance of meeting new people was also diminishing quickly as the two strangers she had spotted both had their heads firmly down, now fully preoccupied with their phones. Bill and Ben, rightly so, were fully preoccupied with each other.

So Maggie turned her attention to looking at the restaurant's decor. She took some comfort in its familiarity; it had not changed since she had first started going there three years previously. But the tastes of the owners, Sukie and her ex-police officer husband,

Samuel ('I was christened 'Samuel' and that's what you will call me – if I had been christened 'Sam', that would have been different, but I wasn't, it's Samuel') were eclectic... or tasteless, depending on your point of view. Sukie, a former insurance sales operator in Ipswich, had been on an interior design course shortly before the restaurant was revamped. Ten years of cold calling had obviously deadened her ears to anyone telling her what and what not to do, because there was no evidence whatsoever that she had paid any attention to her course tutor. The refurbishment was supposedly modelled on a fancy Italian restaurant in London that she and Samuel had been to on their twentieth wedding anniversary, adapted ('with an Essex twist') to suit their meagre budget for setup costs. Rather than displays of extravagant glass jars and bottles of olive oil soaked peppers and artichokes, Sukie had arranged six plastic bottles of budget cooking oil on the shelf above the kitchen hatch. ('Not in a row, staggered, like, so they're artistic'). Pepperoni sticks in individual green wrappers sat upright in a tin next to the till, a nod towards the huge Italian salami that she had seen hanging from iron meat hooks. She had told Samuel to get hold of a pizza peel, so he had bought a shovel from the local D.I.Y. shop and fixed it to the ceiling above where Maggie was now sitting. ('It's more-or-less the same shape.') The red and white of the checked table cloths was a popular choice in pizza restaurants, but these clashed hideously with the wooden floor which had a similar pattern, hand painted in much brighter red squares of various sizes, with loose interpretations of the word 'square'. Sam's only other contribution to this heady continental mix had been to insist on painting the skirting boards green so they had the three colours of the Italian flag. '*Il Tricolore*' was lost to most customers, Maggie guessed, as it was ruined by the yellow seats. His choice of luminous green did not help make the theme explicit either. The whole psychedelic effect gave Maggie a headache if she stared at it for too long. The posters depicting famous Italian scenes were a good idea, but some local wag had straightened up the one by the door to the toilet so that the leaning Tower of Pisa was no longer leaning and was now perpendicular to the ground. Maggie doubted anyone had noticed. That was just how it was.

Despite the design faults, Sukie and Samuel's warm welcome and enthusiasm had been a breath of fresh air to the inhabitants of sleepy Frampton-on-sea, Maggie included, and they had somehow ridden the difficult times to now, incredibly, make a decent profit. 'Sukuel' (a combination of their names) had become a surprising success.

'You alright, Maggie?' Inertia had got the better of her and she awoke with a start. 'You dropped off there for a moment.'

Sukie was standing over her, pen and notepad in hand. Maggie was annoyed with herself. Daytime naps were becoming a regular occurrence these days, and she hated herself for it, especially when it was not planned.

'Sorry. I'm fine, thanks.'

'You ready to order?'

'Yes please. Bulgur wheat and lentil salad with a side of cucumber. Make sure you take the skin off the cucumber. I'm on a diet.'

Sukie laughed. 'Clean out of bulgur wheat. How about gooey French chocolate gateaux instead? Or Dave baked a nice coffee and walnut cake yesterday, if you prefer that? Got a double dose of his best profanities mixed in.'

'Coffee and walnut.' *Nuts are good for you, Maggs.* 'I was going to have the carrot cake, but that sounds so tempting. Nice cup of tea too, please.'

'Is there any other kind? Coming right up, Maggie love.'

Sukie turned and headed towards the coffee counter where they kept the cakes, then doubled back. 'Oops, I nearly forgot. That young lad over there told me to tell you that whatever you want is on him: his treat.'

Maggie looked quizzically to where Sukie was gesticulating. The teenager was sitting right by the entrance, near Betty, and she had walked right past him. Maggie was annoyed with herself for not noticing, disappointed once again in the failings of old age. Years ago she would have memorised every single detail of a place this size within a second or two. Such a quick analysis could have been the difference between life and death back then.

You can add diminishing observation skills to the list of things going wrong with your eighty-one year old brain then, Maggs.

'One of your many admirers, is he? Bit young! Can't be more than sixteen.'

'Who is he?'

'I've no idea, but he has the dosh to pay. He produced a roll of bank notes when he paid for his breakfast earlier.'

Maggie frowned. 'How long has he been in here? I didn't see him when I came in.'

'He's been there all morning. You had your specs checked recently? Mind you, I'm the same, Maggie. My vision is no longer twenty-four seven.'

As Sukie bustled off again, Maggie took the opportunity to study the boy who was busy going through an old satchel on his table. She wanted to catch his eye, hoping she could invite him over to her so that she could thank him... and ask him why he was paying. But, like the other strangers nearby, he had his head down. She found this unusual, bearing in mind his offer. Still, the chance of a free cake and drink from a mysterious young man... well, it was many years since anything like that had happened to her.

Exciting! ... Maybe life is finally looking up, Maggs.

Then, several things happened suddenly. So suddenly that Maggie had no time to process them all properly.

It began with an angry cry: 'No, I won't do it!' and she turned as the man who had been eating the sausages slammed his phone down onto the table. The loud thud was accompanied by an equally loud cracking sound as the screen broke, and bits fell out onto the floor. She barely had time to react to that before there was a shriek from the young woman in the central aisle: 'Aiieeee!' In one smooth movement, the woman leapt out of her seat, up onto her table, and struck a defensive martial arts pose. Unsure where to look next, Maggie found herself making eye contact with Sukie who was standing by the hatch holding a cloth and a squirty plastic cleaning bottle. Her mouth was wide open and she was looking in her direction. She made a subtle nod to the right and raised her eyebrows. Maggie followed her gaze to discover there was a figure next to her. The teenager, who a split second before had been rummaging through his satchel was now by Maggie's side, a gun in his hand making a sweep of the restaurant.

Things seem to slow down when the body is faced with danger – Maggie knew that from experience – and this is what she felt next. There was a huge crash as the sound of breaking glass shattered the air. This was followed by the enormous crunch and crack of plastic and wood ripping apart. At the same time, something large came thundering through the restaurant's main entranceway. A perverse thought flashed through her head – *Well, that's one way to get your trolley in quicker next time, Maggs* – before she replaced it with an agonised shout, as she realised the 'something large' was heading straight for her. The sense of slow motion enabled Maggie enough time to assess that it was a black car, that there was no driver in it and, very worryingly, that she was wedged firmly in her seat. It was not so slow, though, to allow her to do anything about being stuck, and she sat helplessly as the car continued its inexorable path of destruction towards her. The gaudy furniture was doing a good job of absorbing some of the impact, but she was doubtful it was going to be enough to prevent the car from hitting her. She took a deep breath and braced herself with her hands on the table. There was a loud thump, and she closed her eyes, waiting for the inevitable.

But she felt no impact. She forced herself to breathe out slowly, and then tentatively opened one eye. She could now see that the car had ground to a halt at the bench opposite her. *Good old Sukie and Samuel – their furniture is robust, at least.* She was mulling over that thought – and the fact that the colour combinations looked much more acceptable mashed up together – just as Samuel's shovel come pizza peel had one last swing before it gracefully unhooked itself from the ceiling.

On its way down, its handle dealt a glancing blow to the back of her head, and knocked her clean out.

* * * *

Chapter 2

Maggie awoke, disorientated and with the mother of all headaches. She had always considered herself fortunate never to have suffered from tinnitus, but wondered if her luck had run out now as she listened to the hissing and gentle ringing in her ears. Since she had passed eighty, she had viewed each morning awake as a bit of a bonus. But as she looked around and realised she was in a hospital ward, memories of the crash came back to her. Over eighty, yes, but she had particularly good reason to be thankful she had woken up this time. She had been in a lot of scrapes over the years; that had to be classified as one of the closest misses.

Her attempt at '*the scan*' was cut short this time by a sudden and desperate throbbing in her head. The room began to spin and a wave of nausea washed over her. She closed her eyes again and willed the sickness to go away.

She must have fallen asleep again as she became only vaguely aware that someone was speaking to her. The voice seemed a long way in the distance. 'Maggie, Maggie… can you hear me?' She opened her eyes and Samuel's face gradually came into focus. 'Maggie, it's me, Samuel. Sukie's here with me too. Look.' Sukie's face peered anxiously at her from behind his shoulder.

'Ah yes,' Maggie said groggily. 'It's good to see you Sukie… Sam.'

'Er, I was christened 'Samuel' and that's what you will call me – if I had been christened "Sam"…'

There was a wince as Sukie slapped his arm. 'She knows that speech, Samuel. Give her a break, will you?' She shoved herself forwards and grabbed hold of Maggie's hand. 'Ahh, there, there. You okay, Maggie?'

'I don't know. You tell me. Are there any bits missing?'

Sukie let go of her hand momentarily, and looked up and down the bed. 'Nah, I don't think so.' There was a pause while her head disappeared.

'What're you looking under the bed for, you silly moo?' said Samuel.

Maggie managed a half smile at Samuel's incredulous tone and immediately felt comforted. She had often been witness to their bickering at the restaurant; it all added to the entertainment.

'Just checking. Them doctors are not as thorough as they used to be. Health cuts.'

'It's good of you to come and see me. You must have loads to do at Sukuel's. Is it a mess?'

'It's not in great shape, I must admit,' said Sukie. 'A large part of the front section is destroyed. Kitchen's okay, but we need to get the damage properly assessed. Hopefully, the place won't be a write-off. But we'll have to see.'

'Unless we go for one of those open-air cafes like on the continent,' said Samuel. He prefaced it with a chuckle, but Maggie could tell he was concerned. *Understandably, poor things.* They had put their lives into it.

'Insurance assessors are coming later today.'

'Oh, Sukie, Sam, I'm so sorry.'

'It's Samuel.'

Sukie glared at him. 'No one was killed,' she said. 'That's the main thing.'

'Oh, God! How could I forget the other people in there?' Maggie felt suddenly anxious. She tried to sit up, but stopped. 'Ow, that hurts!'

Sukie eased her back into her pillow and spoke gently. 'Shush. You need to rest. You've taken a nasty blow. Bloody shovel.'

That explained a lot. She had been thinking that the pain felt like she had been hit on the back of the head with a shovel. Apparently, she had.

'Pizza peel, you mean,' said Samuel.

'It's a bloody shovel and not a very well secured one at that.'

'How was I to know some boy racer would smash the place up and knock half the walls and ceiling down?'

'You should have thought of that before you dangled it up there.'

'It was your bloody idea! You wanted a shovel.'

'I wanted a pizza peel!'

'And that hurts less than a shovel, does it?'

Maggie shut her eyes as she waited for the pain, and the sniping, to subside.

Eventually both did, and she felt a squeeze on her hand. 'Listen,' Sukie said gently, 'everyone's okay. You're the only casualty as far as we know. Samuel was at the cash'n'carry, and I was in the kitchen with Dave. Bella was the only other member of staff there, and she was out back sorting the bins.'

'What about Betty?'

'Betty's fine. She was away from the main impact. The police found her still in her seat finishing off her cake. It was covered in dust and other bits, apparently, but she was still happily munching away. Told the police she thought it was sprinkles. Which it was, in one way, I s'pose.'

'And the others?'

'Nigel and Darren…'

'Who?'

'You know, the gay couple.'

'Right, Bill and Ben.'

'Who?'

'Never mind. Nigel and wotsit. Are the boys okay?'

'They're fine. Nigel told me he had dropped his engagement ring just before it happened, and they were both under the table looking for it when the car hit. It didn't get that far in fortunately. Barely a scratch on 'em.'

'I'd heard they were hiding behind your plum pudding,' Samuel joked. Then, as an aside to Maggie, he stage whispered, 'The Ministry of Defence have asked for the recipe, Maggie. They're thinking of rolling it out to the general public as protection in the event of a nuclear strike.' He took another blow to the arm. 'Ouch!'

Maggie found her head was starting to clear a little, enough to ask, 'What about the others in there? Three of them I hadn't seen before. There was that lad who was going to buy me a cake and tea.'

'Now, that's the strange thing, Maggie,' Samuel said rubbing his arm. 'Sukie told the police about them three, but there was no sign of them at all. Not a trace. They must have scarpered straight away.'

'What, all of them? Where did they go?'

'Don't know. And the police said the car was empty when it hit. Whoever was in it must have jumped out before it smashed into us.

As I say, you were the only one hurt. A miracle really, although not nice for you.'

'Nigel and Darren were the first ones to you,' said Sukie. 'Looked after you until the ambulance arrived.'

'That was good of them.'

Maggie tried to picture the scene and events leading up to the crash, but they were all a bit of a muddle. Sukuel was on a T-junction, but it was not, as far as she knew, a hotspot for accidents. In any case, as Samuel confirmed, the car was empty. Did that mean someone had deliberately aimed it at the restaurant? Why would they do that? And what about the three strangers who were in there? Where did they go? Surely, most people would have stuck around after something like that.

She thought about the other strange things that happened just moments before: there was the man with the sausage who cried out, then slammed his phone down; the young girl, who looked like she was waiting for someone, that jumped onto the table in the karate pose; and there was the teenage tea-buying boy... with the gun. Or did the boy appear with the gun before the phone was slammed down? It was all so quick, and so incredibly confusing that she was finding it hard to separate the events. There was a lot here that made no sense, no sense at all. *Come on Maggs... pull yourself together and think logically. You can do it!*

There was a weird crackle followed by a sharp pain from somewhere in her head, strangely not at the back where she had been hit. It quickly developed into a throb, and she suddenly felt very tired. She could think later when she had her mind on it more.

'You look knackered, Maggie,' said Sukie. 'We'll leave you now and visit again, after the police have seen you.'

'The police?'

'Yeah, they want to interview everyone who was there. They've already spoken to all of us.'

She watched them turn to go, but called them back. 'Sam, Sukie…' Her voice was tired. 'I'm so sorry about your business. It must be awful.'

Sukie gave her a reassuring smile. 'That's alright, Maggie.' Maggie watched Samuel pull his wife in tight and place his arm around her shoulder. She was vaguely aware of them standing there, looking at her, as she began to doze off, before Samuel whispered, 'Let's be honest; it was a bit of a shit-'ole.'

The doctors were pleased with Maggie's recovery. She had suffered a little hearing loss as a result of the tremendous noise upon impact, but she was told that should return. Her new hearing aid would compensate in the meantime. Tests revealed no concussion which surprised everyone, including Maggie. Her head felt a lot better, but her stomach and thighs hurt where the table was squeezed onto her as the car stopped. She was particularly proud of a large bruise at the top of her right leg. Purple was her favourite colour – she had decided a long time ago that everyone would wear it at her funeral – but she was spoilt for choice of tones now judging by the variety on show on her thigh.

There was a definite up side. People had been kind and, much to her delight, she had had a constant stream of visitors in hospital, including many regulars from the restaurant. She loved the attention, particularly when Bill and Ben came. On the first occasion, Bill, looking somewhat subdued, had presented her with a huge bunch of flowers.

'Why the long face? It wasn't your fault, Bill Love,' she assured him. 'Anyway, you and Ben did a fine job with the first aid, I'm led to believe.'

He livened up when, with a flourish, she pulled back the covers and showed them her bruise. Ben's appalled reaction made them both laugh raucously.

When she was discharged, Samuel collected Maggie from hospital and took her home to her small flat within the Frampton-on-Sea retirement block that she had lived in for the last four and a half years. On the way, he explained that Sukie was in Ipswich having a stand up row with the insurance company over compensation. It was the same company she had worked for previously, but they were playing 'hand ball' as Sukie had described it.

'This is so good of you to do this, Sam, but why aren't you with her?'

Maggie noticed that he had given up trying to correct her on his name, and had, instead, taken to deliberately getting hers wrong, presumably in the hope she would recognise her mistake. It had not worked. Maggie had been called many things over the years, most of them far worse, and it washed over her.

'To be honest, Mavis, I'd lose my rag. She's much better at these sorts of things, and she knows the ropes. She's quite enjoying winding up some of her former colleagues and bosses. Anyway, how did it go with the police yesterday? I haven't seen you since then.'

'There wasn't a lot I could tell them.' *Or that they could or would tell you, Maggs, despite your best efforts. You're losing your touch.* 'They asked for descriptions of the three strangers in there and what they were doing just before the crash. I told them the best I could, but it was all very confusing. You know, it's funny, but up until they questioned me, I realised that I never got a good look at any of their faces really. All I could say about the middle-aged guy with a dark suit and glasses was that he was middle-aged, and wore a dark suit and glasses. Oh and that he had ketchup round his face, which I assume he's wiped off by now. At least, I hope so.'

'Sukie said the same thing. No one has got a good description of any of them.'

'The woman was young, but I've no clear idea what she looked like, and the teenager who had the gun, I'd guess, was about fifteen, but again I just can't recall any distinguishing features at all. I'm normally good at remembering faces.'

Samuel swung into the drive that led down to the Maggie's block. 'I've got a few bits of shopping for you in the boot, Meryl. Just the bare essentials. Give us a call if you need anything else. Now, are you going to be alright on your own?'

'You've been so kind, Sam. Thank you, but I will be just fine.'

'Are you sure you don't want us to make contact with your daughter? She really should know her mum has been involved in an accident.'

'What can she do all the way in Australia? She'll only worry. I really am okay. I will let her know what's happened in good time. Anyway, you concentrate on getting your business sorted out.'

Miraculously, her trolley had survived too, and they transferred the bits of shopping he had bought into it. He insisted on wheeling it in behind her and carrying her overnight bag over his shoulder, while she went on ahead to fiddle with the key to her door.

'There, I'm in. Thanks again, Sam. Do you want to come in for a cuppa?'

'No, best get back. I've got to go to the restaurant. Sukie's already talking about salvaging some of the more decorative pieces from the mess... whatever she means by decorative. We hope we might be able to start it all up again soon.'

'Give Sukie my best, won't you... Sid,' she added mischievously.

It got a smile. 'See you then... Mabel. Take care.'

She closed the door and made her way into the sitting room which overlooked the communal gardens. She stood for a moment, taking in the greenness of the lawn that contrasted well with the splashes of colour around the edges. It was a pleasant garden, one she knew very well having spent many an hour staring out at it. She should have been looking forward to having a nice cup of tea in her own home but, the last week or so had been quite a ride and the flat reminded her that life was... well... normal again.

She decided the tea could wait as she slumped down on her chair by the patio door, and did her best to not think about the dullness of it all.

Within a minute, she was fast asleep.

*   *   *   *

Chapter 3

An instinct, a feeling, no more, but she knew straight away that someone else was in her sitting room. Her memory might have been going, and her bones had slowed her down, but the intuitive side of the job had never left her.

One person, sitting or standing still. *Stay calm, Maggs. Don't make any rash moves, think logically.* If she opened her eyes, the visitor would know she was awake. Then what would happen? She had heard so many dreadful things about attacks on elderly people in their homes. Perhaps she should feign to be dead? No, that would not work. They would already have seen she was breathing. Perhaps she should front up, be aggressive? That was not a good idea either. *Remember Maggs, you are eighty-one.*

She tried not to panic. *Think, Maggs, think!* Then it occurred to her that if they wanted to harm her, they would have done it by now. A small sigh of relief escaped her lips at that thought, quickly replaced by an attempt to stop it as she realised she was supposed to be pretending to be asleep. The resultant half sigh, half snore, accompanied by a shake of the head as she admonished herself for the half sigh and snore, gave it away.

'You're awake! That's good.' The voice was a lot younger than she had expected. In her head, she had envisaged an older man as her would-be mugger. Someone in his fifties, skinhead haircut, and scars about his face from all the encounters he had had in dark alleys. The sort of man she might have had dealings with years ago. This voice was a lot lighter, kind, almost chirpy. Encouraged, she opened one eye to see a diminutive figure perched opposite her on her kitchen stool.

Opening both eyes, she leant forward and scrutinised him from over her glasses. 'I recognise you now. You're the boy in the restaurant.' He sat there patiently as she looked him up and down. 'So that's what you look like! How did you do that?'

'Do what?'

'Back in the restaurant. How did you look so inconspicuous?'

She was met with a shrug. 'You should know. I've heard you're a bit of an expert on that kind of thing yourself.'

She ignored his comment. 'No gun this time?' He shook his head. 'Anyway, aren't you a bit young for that sort of thing?'

'Maybe.'

She sat back and folded her arms. 'What is it that you want?'

He smiled a half smile. 'Quite simple, really. I'm calling you in…'

'What?'

'Agent Maggie Matheson, 6125... we need you to come out of retirement.'

'I've not been called Agent Matheson for ages. Not since...'

She was interrupted. 'Were you going to say, "Since the Madrid job", Agent Matheson? 15th February 1994, 22:06? On the steps of the east side of the roofed marketplace, the Mercado San Miguel. The Mariana Rodriquez affair. Two foreign agents killed, three injured. Your quick actions are legendary in the world of covert operations. You helped prevent a major incident with the Russian embassy in the city and saved many more lives. Your last job before retirement.'

'No. I was going to say since the year before last when I asked my Sharon to stop writing it in my Christmas and birthday cards. June's a nosy bugger and always looks inside my cards when she's round here. I had to lie and say that Avon agents carry on being referred to as agents, even after retirement.'

She needed a moment to take this all in, so she eased herself out of her chair, shuffled into the kitchenette, and began to fill the kettle from the tap. 'I'm truly gasping for a cup of tea now. Do you want one?'

He followed her and stood at the door, casually leaning against the doorframe with his arms folded. 'No, thank you, Agent Matheson.'

'Youngsters don't seem to drink hot drinks much these days. Would that be fair to say?'

'Could be right. I don't tend to mix with many people my age so I don't really know. Me, I love a cuppa, but I had one while you were asleep.'

'Really? You made a cuppa?' She could not help feel disappointed again. 'And I didn't hear anything at all. I am going so deaf.' She fiddled with her hearing aid. 'Perhaps I need to see my specialist again. It's a bit fuzzy. I'm missing so much these days.'

'You took a bad knock. The hearing will settle down, I'm sure. Anyway, we're trained in these sorts of things. First lesson we learnt at spy school: how to make a covert cup of tea.' Maggie looked at the mischievous grin which had crept over his face. She had decided, already, that she quite liked him. She returned the smile before busying herself with looking for a cup and saucer. 'Can I do your tea for you?' he asked.

'No, I'm fine. I need to keep on the move. Thanks for putting the shopping away. Did you learn how to do that at spy school too?'

'Second day, just after the lesson on: *How to iron perfect creases in would-be-assassins' trousers without them noticing.*'

'My word, they do push you these days, don't they? We didn't do that until week two!' She straightened out her back while waiting for the kettle to boil.

'How's the head?'

'It's okay. Tinnitus is gone too. It's the arthritis in my lower back that bothers me. I'll be alright in a minute. Couldn't go to my hot yoga class while I was in hospital, so it's got a bit stiff.'

'Hot yoga? Isn't that when they put you in a specially conditioned room and make you twist yourself in knots?'

'Well, I say hot yoga. That's what I call it. Gladys Tilson makes us wave our arms and legs about for half an hour at the church hall before the bingo. I do wish they'd switch the radiators off, especially in the summer.'

Maggie could do social chitchat for England, yet she was also keen to know what this boy was doing here. He had said they were calling her in. 'They' being who, exactly? The Service, presumably, but who specifically? Calling her in to do what? When and why? No doubt it had to be connected with the accident at Sukuel's. But what possible use to the Service was she now? *Patience, Maggs. You'll find out soon enough.*

The tea made, Maggie indicated to the boy to go back into the sitting room, where she sat down and took the opportunity to study her visitor over her cup as she sipped her tea. Her original thought that he was about fifteen was possibly an overestimation. *But then, maybe not.* He could just as easily be thirteen or fourteen as seventeen or eighteen; he had that indefinable look about him that many of his age had. He was skinny with blond hair that covered his ears, long enough for one side to curl outwards slightly. He had a side parting and a fringe which was swept back, gel used to hold it in place. A blue suit with an open necked white shirt and brown brogue shoes were not so much worn as placed around and on him. The suit was a little too large. It was not the most fashionable of styles, yet Maggie could imagine that his impish face, sparkly blue eyes and non-cool alternative style would make him attractive with some girls. *Or boys, Maggs.*

'Were you dressed like that at the restaurant?' she asked.

'No, this is my posh outfit. The boss told me I had to put something smart on to convince you of who I was. She's a bit on the traditional side.' Rather embarrassed, he added: 'I lost the tie.'

'Expect you used it to escape from the third floor window of a terrorist cell in Afghanistan, did you?' she asked with a twinkle in her eye.

'Either that or I left it on the counter in Marks and Spencer's.' They both laughed.

There was a pause during which Maggie let her impatience get the better of her. 'So, are you going to tell me your name and what this is all about?'

'My name, yes. I'm Agent Harley. Joshua Harley. But I can't tell you what this is about. That's down to my boss. She wants to speak to you directly over the net, now that I've finally made first contact.' He produced an iPad and stood next to her. 'Listen carefully and I'll explain what to do.' Maggie switched to polite, listening face – the one she used in the bank when the cashier extolled the benefits of internet banking – as Joshua held the screen up. 'Swipe here after I'm gone. Email is already open. Scroll down to the attachment at the bottom to open that too. It's password enabled, so you will need to toggle to the notes app and click on that. That also has a password on the second file which is your birthplace. Open that and it will give you the password for the original attachment in the email. The file is encrypted so you will need to verify it by going on Google and searching on the word "Demonsky"... with a 'y' at the end, rather than an 'i'. Click on the second website that comes up on the search, and that will take you to a page which has two photos on it. Click on the hyperlink under the second photo. Once you've done that, toggle back to the original attachment and that will open automatically now. That attachment has the contact details for the boss. Copy and paste those into the address field. You will obviously need to open up Videocall first. From there you can speak face to face.' He handed her the tablet, straightened up, and buttoned his jacket, ready to go.

'That's nice, dear. Thank you.' She set her cup and saucer on top of the tablet which she had placed on her lap. 'Before you go... just one quick question, if I may?

'Sure.'

'You said something at the start about wiping something. Will I need a special cloth for that?'

Joshua started to go through the iPad instructions again, but soon gave up.

'Would it be fair to say that your computer knowledge is limited, Maggie?' he said.

'Limited would be an overstatement. I've only just worked out how to use the remote on the telly, dear. That took a lot of getting used to, believe me. When I first got it, I spent half-an-hour going up and down in my recliner before I realised I had the wrong control.'

Joshua explained that, as per protocol, all agents had to be briefed separately, and he would be in trouble if he stayed for her briefing.

'That's just about ready now,' he said after he had set up the iPad for her. 'There you are.'

'How exciting! Sharon has been nagging me for ages to get one of these paddy things, so we can talk over the airwaves. I might have to invest in one now. Thank you for your help, dear.'

'Probably best to call me "Agent Harley", if we're going to be working together.'

'Oh, well, no offence, Agent Harley, but we'll have to see about whether we are working together or not.'

Joshua left her ensconced at her kitchen table with strict instructions to only press the call button after he had left. Maggie listened to the trilling sound the tablet made then frowned when it stopped and began to make the connection. 'Blast, I've broken it.' She started to shake it and was about to lift it to her ear when, suddenly, an austere face flickered onto the screen.

'Good afternoon, Agent Matheson.'

Maggie leant forward and frowned again. She took off her glasses and gave them a rub on her cardigan before putting them back on again to study the screen. 'Is that you, Tina? Tina Sheldon? You've put on a bit of weight since I saw you last. Nearly as bad as me! Good God, Woman. What have you been eating?'

Sheldon shuffled somewhat uncomfortably in her seat. 'A bit of respect please, Agent Matheson. I am your superior after all.'

'No you're bloody not! You weren't my superior when I was in the Service and you're certainly not now. You used to be my line manager – you were never my superior.'

'Semantics, Agent Matheson.'

'Maggie. I'm called Maggie, or Mrs Matheson, if you prefer. I'm no longer an agent. You retired me, remember? The young man you sent to see me called me "Agent Matheson", but he was too nice for me to get shirty with. I'll get as shirty as I like with you coz I don't care two flying hoots what you think.'

'You haven't changed much, I see. Still as blunt as ever.'

Blunt, yes, she reflected, and always willing to question and challenge people when needed, Sheldon included. It was part of what had made her such a good agent. That, and the fact that she could split a pea from one-hundred metres away with an automatic rifle.

'Bit older, a bit wiser, but, apart from that, I'm still Maggie Matheson. Anyway, what the hell are you playing at, Tina? That young lad of yours mentioned I'm being called in. You can't bloody well do that.'

'Oh, we can, Maggie. Read the small print.' She pressed a button and a message popped up on Maggie's screen. 'Go on; take a look at the attachment. It's all in there. When you signed the contract nearly sixty-three years ago, you signed your life away to the Service. We have the right to call you in at any time we like. Even after retirement.'

Maggie enjoyed the occasional 'bristle'. She was good at it, having spent many hours trying to perfect it in front of her bedroom mirror. It had distinct component parts which she had got down to a fine art. It always kicked off with the tilting down of the head, ever so slightly, and the mustering of a very stern look over the glasses. This was followed by the tucked in chin and, if she felt confident, the option of the raising up of one disapproving eyebrow. (She could not always get just the one brow up successfully, so often missed that step out – two eyebrows going up by mistake ran the risk of her looking suddenly surprised at a time when she was trying to build some momentum in the direction of rebuke). Then – and this was the part she had particularly worked hard on – the deliberate clasping of one hand in the other and placing them onto the stomach, with elbows tucked in tight. The last component was her favourite part: the lean back and shake of alternate shoulders, coinciding with a wobble of the head. This was what really distinguished it as a 'bristle' rather than the less serious 'glare'. (The common-all-garden glare was reserved for teenagers who cycled on the pavement with their hoods up and headphones on... or Tory politicians).

It was the full 'bristle' she employed now.

'If you think you can start baffling me with all this fancy technology and quoting the riot act at me in the form of a bloody file I can barely see, let alone open and read, you've got another think coming. I might have known you'd revert to something as sneaky as this. You were known as the "The Spy Who Shafted Me". Did you know that? "Shafter Sheldon." Willing to do anything to get what you wanted, no matter the consequences for other people. That's you all over. Doesn't the Service do gentle persuasion anymore?'

Maggie was disappointed to find that she needed to take a breath; a sign she was out of practice with this sort of thing. She caught herself just as Sheldon was about to interrupt. 'You send a very personable young man, and then basically tell me I've got no bloody choice. What a waste of time! I'm surprised you didn't get him to go straight into doing a bit of water boarding on me.'

Maggie could tell she had hit a nerve with regurgitating Sheldon's old nickname. Disconcertingly, there was less of a reaction to the water boarding jibe. Having vented, she decided to calm down a little. 'By the way, how old is Agent Harley? Is he qualified to do this sort of thing?'

'Old enough. Agent Harley is one of our best agents.' It was clear Sheldon would divulge no more. It was also obvious that Sheldon was confident she had Maggie over a barrel, as she continued, 'So Maggie, now that you're gainfully employed once more, why don't I tell you what this is about?'

Maggie considered another bristle, but she held off. Because a part of her was intrigued. Very intrigued indeed. When Joshua had referred to her as "Agent Matheson, 6125", she had felt something she had not felt for many years. Excitement. Pure, unadulterated excitement.

She had to admit, as she listened to the start of Sheldon's briefing, it felt good to be back.

*   *   *   *

Chapter 4

Maggie gave up trying to work out how to switch off the iPad. Eventually, she cast it aside onto the kitchen table and was quite relieved when she heard a click sound which she took to mean either it was switched off, or it was broken. Either way, she was content not to have to keep peering at the small screen which hurt her eyes. And the terminology Sheldon and Joshua kept using was so confusing! *Open this, tab that, goggle the other.* In her day, a note written with invisible ink, rolled up inside a fountain pen was just as effective as anything. And why did Sheldon do it over the internet anyway? *The stuck-up cow was probably only round the corner.* She could just as easily have popped in.

The whole experience had certainly made her think about how much things had changed since she had left the Service… and how much she might have to learn if she was to have any sort of impact in the modern world of covert operations. It was a daunting prospect.

Joshua had also left a smart phone, which she was now examining. She bent down and pulled out two beer mats which had been folded in half and tucked under the kitchen table leg. She replaced them with the phone, then put her hands on the table and rocked it, testing the stability.

'That's better,' she said out loud. 'Now, where's that card for the taxi?'

Less than an hour later, she was back in the centre of Frampton-on-Sea, standing outside what remained of Sukuel's entranceway. The main door had been boarded up, but she could see the devastation inside when she looked through one of the side windows. Most of the mess had been cleared up, although a few tables and seats remained scattered about and there were still smatterings of glass on the floor. Bags of cement and a skip nearby suggested that builders were preparing to perform repairs.

The car had obviously been removed straight away by the police, but there was further evidence of the pathway it took when she looked down the street. Sukuel was handily placed for passing trade directly on a T-junction, its front facing down a less busy road that led down to the sea, one of several that came off the main drag. She reasoned that the car would have been driven up this road at speed towards the restaurant. The stop sign was bent where it had been clipped, and there were black tyre marks on the kerb, meaning the driver most likely jumped out of the car before it passed over the main road and crashed through the entrance. It was a feat of no little skill, bravery and dexterity, not as easy as the films made it look. Maggie knew that because she had done it herself once or twice in other scenarios: Oslo fish market, 1981, for example. *Haddock, pollock and prawns all over the place.*

A gust of cool, autumnal air from the sea stabbed the nape of her neck, and she tightened her headscarf. How many times had she and her friends commented about feeling the cold so much more 'at their age'? She pushed that thought firmly to the back of her mind. 'Old Spy-ce' she may be – cheekily so named by her two teenage granddaughters out in Brisbane – but she had to try to change the emphasis now: *Be positive, Maggs: less of the 'Old', more of the 'Spy'.*

She took a deep breath and fastened the top button of her grey-black coat. A final glance at the restaurant, then she set off on the short walk towards Frampton-on-Sea railway station, very pleased to be wheeling a suitcase behind her rather than a shopping trolley.

Maggie had always enjoyed travelling on trains. It was her favourite mode of transport, by far. She had met her future husband, Frankie, on a train in 1953, on her way to work in a shop in the West End of London. Frankie had sat right next to her and immediately started to woo her with his charm; enough wooing and enough charming to persuade her to go on a date, marry him six months later... and eventually join him as an agent in Her Majesty's Secret Service.

In comparison, trains were a lot busier these days, and she was struggling to find somewhere to sit. Eventually, a kindly looking man caught her eye from further down the carriage and indicated she should take his seat. She was grateful for the offer; standing was doing her back and knees no good at all.

Comfortable at last, Maggie stared out the window, watching the world flash by and enjoying listening to the rattle and rumble of the train over the tracks. Unfortunately, the noises were soon drowned out by an infuriating hiss escaping from the earphones of the smartly dressed young man opposite her. She could see other commuters surreptitiously glancing up and shaking their heads, clearly irritated too, yet clearly failing to do anything about it. She loved music of all types, but this was unpleasant, and very loud.

She leant forward and gently tapped the young man's knee once.

Up until that point, he had been obsessed with flipping though his phone, but he looked up, rather startled initially, and took out one of the earpieces. The noise was even worse as it hung limply over his tie. 'What?'

'Sorry to disturb you, but would you mind turning your music down a little, please? It's quite noisy for the rest of us, even through your headphones. Thank you. I do so appreciate it.'

He sneered. 'Bollocks.'

His response startled her. She quickly decided the smart suit was not as expensive as it first looked and that, far from him being the highflying executive on his way to a powerhouse meeting in the city that he first appeared to be, he was, in fact, a wide boy thug in a cheap suit. An extremely rude, wide boy thug in a cheap suit, at that.

'I beg your pardon?'

He stared levelly at her. 'You deaf? I said: bollocks.'

'There is no need for language like that. I asked you politely. This is a designated 'quiet' carriage, and your earphones are causing quite a disruption. I respectfully ask that you turn it down a little, please.'

She was aware of the other commuters shuffling uncomfortably in their seats, looking across and away again – behaving like all passengers tend to, in similar circumstances, who are intent on pretending they have not heard the confrontation going on nearby, but nevertheless are determined to witness how it develops so they can relate it to their family and friends later.

'Piss off, Granny.' At that point his phone rang, and he began to speak loudly into it with exaggerated guffaws, punctuated with foul expletives.

He's worse than Dave! And with none of the good humour and charm.

She waved to attract his attention again.

'Just a minute, Louis mate. I've got some cow here winding me up. I'll call you back.' Menacingly, he bent forward so that their faces were barely inches apart. 'Listen, you stupid old bitch, I'm on the phone. Shove your moaning and groaning up your fat, baggy arse.'

Maggie pointed to the 'quiet carriage' sign and was about to explain her position again, when she felt a sudden and violent squeeze on her wrist. This time he was grinning as he talked, his voice lowered. 'I won't say this again,' he said through the phoney smile. 'Piss off or else I will actually beat the crap out of you when we get off the train.'

Maggie glanced down at her wrist, and then slowly raised her eyes so she was looking directly into his. 'Please let go.'

'Why should I?'

'Because if you don't, the knitting needle I have just pierced your trousers with will go in another inch or two and skewer your testicles, which I will then pluck out and put on display to all our fellow passengers.' She smiled. 'Did your little prick just feel that little prick, you Little Prick?'

'Ooh, ouch…Yes, it did.'

'Good. I love a kebab, don't you? Meat and two veg on a stick. Can't beat it. Now, I'm asking you politely for the last time to please switch your music off. I suggest you also refrain from talking into your phone, just as the sign advises in this particular carriage.'

The man nodded slowly, shuffled back into his seat, and then switched off his phone and music. With nowhere else to go on a packed train, he took to staring uncomfortably at a spot on the floor.

Maggie also sat back and started to do some knitting, as she mulled over the mission she had been sent on. *Yes, you're on a job, Maggs. Back in the game ...* she took a quick look up at the man opposite who flinched just as she gave a loud clack of the needles.... *and you've obviously not lost some of your old touch!*

She had no real idea exactly what the Service might want her for – full details were yet to come – but Sheldon obviously had faith in her. She had indicated that she needed someone with Maggie's experience and unique characteristics. The prospect of international travel made it all the more enticing. Maggie had butterflies in her stomach just thinking about it.

The rest of the journey was uneventful and, with the new respect she had earned, Maggie had many offers to help her with her bag as she got off at Liverpool Street in central London. She made a point of thanking everyone for their kind offers. The young man who had caused the trouble disappeared before she was on the platform.

She checked the station clock that dominated the concourse – nearly half past three – and decided she just had time for a quick cappuccino before she met her contact. She would need the caffeine to make sure she was as alert as possible. The prospect of a long evening – possibly way past her usual bedtime – lay ahead of her.

*   *   *   *

Chapter 5

'I wasn't expecting to see you, young Joshua! Sheldon told me it would be another contact, but all I was given was a name and told she would find me. All this subterfuge takes me back a bit. Meetings with men in pinstripe suits carrying a red rose in their right hands, copies of the Times under the arm.'

'We don't do it that way anymore, Agent Matheson. A text with a photo normally does the trick, as you would know if you bothered to switch the phone on I left you. I've been trying to contact you for the last hour. I was getting worried.' His voice showed urgency she had not heard in him so far. He had seemed so laid back at their last meeting. 'Haven't you got it with you?' She shook her head. 'How do you cope without one?'

'I agree they're indispensible. Just the right thickness.' She ignored his puzzled look. 'Now, why are you here? I thought I was meeting Agent Misha Summerbee.'

'Agent Summerbee has been taken out.'

'Taken out? Dead?'

'No, she's been taken out. It's her fortieth birthday next week and her husband, who has no idea what she does as her day job, sprung a surprise on her at her undercover workplace in the Job Centre. He confiscated her phone saying that it was just the two of them for once, and literally whisked her away to some swanky restaurant.'

'Why didn't she call someone from a telephone box?'

'A what?'

'You know. One of those red things with phones in them?'

'The things that people put on their patios and fill with plants, you mean?'

'I take your point, Agent Harley.'

'The fact she didn't report in automatically generated a Code Seventy-two.'

'Isn't that the Agent Missing code? Blimey! It must have all kicked off.'

'It did. We've had agents running around everywhere. They've found her now, three quarters of the way through a bottle of Prosecco, having a lovely time, apparently.'

'Shafter Sheldon won't be happy.'

'I suspect not. Anyway, the upshot is that I've been diverted to here to meet you now, rather than in Vienna as planned, to fill you in on the details Executive Sheldon left out of her briefing. I was supposed to catch the earlier flight from Heathrow to help prepare the way for your visit.'

'Prepare the way? Sounds like a lot of fuss to me.' She patted his arm. 'Still, I'm sure you all know best. Well, dear, it's nice to see you again. You can tell me all about it now instead, can't you?'

'Yes, but not here. It's too public. We might get a chance to go through things on the tube, if it's not too busy.'

'Shall we go then? Perhaps you could bring my case for me.'

They set off towards the steps which led down to the tube station, she, holding onto his arm, and he, looking slightly embarrassed, pulling along a bright pink case covered with white spots. They descended into the bowels of London with no idea they were being tailed by the young woman from the café with the red clutch bag.

Had Maggie known she was there and been able to take a look

inside her bag, she would have seen that it contained the usual bits and pieces any young lady might need for a day out in London: makeup, purse, phone, tissues, sunglasses… gun.

The yob that had caused all the disruption on the train earlier looked more than a little disconcerted when Maggie and Joshua got onto the same tube carriage on the Central Line. He was sitting in the seat reserved for elderly passengers and those with limited mobility. Although the train was not at all busy, he seemed more than happy to give up the seat and dash to the other end. Maggie watched him struggle with the two sets of doors between the carriages as he frantically moved further down the train.

'Something you said?' asked Joshua. 'I've heard of people giving up these seats for those that need it, but not give up the whole carriage.'

Maggie looked up and down. It was indeed empty; a rare occurrence on the Underground. She shrugged. 'Well, now that it's quiet, are you going to fill me in? All I know from Sheldon is that it's all kicking off in Vienna.'

'Is that all she said?'

'Well, there might have been a bit more, but I knocked the pad thingy over, and when I put it back up again it said she was on mute. She was jabbering away and I couldn't hear any of it. It was quite funny to watch. Eventually, I gave it a bit of whack, like we had to do with our old tellies, and that seemed to do the trick. That's when she told me where and when to meet my contact, and said I had to take my passport because I was off to Vienna.'

Joshua gave her a quizzical look. 'You like to play it all naïve, don't you Maggie, but there's a lot more to you than meets the eye.'

Maggie put her finger to the side of her nose and tapped it, raising her eyebrows up and down at the same time. 'That's my enigmatic spy look I just gave you. Like it?'

'No-one would guess you were a spy. You are definitely the mistress of mystery, Maggie.'

'I like the alliteration and you're calling me "Maggie". That's good. More friendly. Now… before we start the briefing, I need to check something with you. Did you know that car was going to pay a visit to Sukie and Sam's restaurant?'

'I didn't. I was there to meet you and discuss bringing you back to the Service.'

'So, which bloody idiot doesn't know that their place isn't a 'Drive-thru'?'

'I have my suspicions, but the short answer is I don't really know. They were certainly intent on attracting the attention of others inside, maybe even out to get you.'

'Get me?'

'Yes, it's possible.'

Maggie had been out of the Service for nearly two decades now. Old age had caught up with her in many respects, and a sedate lifestyle in Frampton may not have helped her maintain the edge she once had. However, she still knew the score. Phones being smashed, martial arts action, guns drawn and cars destroying restaurants, all happening around an ex-member of H.M.'s Secret Service, was surely no coincidence.

'Can I talk to you about the information missed from the boss's briefing?'

'As Van Gogh's mate said when he opened Vincent's surprise pressie to him – I'm all ears.'

'Do you remember a job you did back in the hot summer of 1976, based here in London? You were undercover, working as a tally clerk at Billingsgate Fish Market.'

'Yes, I do. I seem to have a thing about fish markets. Can't get enough of them.'

'Ah, the Oslo job in 1981.'

'Do you know everything about me?' She chuckled as he put his finger to his noise and raised his eyebrows. 'Touché.'

'Anyway, the 1976 case involved an intricate network of double agents working out of East Germany.'

'That's right.' She paused as the train pulled into a station, and watched the young man sprint past, eyes fixed firmly ahead. A mother with her toddler in a pram got on and sat at the other end, far enough away to allow Maggie to continue unheard. 'I was based in Bonn to begin with, and then transferred back to here. As I recall, there were three main people involved; Thingamy Wotsit, Someone doo dah and Lena…now, what was her surname? Or was it Liza?'

'Christian Neumann is one of the names from that vague list and the one you need to focus on. He's still alive, but now goes under the name of Chris Voigt. Obviously, he's no longer working for the East German government, since that doesn't exist anymore. He has different loyalties now.'

'The Russians?'

'No. He doesn't work for any government. He… are you alright, Maggie?'

Maggie had started to wriggle in her seat. 'Yes, I'm fine. Carry on, I am listening.'

'He's… he's freelance now, part of, how can I put this, a company – an organisation – which has motives that run contrary to the interests of the British government. He's based in Vienna, amongst other places in Europe, and his prime function is… are you sure you're alright, Maggie? Is there anything I can do?'

Maggie grimaced as she shuffled backwards and forwards on her seat, her hands holding on to the seat rests.

'I'm a bit uncomfortable; one of the hazards of having a big backside and knickers that don't fit properly. A dress malfunction this morning in the dark. You've got my full attention, really you have. Do continue, but I must sort this out, otherwise it will drive me mad.'

'Right… okay. Well, we think Voigt is heading up this organisation, building up a network of highly trained specialists who are capable of launching a direct attack on the institutions over here.'

'You mean terrorists? Bombs, missiles, that sort of thing? I didn't think he was into that from what I can remember about him. More of an intellectual type, wasn't he?'

'No, not that kind of terrorist.' Joshua was looking quite embarrassed at Maggie's antics which had started to attract the attention of the young mum and daughter. The girl, in particular, could not take her eyes off of Maggie, who was now bouncing up and down. Her mother was trying, and failing, to distract her daughter with a book.

'It's no use, Joshua. Your briefing is very good and I want to do it justice. Give me a sec to get this untangled.'

'I wish you would. We're pulling into Holborn station shortly, and that's going to be busy. Look, let's get off there, grab a coffee, and we can continue the briefing somewhere else in peace.'

As the train pulled in, Maggie stood up, gave a cheery wave to the toddler with one hand and with the other, extracted the offending article.

'Better, now?' Joshua said as he guided Maggie through the sliding doors into the throng of travellers,

'Yes, thank you for asking.'

The coffee shop was close by, and once they had their drinks and were sitting down again, Maggie was more than ready to find out more. 'If not terrorists, then what?'

'Computer experts. Hacking. Viruses. Anything I.T. related that can cause turmoil. These guys he is recruiting are serious about messing up the whole infrastructure, not just in the U.K., but in other countries.'

'Oh, well, you've come to the right place. With my skills, I'm just the person you need...you know what a trekky I am.'

'I think you mean "Techie". Trekkies are Star Trek fans. Anyway, we don't need you for your I.T. experience, Maggie, you'll be pleased to know.'

'What then?'

'We need you to go undercover directly inside his operation. It's a classic job: infiltrate, assess and disrupt. I've heard you're good at that.' He smiled again.

'I may be good at that, but you've seen how bloody awful I am with computers. They'll sniff me out as an interloper when I fail to work out which button to press for the doorbell.'

'Computer guru you are not, I agree. You've just got to get in and mess things up a bit. Divert Voigt so that he takes his eyes off the ball. We'll come in and do the rest.'

'And how do you suggest I get in?'

'I'm counting on you being welcomed in with open arms.'

'Eh?'

'Voigt will want you there.'

'He will, will he?'

'Yes, Maggie. You see, Voigt thinks that you're his mother.'

*   *   *   *

Chapter 6

'Mother? You want me to be his mother? Cheeky sod. How old do you think I am?'

'Keep your voice down please, Maggie.'

'This is down, believe me, especially when I'm a bit tacked off about something. That bloke, Neumann – Voigt, or whatever he's called – wasn't that much younger than me. Ten, twelve years at most. In any case, if I'm supposed to be his mother, won't he be a bit suspicious? An old woman turns up on his doorstep from London, only ten years older than him, looking nothing like him, not to mention nothing like his mother, and says to her German son: "Gawd blimey, fella, I'm your old Ma, ain't I? Why don't you take me up the old apple and pears to the kitchen and make me a nice cup of Rosie-Lee?"'

'You've reverted to stereotypical cockney, Maggie. A female Dick Van Dyke.'

'Careful what you say. A much maligned cockney was Mr. Van Dyke. You take my point, though? I'm quite English.'

'I do, but you really are a stunning likeness to his real mum. We've compared photos of you both from years back. The resemblance is uncanny. She and Voigt parted on rather bad terms about forty years ago, and have had no contact since. Some disagreement about which side Voigt came down on: his loyalties to his father's German East, rather than to her roots in the West, possibly, but we don't really know for sure. We do know they just drifted apart as he became more embroiled in the Cold War and the Iron Curtain went down. As far as Voigt's concerned, she was – or rather, you were – dead.'

'A dead cockney, then. Even better!'

'We've planted a few subliminal ideas to hint at her still being alive. It's all very clever but, basically, we've been putting things out on social media… that's the thing some people use to talk over the internet…' He took a deep breath. 'The internet is…'

'I know what the bloody internet is, Joshua! I just don't know how to use it. I also know what social media is.' When she realised she only knew what those two words meant individually, and not as a whole, she added an embarrassed, 'Well, sort of.'

'So, we've put stuff out on local news items and Facebook about you, his mother. Subtle things to do with clubs and societies, nothing major that would make him suspicious, but enough to hook him in and make him realise she is still very much alive. The biggest item was to do with an evacuation of a nursing home near San Francisco following a flood. We edited a recent photo of you into it and listed his mother's name as one of those affected.'

'I really do look like her, then?'

'You really do. You are a very convincing version of an older, and indeed a younger, Mrs Neumann.' He got his phone out and showed a black and white picture of a woman posing in front of a castle. 'That's her forty or so years ago.' She stared at it. Apart from the crooked nose, she had to admit it could have been an old picture of her. 'You'll need a bit of face work done, a quick nose job. That's partly why we're off to Vienna.'

'You said she's from San Francisco? That's good; I can do an American accent.'

'Is it as good as your Dick Van Dyke impression?'

'Better. Would you like to hear me sing 'Annie', gushy American accent an' all?'

'No thanks. An American accent won't help. She's Italian.'

Maggie flung her arms into the air. 'Mamma Mia!'

'Oh God… Anyway, we think Voigt's taken the bait. Feedback on the various sites usage is positive, suggesting there may be lots of hits from him. We're confident they are from his various bases dotted around the continent. He has a big one in Belgium too, amongst others. We're convinced he is now actively searching for her at the same time as setting up his illicit operation.'

'You said he has a base in Vienna. If you know where he is, why don't you just arrest him? Lack of evidence?'

'Exactly. That's where you come in.'

'What makes you think I can get what you need? Look, I'm being serious now, Joshua. I'm a good spy – was a good spy – but I'm out of touch. Even if I can get into his circle, I won't be able to understand the computer stuff.'

'We don't want you to collect technological evidence. Remember: infiltrate, assess and disrupt. The emphasis here is very much on the 'disrupt' part. Voigt won't know what's hit him! He'll make mistakes, take his eye off the ball, and that's when we swoop.'

Maggie took a bite of the chocolate brownie and stared at her cappuccino, momentarily diverted by the size of her drink. Why did they serve coffee in containers she could swim lengths in? Who could possibly drink that amount of coffee in one sitting? She was a prolific tea drinker – taking it in standard cup sized quantities – and rarely dabbled in the dark arts of coffee because it tended to have a diuretic effect on her. But she had panicked when they had entered the coffee shop. Confronted by the huge array of beverages, she had picked the first thing on the list. Now, having sipped a few gallons, her bladder had interrupted the flow of conversation to remind her she had to deal with a more pressing flow.

Maggie told it to wait, as her brain switched back to the matter in hand. 'Hang on a minute! Did you say you put images of me into those pictures of people being evacuated?'

'Yes. It's all done very professionally. It looks like you were actually there.'

'And you say you've been putting stuff about his mother on the internet for some time?'

'Yes, for about eight months now. We had to build up a pattern discretely so he thinks she is alive and won't be surprised when you turn up. She may actually be dead by the way. At least we think so.'

'So if I'd said "no" then, you would have used some other old lady?'

'Unlikely. We need someone of your experience and likeness. Someone who can carry it off.'

'So it's a good job I said yes, then? Otherwise you'd been wasting your time.'

'We knew you'd say yes, Maggie, and not just because the boss pretended your contract said you were tied to the Service.'

Maggie was close to bristling again, but decided Joshua was too young to appreciate its full impact. She opted for a growl. 'Pretended?'

'You didn't actually read the contract, did you, Maggie?'

Maggie also did 'sheepish' very well, when she had to. 'No, I didn't know how to open the file.'

'Regardless, I knew you would do this job.'

She was being manipulated. 'You're winding me up now, young man. I like you, but I don't like what you and the Service are doing here.'

She wanted to storm out. But it would take a minute to get out of her seat, plus a couple more to get her things together, before marching towards the door on her arthritic legs. Then she would have to come back in to go to the toilet. She hated being old sometimes; grand physical gestures did not work as well as they used to.

'Give me one good reason why I don't just forget about this whole damn thing, Joshua. One good reason.' She tensed, ready to stand up to have a go at the theatrics, at least.

'One good reason, Maggie? Apart from the fact that you love this work? Okay. I'll give you a good reason: do it for me.'

'For you?'

'Yes, for me. You're a legend in the spy world, but you're so much more than that to me personally.' He smiled, what she had decided the first time she saw it, was a winning smile. Deliberately spinning out the moment – someone else who obviously enjoyed the theatrical – Joshua took a sip of water, paused, before holding her gaze and saying: 'You wouldn't deny a great grandson the chance to work with his great granny, would you?'

Not many things surprised Maggie. Cars smashing into restaurants would certainly be on the list, as would being whisked away by George Clooney to a deserted island (it had not happened yet, though she lived in hope). But Joshua's revelation did knock her sideways, literally as it turned out. She had used her arms to straighten up from her seat when her hand slipped on a splash of coffee. Fortunately, Joshua was on hand to catch her and ease her back into her seat.

Maggie mopped up the spill with a serviette, busying herself while she collected her thoughts. There was an awkward minute when nothing was said. Eventually, Joshua broke the silence.

'I expect you have some questions.'

Maggie looked at his face again, this time from a different perspective. Was there a family resemblance? She could not see it at the moment, but, then again, he was three generations down. That in itself brought out a whole load more questions. Since her daughter was late to motherhood and her grandchildren were still young, she knew where that line of enquiry regarding lineage would have to start. It was a box of pain she was now being forced to open.

'Peter's your granddad, is that what you're saying?'

Peter, her precious son, older than Sharon by fifteen years. The Service had been Maggie's life, so much so that she had been forced – she and Frankie had been forced – to give up Peter for adoption at a time when the world was a very dangerous place. Their cover as agents had been compromised shortly after he was born, when she and Frankie were on a joint mission in South America. The Service arranged for them to go into hiding there. With no close family alive – Peter had been staying with a friend while they were away – he was placed with foster parents. It was some time before the danger passed. Desperate to get back home, but physically unable, she was constantly reassured he was safe and happy. When they returned some seven months later, she was advised against an early reunion with her baby because he was 'well settled' and the time was not right. Another security breach pulled the two of them away again for three more months. As hard as it was, she eventually had to accept he was better off with his new family who agreed to adopt him. It ranked as one of the darkest times of her life; that and losing Frankie to lung cancer nine years ago.

Sharon had come along much later than Peter. Even with Sharon, Maggie had had to make sacrifices she now regretted. Too many days, nights and weeks away from her daughter, reliant on neighbours and friends to help out when Frankie was also away. But she had poured all of her love, including that she had reserved for Peter, into her daughter. *Too much though, Maggs. You forced her away to the other side of the world.*

She fought back a tear. 'Bloody cataracts,' she lied. 'They get sore.'

Joshua waited until she had composed herself before replying, 'Yes... Peter is my granddad.'

Is? Still alive then, although he must be getting an old man himself now. 'My, my. You've rather thrown me. This is a lot to take on board in one go, I'm sure you understand.'

'I've been doing some digging around. Just like good spies do.' He smiled, but Maggie was in no mood to share a joke at this stage. Her mind was in a whirl. Joshua continued, 'The link was not obvious because of his name change to that of his adopted parents. It turns out that he had a relationship with my grandmother, but left before my mum was born, then disappeared off the radar. Granny married a nice bloke who, as far as my mum was concerned, was her real dad and my granddad. When I found out that Mum's original birth certificate was lost, I decided to make some enquiries and dug up a copy. My Nan had put Peter's name – adopted name: Saunders – on the certificate. More digging around through the archives eventually led me to you.'

She sat in silence for a moment while she digested that information. Joshua had done something she had not been able to bring herself to do – trace Peter. Her fear that she would disrupt his new life had stopped her, although she had come close many times. So close, so many times. It hurt to think about it, so she went down another track.

'You could have told me you were my great grandson anytime you wanted to. Why have you waited till now to tell me this?'

His uncertain pause and the reaction in his face showed a mixture of contrition and anxiety.

'Ah, I get it. She doesn't know you're telling me all this, does she? Shafter Sheldon, she doesn't know. Either that, or she knows we are related and she's told you not to tell. Which one is it?'

'The Service's background checks never made the link because of his name change. I've kept it quiet.'

'You still haven't answered my question: why tell me now?'

'I couldn't believe my luck when the boss told us the plans for this job and how she was going to involve you. She didn't need a lot of persuading to let me be one of your co-workers – I'm told that I'm very good at my job, and the boss wanted me to be involved.' The way he said the last part came across more as a fact rather than a boast, but there was another pause before he continued. 'I've told you now because…'

Maggie could see he was struggling to find the words. She was keen he pressed on, for many reasons. 'You need to talk, Joshua, and soon. Victoria Falls is going to seem like a leaky tap compared to me in full flow. Why now?'

'Right. Well, I've told you because I thought you should know what you're letting yourself in for... before you go much further.' Joshua swallowed and then went on. 'Okay, here goes. The Service suspect that Chris Voigt is not acting alone. He has a right hand man by the name of Peter Saunders.' She stared blankly at him for a moment, and then it clicked, just as he said: 'Your son, my granddad, may be an international criminal.'

Maggie only just made it to the toilet in time. Even when she arrived, she still had to cope with the fumbling of the skirt, tights and knickers. *I've come across secure governmental safe houses that were easier to break in to.* Eventually, she plonked herself down on the seat, breathing a huge sigh of relief, and tried to process what Joshua had just told her.

What he had said was entirely plausible. Incredibly difficult to accept, yet plausible. Peter had had another life, away from her and Frankie. A different upbringing, different influences, none of which had been within their control. A lot could have happened to him: bad things could have happened. He was effectively a stranger to her. *He wouldn't be if you had tried harder to find him, Maggs. Maybe he wouldn't be doing what he's doing now.*

Feeling very upset with herself, she scrabbled away behind,

aiming to take out her frustration on the toilet paper. Why was it always in such an awkward position? She just was not designed to bend round like that these days. She grunted and strained until she had gathered several bits, did what she needed to, then sat exhausted waiting for the energy to start doing battle with her garments again.

The big question was: did she have enough energy to do battle with everything else this mission would entail?

After leaving the cubicle, she washed her hands, and then stopped to take a long hard look at herself in the basin mirror. Unbelievably, her face seemed to have acquired a few more wrinkles since she last checked that morning. She opened her compact and smothered as much powder on as she dared without looking like Coco the Clown, shrugging as she realised she already had, and that the red lipstick only served to complete the look. *Just need to leave the loo on a tiny bike juggling plates...*

Joshua was already on his feet, her suitcase by his side when she came out.

'I've sorted the bill. We best be off to catch our flight.'

'Hang on. You are assuming I still want to be part of this.'

He looked surprised. 'Don't you?'

'Listen, Joshua, I like you, but you've made a mistake here. You've made the rather large assumption that I would still come, without considering other possible options. I was initially wooed by the thought of rejoining the Service. A last fling for an old lady, before she joined the rest of her friends and elderly relatives either in a nursing home or pushing up the tulips. Before you correct me,' she held up a finger, 'I've never liked daisies. Like surprises, they tend to crop up where they're not wanted. I was even tempted by the thought of working with you, my great grandson. What a lovely idea, a final swansong with a long lost relative!'

She could see Joshua was waiting, with some concern, for the 'but'. She did not like to hurt his feelings, and she wavered for a moment before continuing with some resolve. 'But…the possibility of meeting my Peter again is tough enough. The thought of possibly having to turn him in because he is wrapped up in criminal action feels wrong and just unbearable. That was a strange assumption to make, Agent Harley, the thought that I would be okay with it, just like that.'

'But I thought you would want to know everything. I didn't think it was fair you didn't have the full picture. I thought you would want to find out what happened to your son. For good or bad.'

Maggie lifted his hand and held it. 'And for that I admire you, and thank you. You could have quite easily gone ahead with all this, hiding critical information from me. I appreciate your honesty. You've gone out on a limb for me by not revealing to the Service my – our – connections to the suspect.

Look, Joshua. I may seem as tough as old boots, but I'm not. And don't be fooled by my Wonder Woman-like physique. I'm not as fit as I used to be. It's hard to believe but underneath my superhero garb, there's a pair of sagging tits and a belly with more folds than my local laundry. There's also an old woman who is now thinking that this is all a bit too much. I'm sorry, Joshua. I think it best for all of us... I want to go back home.'

* * * *

Chapter 7

Even before she was fully through the door to the restaurant, Ben was on his feet and rushing over to her. 'Maggie! Thank goodness, you're back!'

Joshua had done the decent thing two weeks before, on the day Maggie had changed her mind. He had taken her straight back to her small flat, and immediately arranged a delivery of shopping so that she could hole up for a while, respecting her wishes that no one should know she was back in Frampton-on-sea. She put in an order for frozen ready-meals, but also sent him out for a few extras. ('The corner shop is doing chocolate Hobnobs on *Buy One Get One Free,* Joshua. Get twenty.').

'Will you be able to sort it with The Tyrant?' she had asked him later over a cup of tea and a biscuit. 'You could always tell her I just got lost. It wouldn't be the first time.'

He had asked her not to worry and left, promising to get back in touch again when the case had been resolved.

As soon as he had gone, she had booked a taxi to take her to the bus station in nearby Walpeth. From there, she had used all her experience to disappear for a while, figuring she would get no peace from her neighbours; figuring that she wanted to be as far away as possible from the Service. She eventually ended up in a quiet B&B in Torquay where she had done what she had set out to do: think.

Needless to say, she got incredibly bored.

Back home, her flat had given her no relief, so now she was back in Sukuel's, keen to see what had been done to the place and hoping for... well, she did not know what she was hoping for, but whatever it was, it was not in her flat... or in Torquay.

Ben steered her over to the table where Bill was waiting, arms open in welcome, and with relief writ large over his face. 'We've been so worried about you, Maggie. Where have you been? You just disappeared off the face of the Earth.'

'Oh, here and there, Bill. You know how it is.'

'Are you okay? How's the head now?'

'Head's fine.'

'And the ear?'

'What was wrong with my ear?'

'You said you had tinnitus or something.'

'Oh yes, so I did. That's fine too, thanks. Bruise has gone on the thigh. Do you want to see how it's doing, Ben?' She started to hitch her skirt up, but Ben held his hand up, laughing.

'Join us, Maggie,' he said. 'You won't find another spare seat at the moment.'

'My, you're right. It's busy in here. They've got this place up and running again well, haven't they? So soon too – I can't believe it!'

As she sat down, Sukie emerged from the kitchen carrying two bowls of pasta lathered in some sort of thick brown sauce. She placed them down on the table nearby with a family of four seated at it, drawing a polite thank you from both the parents. Their twin girls were already tucking in to their pizzas, giggling as the stringy cheese extended from the slices to their mouths, and then broke, flopping down against their chins.

Sukie rushed over when she saw Maggie, and gave her a huge

kiss on the cheek. 'We've missed you, Maggie.'

'I've missed you all too.'

'Do you like what we've done?'

Maggie looked around. It seemed to be exactly the same. 'It's lovely, Sukie.'

'Ah, thanks. Scuse me, won't you? It's like Piccalilli Circus in here today.' She hurried off, prompting Maggie to lean forward.

'Educate me, boys. What's changed?'

'Nothing really, 'said Ben. 'There's a photo of the scene after the crash on the back of the menus, and they've re-launched the business as – and I quote Samuel from the interview he did for the local press – "A safe, family restaurant where you will have a *smashing* time". It's the same table cloths, same crappy plastic chairs, same coloured walls, same badly painted floor.'

'We're pleased,' said Bill. 'It's still the ultimate in kitsch, and that's why we love it.'

Even the old posters were up, Maggie noted. She wondered how they had survived the crash and being open to the elements. The Tower of Pisa had been put back up at the same angle, maintaining its perpendicular status relative to the floor. She looked up at the plastic oil bottles. They were still there too, though the shovel had gone, she was relieved to see.

'There's a load people in here,' Maggie remarked. 'More than ever.'

'Word's got round about what happened, and now they're all enticed by the thought of danger, apparently,' continued Bill. 'The idea that something might come crashing through the door at any point seems to attract them. Dave's been given a bit of latitude with his swearing, too. Samuel says it gives the place an urban edge.'

Maggie had to smile. She was pleased for Samuel and Sukie. They worked hard and were a lovely couple. They deserved it.

On cue, Dave poked his head through the door and called through to Sukie who had reappeared and was making her way down the aisle with a tray of drinks. 'Can I say, "fuck" yet, Sukie, or do I have to wait a bit longer?'

The girls with the pizzas almost choked on their cheese before collapsing in a fit of giggles. Their parents continued to suck hard on their spaghetti, pretending to be unconcerned.

'Not yet, Dave. It's only just gone six. I'll tell you when. And remember, even then, you're only allowed a maximum of three F-words every hour.'

'Shit, bugger, sorry Sukie. Sorry kids. Sorry to everyone.' He nodded an apology to the restaurant in general before wiping his hands on his apron and disappearing back into the kitchen.

Bill and Ben were keen to know what Maggie had been up to, so she chatted with them without giving much away, until Sukie clopped over on her high heels to take her order. 'What's it going to be today, Maggie? We've got a special we haven't advertised on the board yet. We're hoping our regulars might try it and let us know what they think.'

Maggie glanced across at Bill and Ben who were surreptitiously making throat cutting signals and shaking their heads.

'Dave's been experimenting with a fusion of Italian food and good old East End of London grub. He's thinking of calling the line, "Bow Bella Pasta". His latest dish is jellied eels served on a plate of fusilli, topped with basil and shavings of parmesan.' The two men, by now, had slid down their chairs, hands clasped round their necks, making choking noises. It caught Sukie's attention and she sighed. 'The boys are probably right, to be honest. It's not really "oat quizzing", as they say. More like sick on a plate, but I want to encourage artistic flair while the place is hot. Got to keep innovating, haven't you, to stay at the top. This sort of "haven't guard" thing will keep bringing them back.'

'It'll certainly bring something back, Sukie love. I'll stick to the regular menu, ta.'

Having had her fill of traditional English food at the B&B, Maggie ordered a leek and asparagus risotto with tomato salad. She knew people of her own age who might have baulked at eating such 'foreign muck' but she was well used to it. She had been eating delicious meals in exotic places as part of her international assignments for years, long before the budget airlines started exporting Brits to gorge themselves on fish and chips next to sun kissed beaches on the Med.

'I'll wash that down with a nice cup of tea.' *Exotic, Maggs! Hark at you!*

The food arrived promptly, and she worked her way through most of it before excusing herself from the table to use the facilities. When she arrived, one of the cubicles in the ladies was out of order, the other occupied. So she took the opportunity to repair her face, groaning as she looked in the mirror, wondering how long she had been sitting there with the remnants of a cherry tomato lodged in her collar.

She removed the offending article, and began searching for more bits of food down her skirt. When she looked up again, a gun was pointing directly at her temple. On the end of it was a black gloved hand belonging to a middle-aged man wearing large spectacles. She quickly realised it had to be the same man who had been in the restaurant during the crash.

His words sounded gruff but forced, as if he was trying to either sound tough or disguise his true voice. 'You're an elusive woman, Agent Matheson. Hard to track down.'

Who said life in Frampton was boring? 'That's strange. I've been sitting at home with my feet up watching T.V. Did you try there?'

'Shit, no. You're kidding me? At your flat? Really? I went there.' The voice rose an octave, revealing what Maggie thought was probably something more akin to his true voice. The gun dropped a tad, and Maggie briefly wondered whether she was agile enough to wrestle it from his grasp. Her brain, though, was quick to realise that, even if her assailant seemed a little hesitant, it would have been very foolish. He was much bigger, considerably younger and in a better position.

'No, I wasn't really at home. I've been away. Perhaps you should have phoned and left a message? I would have picked it up when I got back.'

She saw his cheek twitch a little. A sign of nerves, probably. *A sign he's not used to doing this sort of thing: an amateur, almost certainly, but keep talking, Maggs, till you know a bit more.*

'Those answering machines are handy,' she said chattily. 'Mind you, if I'm there and I think it's one of those nuisance callers, I take it off the answer phone and just let it ring out. I don't want any silly messages, but these people can be so difficult to get rid of if you pick up, can't they? Try to sell you anything, and always try to kid you into thinking it's some kind of survey. That's how my friend Harry got caught out.'

The cheek twitched again, and the man opened his mouth as if he was about to interrupt. She did not let him. Once a spy, always a spy. *Observe and evaluate body language. Observe and evaluate, until you know more about what and who you're dealing with.* 'What started out as some straightforward questions about lifestyles ended up with him buying a year's supply of Viagra. At his age too! His hearing is a bit like mine, and he got the wrong end of the stick. Apparently, one of the questions asked if he had trouble getting it up. Harry thought the caller said, "Do you have trouble getting up?" He told them that he did... every morning. Before he knew it, he'd given out his credit card details. A box of pills turned up a few days later. It was a month before he realised his mistake. Maureen, his wife, didn't know what hit her! Literally, in some cases. Lucky girl."

'Do you always talk this much?'

'Oh yes. I'm quite the chatterbox.' She tried to catch his eye, but he refused to reciprocate, concentrating instead on looking at the trigger of the gun. His hand was shaking. *Definitely nerves, but be careful, Maggs. Nerves can make people do rash things.*

'Look, is all this palaver really necessary? I'm running a bit late. The lady who cuts my toenails is due round mine this evening. It's very difficult to get an appointment. She's so in demand round here. A late one was all she had this time.' He put his thumb and index finger in his eyes, and gave them a rub, before blinking several times and opening them wide again. *Eyes off the target; he definitely doesn't know what he's doing*. 'I'm not surprised she's so popular; she does a smashing job. Clean cuts, straight lines, and she takes all the clippings away with her too! Mind you, I don't know how she has the strength to get through my toenails sometimes. They're like granite. I suppose it's the equipment: she uses bolt cutters. I joke, but you take my point. Like any good tradesman, the better the tools you have, the better the quality of work.' *Unlike you, young man. That semi automatic SIG Pro you're holding has seen better days.*

'Stop talking!' His rough voice had returned. 'Now, we're going to take this nice and slow. I want you to go out the back, and I'll follow. I'm going to be pointing this gun at you the whole time. One false move and you've had it.'

One false move...? Who says that these days, except on the telly?

'Are you the man who was in here when the car crashed into the restaurant? The one who broke his phone?'

'I'll ask the questions round here. Now stay right there, while I check if it's clear outside.'

He backed out with his hand still on the gun, pointing in her direction, and had a quick look outside the door. She took the chance to grab her handbag by the sink then followed him out.

'That's it. Nice and easy. One false move and you've had it.'

'You've said that.'

'Said what?'

'That, if I do a false move, I've had it. You said that already.'

'So, we're counting now, are we?' He pointed her towards the exit that led onto the courtyard to the rear of the restaurant. 'Just do as I say and no one will get hurt.'

"No one will get hurt!" He really likes his clichés. With her handbag in front of her chest, she shuffled along until they got to the exit door. There were glass panels either side with a clear view to the small courtyard. It was devoid of people; she knew Samuel was probably helping Dave in the kitchen, and Sukie and Bella were busy waiting at tables.

'Okay, the coast is clear, let's go,' he said, pulling the latch down and shoving her through. *More clichés.*

'The car is parked down the side the street. You're going to get in the driver's side, easy does it, keeping your hands where I can see them.' *"Easy does it!"* 'I'm going to get in the passenger side. You will drive, following my exact instructions. Is that clear?'

'Perfectly clear, although I hope you don't mind me pointing out that there is a fundamental flaw in your plan. Two if you include the fact that we can't get out onto the street this way.'

The man looked frantically around. It was true; there was no exit onto the street from there, just a washing line full of red and white table cloths drying in the autumn sun, and an area where they kept the bins, all surrounded by a high wall.

'I should've checked. Sod it! I just assumed it would lead onto the side street. I saw a gate.' His voice had returned to its natural tone, all pretence at gruffness gone. 'Right, okay. Plan B then… Hang on. Did you say there were two flaws?'

'Yes, two flaws. Flaw number one: no way out. Flaw number two: I don't know how to drive.' *You can still lie like a good un', Maggs.*

'Really?'

'No, never needed to.'

'I thought all spies could drive.'

'You've watched too many Bond films. You'll have to do it. Perhaps I could hold the gun for you and use it to point out which way to go?' *Don't be too sarcastic, Maggs. It might wind him up.*

'No, that won't work.' *A literal man, I see.* 'Okay, right…' He looked genuinely flustered now. 'Okay, I can do this.'

'Can you?' she said gently. 'Are you sure?' She turned round and studied the eyes behind the glasses. They were not the eyes of a killer, let alone a kidnapper. They were the eyes of a desperate man, hopelessly out of his depth. 'Look, young man. Can I give you some advice?'

His head dropped, and he lowered the gun. 'I'm sorry. I'm not great at this sort of thing, to be honest. What would you suggest?' She eased the gun out of his hand, and looked to see if the safety catch was on. It already was. She popped it into her handbag,

'Well, what I suggest depends on your intentions. Why don't we have a nice cup of tea and talk about it?' She steered him back towards the restaurant. 'I just need the loo first.'

Chapter 8

Ben looked somewhat startled when Maggie returned to her seat, inviting her would-be kidnapper to join them. Ideally, she would have sat somewhere else, but the restaurant was still full, and she was not prepared to leave the place with the man until she had found out more about him.

'Bill, Ben… this is… er…'

'Um… call me, "Steve".'

'This is Steve. I met him in the ladies' loo.'

Bill looked considerably less startled than Ben, although still a little worried. He seemed to recover his composure quickly and offered his hand out to be shaken. 'Pleased to meet you, um, er… Steve.'

Ben followed suit, but failed to close his mouth which had opened as soon as Maggie had said she had met him in the ladies' loo.

'Two teas, please, Bella,' Maggie said, catching the young waitress as she went past. 'Is it too early for a glass of Chianti for you two?'

'We were about to go,' said Ben. 'We have an appointment to go through some of the reception arrangements at the Ivy but...'

'... we can cancel that,' Bill continued. 'Perhaps we should stay.'

'Yes,' said Ben. 'We can go another time.'

'No, no. I won't hear of it. You go off. You can't miss that. Besides, me and... Steve, was it? ... have a few things to discuss in private.'

Bill looked doubtful, but he nodded. 'Okay then,' he said. 'Ben, let's go and settle up with Sukie. Nice to meet you… um… Steve.' He leant over and whispered into Maggie's ear, 'You don't know this man, I assume? Take care, okay?'

Maggie was not good with whispers, but she nodded an acknowledgement, and smiled the smile she always did when people said something about which she had no clue on content, yet knew was well intentioned. Bill dragged away Ben who was still gaping at Maggie's new companion. She watched them leave and heard Ben mutter, as he went, 'Did she say she met him in the ladies' loo?... The ladies' loo! Actually in the loo?'

She turned to her new companion. 'Now, Steve. What's this all about? Why did you want to kidnap me?'

'I didn't really, but I had no choice.'

'We all have choices, Steve. By the way, is that actually your name?'

'No. It was the first name that came into my head. I'm Carlos.'

'But that's not your real name either, am I right?' She glanced up. 'That was quick! Thanks, Bella.'

'Are you alright?' Bella discretely mouthed.

Maggie nodded cheerfully, and waited until Bella had taken the tray away before continuing, 'So, you're Carlos. Carlos who?'

'I won't tell you my full name. Leave me with some sense of credibility, Agent Matheson.'

'Yet you're quite happy to use my surname?'

'Yes.'

'And you think I'm an agent of some sort?'

'Yes.'

'Travel or Estate?'

'Neither. Why would I want to kidnap a Travel Agent?'

'Why would you want to kidnap anyone? Especially an old woman. That's what I'm interested in.'

'Except you're not just any usual old woman, are you?'

There was a moment's silence while Maggie poured the tea and they both helped themselves to sugar.

'Ah, that's better,' said Maggie. 'You can't beat a nice cup of tea!' *Talk about clichés, Maggs: the oldest old lady cliché in the book.*

She took the opportunity to assess his features in more detail. The glasses, which she could now see were designer ones and probably cost a lot, hid what was quite a pleasant but wholly unremarkable face. If the glasses were a disguise, she decided, they had the opposite effect because they were the only thing about him that stood out. He had mousy-brown hair, greying at the sides and with just enough on top to allow it to be brushed back. His eyes, beneath eyebrows that were neither bushy nor pencil thin, were a hazel colour, his nose was an average size and shape, and his cheeks and chin were clean shaven. He wore a brown jacket, no tie, complemented by a plain magnolia coloured shirt with the top button undone. All in all, no distinguishing features – which was why she had not been able to identify him to the police when he had been in the restaurant that day, other than to say that there was a man with glasses.

She concluded that when he was not busy wielding guns and attempting to kidnap old ladies, he was probably either an English teacher or a civil servant at the tax office.

'As you might have guessed, I'm not used to this sort of thing. I used to be a maths and computer teacher in a secondary school in Slough,' *Close! You've not lost it, Maggs*, 'but I lost my job and access to our two teenagers after the divorce. Since then, I've been trying to scratch a living as a temp on I.T. projects in the civil service. *You definitely haven't lost it.*

'A word of advice, Carlos. If you don't want to get caught doing illegal acts such as kidnapping, don't give so much away. You've told me enough information there to not only trace your current address, bank account details and family history, but with a bit more digging around, your blood group, favourite TV programme and probably whether you prefer Coco Pops or Weetos.'

Carlos sighed. 'Neither, actually. I'm a celiac. Although, I do love pizza.'

'Why did you pull a gun on me?'

'I'm desperate. I'm wrapped up in something big, and I can't find a way out of it. I'm being blackmailed.'

'Who by?'

'I can't say. Listen,' he said, leaning forward and staring at her intently, 'I need you...' He hesitated, glancing from side to side.

'Need me? Well, it's a long time since I've been propositioned like that, Carlos. There are other ways to woo a woman other than shoving a big weapon in her back. Although, I must admit, that's not a bad start.'

'No, I need you... to come with me. If you don't, I may never...' He stopped.

'Never what?'

'Never... never...'

Whatever it was he may never do was obviously so upsetting he could not bring himself to finish the sentence. However, his lack of openness was beginning to annoy Maggie. She was willing to forgive him threatening her with kidnapping, but only if he gave her something in return. Sadly, that thing – information – was lacking at the moment. She said as much.

There was another short pause and then he spoke, softly. 'That girl in the restaurant... before it was struck. Remember her?'

'The karate kid? The one who jumped on the table just before the crash? Of course.'

'She's involved in this too. But she's just one of many other dangerous people around. All are after the same thing. And you've got it.'

'I really have no idea what you are talking about.'

'You have the data chip. You know…,' he lowered his voice and she had to lean right in and turn her good ear towards him. '… it holds the access codes... to get in... into...

'Into what?'

'I can't say... Look, I need you to come with me so they can secure the data chip and use those codes... before the girl – or anyone else – gets to you.'

'Who is this girl? And who is "they" you refer to? Who do you work for, Steve-Carlos?'

Maggie noticed the bead of sweat running down the side of his temple. 'I can't say.'

'There's a lot you can't or won't say. Look, I haven't the foggiest idea about any data chip. Data sounds a bit computer-ish to me. People who know about these things tell me I may be computer illiterate, an unfortunate condition which I fear may be terminal.' She began to stand up, irritated with his lack of transparency. 'I don't think I can help you. I don't know what you are getting at, and you obviously "can't say"! I'll get the bill for the teas as I've got other food to pay for. I wish you a good day.'

'Don't go. I need you and, frankly, you need something too. I know you do.'

'What makes you think that?'

'Please... you wouldn't be talking to me now if you didn't need to... need to...'

She folded her arms, ready to stamp her foot if so required. This man was so frustrating! 'Need to ... need to... You keep saying that. Need to do what?'

'Need to find out ...' There was another infuriating pause when he seemed to be fighting over how much he should say. She waited, foot still poised.

Finally, he said, 'Like you, I know what it's like to be separated from my children.'

'What?'

'Maggie. I know you want... you need... to find out more about your son, Peter.'

* * * *

Chapter 9

Half an hour later, Maggie found herself back home again, letting a complete stranger into her house. Except that he did not seem like a complete stranger anymore. On the way back, Carlos had revealed a lot more about himself: the fact he loved his kids; that he had a very domineering wife; he was in a job he hated, and he opened up about the desperation he had felt when his wife threw him out of the family home. Unless he was a very good actor – and Maggie had come across plenty of those in her time, so she was still a little wary – his recent life had sounded absolutely terrible. In truth, she was a sucker for the sob story. From the first time she had seen him in the restaurant and felt the urge to wipe the ketchup from his mouth, her mothering instinct had kicked in. She wanted to make things right for him. She had to help him.

But some things bothered her: Peter for a start. Carlos resolutely refused to say how he knew about Peter, yet he obviously did. That led her to think that Carlos might be connected to Voigt in some way. In which case, did that mean that Voigt was onto her and the mission? Perhaps Carlos was connected to karate girl, and he had mentioned her as a double bluff? Many questions, but Carlos raising Peter again had hit a nerve, and been yet another reminder of the hurt of having to give him up.

She was unclear on the main issue too: what exactly was this data chip, and why did Carlos and his blackmailers (whoever they were – he still would not say) think she might have it? If he and they believed that, was it wise to keep Carlos close to her? Indeed, there had been a moment in the car when Carlos had made her question the wisdom of her decision to take him back to her flat. They had begun to discuss what the next steps might be when Carlos suddenly seemed like he needed to try to assert some authority.

'Of course, what's to stop me drawing my gun again and forcing the information out of you as soon as we walk in the flat?' he had said.

He had then gone rather quiet when she pointed out that that eventuality was most unlikely to happen now because his gun was at the bottom of her handbag, nestled between the packet of pills she took for her thyroid problem, and 'The Lady' crosswords she had cut out with her nail scissors and squirreled away when she had been at the doctor's surgery the other week.

'And before you get any other bright ideas about snatching it from me, I have dismantled the gun as we have been talking. It will take you half an hour to put it back together again. That's assuming you even know how?'

'You have a point; I don't know how. Sorry.'

The incident actually only served to reinforce his vulnerability.

In the flat, she led him through to the kitchen and pointed to the floor. 'See that phone under the table leg? Do you think you can pick it up without smashing it all over the place?'

'I don't smash all phones, just that one in the restaurant.'

'And why did you did you do that?'

'I was frustrated because I was told I would need to come over heavy-handed with you from the get go.'

'And you smashed the phone because you didn't want to?'

He nodded, rather sheepishly. 'I don't like threatening anyone, especially old ladies. It's not my style. I felt they were constantly moving the goalposts, pushing more and more. I was angry.'

'But you changed your mind. Decided to kidnap me after all?'

'I can't bear the thought of not seeing my kids. I had to do something.'

It was her turn to feel like she was being evaluated, as he paused for a moment and eyed her up and down. 'Maggie, do you really not know anything about the data chip?'

'I'm totally in the dark. But I think I know someone who will be able to help. You've got to trust me, but, more importantly, I've got to be able to trust you. Let's start with your real name, shall we? "Carlos" doesn't really suit you.'

He looked hurt. 'No, that's my real name, honestly. My grandfather was Spanish. Why doesn't it suit me?'

'It's got an exotic ring to it. Hope you don't mind me pointing out, Carlos, there's not much exotic about you. There's nothing wrong with that. You seem a nice bloke. I would stop the kidnapping attempts though; it's not a nice habit, and you're hopeless at it.'

'I agree.' He held up the phone. 'You do know you're not supposed to put these under table legs, don't you? It's got a bit scratched.'

'Does it say somewhere that I can't? Pop those beer mats back under, will you, and do me a favour and switch the phone on. I'm hoping the number of Joshua might be in there somewhere.'

'Joshua?'

'He'll help us sort this out. Look, stick the kettle on, Carlos. I just need a moment to think.'

She took the phone from him, went through to her bedroom and sat on the edge of the bed. Putting the phone behind her, she reached for the cloth from her spare glasses case on the bedside table. She took off the ones she was wearing and sat there giving them a good wipe, letting her mind think about her next steps. There was a lot to consider, so many inconsistencies, so many gaps in her knowledge. An incompetent kidnapper; apparently ruthless blackmailers; a call back to the Service, out of the blue, to go on a mission; a link to her past, an emotional one, and one that was sure to test her mettle; an attack on the restaurant – that car had been sent to kill her, hadn't it? Then there was another player in the game she was aware of, but knew little about: the girl. Maggie had seen her jump up, ready for an attack, about the same time as Carlos received a call or text, and just before the car smashed through. He apparently knew of her, but knew little about her, unless he was hiding something? Did she work for the Service? That was possible. Was she in with whoever drove the car – knowing they were about to drive into the restaurant – on hand, ready to pick up any pieces if the attack failed?

But the attack had failed. Maggie was still alive, so why was that? Surely, if someone had wanted her dead, they would have had ample opportunity to kill her. If the girl had wanted her dead, there would have been a chance to finish her off in the chaos afterwards. But the girl, Carlos and the driver of the car had all disappeared quickly. Perhaps the attack was a warning then, a shot across the bows. But from whom?

Danger, unanswered questions and scope for double and triple crossings… it was becoming a typical Service job. *Lovely! You're committed now, Maggs.* If truth be known, she knew she was committed, despite her reservations, as soon as the car breached the restaurant's glass door.

'Right then,' she said out loud to herself. *Get back in there, Maggs*. She was about to get up to ask Carlos how the phone worked, when her heart nearly gave up the ghost. The parcel bomb that exploded unexpectedly in the next door hotel room in Karachi one baking hot July in 1972 scared her less than the sudden loud ringing behind her on the bed. She fumbled at it, pressing random buttons.

'Maggie, Maggie… is that you? Can you hear me?'

'How do I talk into this blessed thing? Right… the green button… hello? Hello? I've already pressed that I think… hello, can you hear me? Why is it making those beeping noises?'

'Maggie, it's Joshua. Just hold it up to your ear and talk. Or put it on speaker phone. No, scrub that idea. Just hold it up to your ear.'

'Bloody thing. Which way up does it go? Where's the mouthpiece?... Hello?'

'There's a volume button on the side. Two actually. The top one turns it up; depending on which way up you have the phone, of course. Second thoughts, scrub that idea too. I can't shout. I'm on the train. Oh, sod it. MAGGIE! HOLD IT UP TO YOUR EAR! CAN YOU HEAR ME?'

'Of course I can hear you, Joshua. I just needed to get used to it. These would be much better if they had a clear piece for your ear and another piece you could talk into. I don't even have one of those portable handset ones here. I much prefer the plug in ones. I know where they are, and they look like proper telephones. I've got one in the kitchen and one by my bed. My friends keep losing theirs. Diane from the Bridge Society left of one of hers in the middle of a large steak and kidney pie she had frozen and reheated for her Book Club friends. Caused an awful mess in the oven, apparently. No change there, I say, having tasted Diane's pies before.'

'Maggie, listen. We need to talk.'

'Sorry, Joshua. Technology makes me nervous. I'm waffling.'

'Yes you are, but I'm glad you've finally switched the phone on.'

'How did you know that I had? What made you ring me?'

'I got an automatic text through. It's not high-tech stuff, Maggie, despite what you might think.'

Maggie considered a semi-bristle for his dig at her ignorance, but realised that would be wasted without anyone there to see it. She said nothing in the hope that a brief stony silence would not go unnoticed. It did.

'I've been hoping you might reconsider your decision and rejoin us. Can I take it that you have?'

'Maybe,' she said cautiously. Since she had invited Carlos back to hers, her intention had always been to contact Joshua. Her initial instinct had told her she could trust Joshua, probably because of the family connection. But here he was contacting her, and trying to pick up from where he had left off back in the café in London. He was assuming she was back on board – and she yet might be – but wasn't he being a bit too pushy? It came down to who she should put her faith in. She opted for Joshua, at least for the moment. There was something about him…

'Are you alone, Maggie?'

'No, I'm with Carlos. You know the man with tomato sauce around his mouth.'

'Carlos? Tomato sauce?'

'Sorry, I'm probably being a little too specific. Carlos was the man in the restaurant I told you about with the glasses who disappeared straight after the crash. He tried to kidnap me at gunpoint this afternoon, but don't worry; it's all sorted now. He's making tea in my kitchen. He seems very nice.'

'Did you just say that he tried to kidnap you? My God, Maggie! Are you alright?'

'Of course I am, dear. Why wouldn't I be? I'd hardly be talking to you on the phone now with him making the tea if things weren't okay, would I? I've got his gun in bits in my bag. I'm just thinking of changing into something comfortable, and then we're going to sit down for a nice chat. First though, I need to know where you stand. Are you telling me everything, young Joshua? I feel this is a bit more complicated than you first intimated.'

'How do you mean?'

'Come now, you can't kid a kidder. There's more to this than meets the eye.' *A day of clichés, Maggs...* 'This isn't just straightforward espionage – our government versus the baddies. I've seen plenty of those before.'

'I told you there were other governments involved. It's a concerted effort from lots of government agencies against this organisation. We're all under threat.'

'Hmm... Are you sure about that, dear? If that was the case, why were you so keen to hide our connection to people in our own Service? Surely, it would be better to be upfront with everyone. Isn't there a danger this could all go tits-up on us – or in my case, tits-down – if someone else finds out the bad guy is my son and your granddad? Carlos knows Peter is my son, so someone else knows, at least.'

'Look, who is this Carlos?'

'I was hoping you could tell me.'

'Maggie, I don't know anything about him.'

'Okay, well, is there anything else I should know? Anything you haven't told me?'

There was silence from the other end for a good thirty seconds. Maggie was tempted to break it, but she needed to let this line of enquiry run its course. Whatever Joshua said to her next would all add to the pot of information she did not currently hold, whether it was true or false. The Service had always taught her to accumulate whatever information she could. Like publicity, there was no such thing as good or bad information. It was how you used it that counted.

'Okay, Maggie. I haven't been totally straight with you. I couldn't be, but I will be now, I promise. I have it on strong authority that everything I said to you about Peter being your son is true. As is the fact that he is connected to this organisation in a high profile way, working for Voigt. So we think, anyway. However, this runs much deeper than that. We're talking about corruption on a big scale. We're talking about… what's that noise?'

'I'm sorry, Joshua dear. I think I pressed buttons on the phone that I shouldn't have.'

'Is that the Archers theme tune?'

'Yes. I think I've started something by mistake. How do I switch it off?'

'Never mind. Look, this will be easier face to face. I'm a bit worried about you spending time with this guy who kidnapped you, though. Can you get away from him?'

'It's best I keep him with me. You need to talk to him too,

Joshua. He might be able to help. He's got such a nice car too. Heated seats. I'll get him to drive us somewhere.'

'I don't like it, Maggie.'

'You don't have to. Just name a time and a place and we'll be there. I'll bring my passport, just in case.'

* * * *

Chapter 10

'I used to watch that programme, too, when I was a kid. I could never remember which one was Bill and which one was Ben. They looked so similar. You two don't look similar at all.'

'Well Carlos, that's coz we're not blood related, and we don't wear flower pots on our heads,' said Ben rather grumpily. 'Plus the fact that my name's not actually Ben, and he's not Bill. That's just what Maggie calls us.'

'You sound like you three are getting on okay.' said Maggie as she lowered herself into the passenger seat next to Carlos and adjusted her belt. She turned around to address her friends. 'You know, I really was fine going with Carlos on my own. There was no need to follow us back to the flat.'

'It's not a problem,' said Bill. 'We were a bit worried about you going off with someone you had only just met. We weren't sure of his intentions. No offence, Carlos.'

'None taken.'

'Then when we saw him loading your suitcase into the back of the car, we thought we'd better intervene and check you were okay.'

'I appreciate your concern, but if I was being whisked off against my will, he's hardly going to allow me to go home and pack first, is he?'

'You've got to admit it's a bit strange,' continued Bill. 'You go to the toilet, come back with some bloke you've never met before, and then decide to take him back to your flat.'

'He really could have been kidnapping you for all we knew,' said Ben. 'No offence, Carlos.'

'None taken… I was trying to kidnap her, actually.'

There was a short pause, before Ben broke out into a slightly nervous giggle. Carlos put the car into gear and sped off down the drive in the direction of the main road.

'It's good of you to accompany us to Harwich,' said Maggie. 'How are you going to get back, Bill?'

'We can get a late train or a bus. We could even stay the night somewhere. There's loads to do in Harwich,' he added with an embarrassed cough. Maggie spotted Ben's rather pained look in the driver's mirror, a clear indication he had been to Harwich before.

Carlos seemed happy enough to meet Joshua when she explained to him that he could help. She could almost see the weight of responsibility fall off his shoulders, but he had still resolutely refused to explain how he was wrapped up in the quest for this data chip, or how he knew Peter. Until he was totally forthright with her, there would always be an element of doubt in Maggie's mind about him. She was fairly convinced that he was harmless. Nevertheless, some insurance in the form of her favourite couple would do no harm. They could go their own way as soon as she had met Joshua.

Bill and Maggie kept up an incessant chat the whole way. Occasionally, Ben would chip in with some dry remark to Bill about how boring the Essex countryside was compared to his home county of Derbyshire. Carlos remained quiet throughout, a fact that Maggie only really noticed when they were in sight of the red and white flashing lights that lit the tall cranes of Harwich port.

'You okay, Carlos?'

'Guess so.'

'You don't seem it. What's wrong?'

'I...I...'

Maggie did not have a chance to find out straightaway as Ben suddenly raised his voice. 'It's so bloody flat here. There's nothing to see. In the Peak District we've got beautiful hills, streams, lovely places to walk, quiet country pubs nestled in valleys and villages.'

'Rubbish!' said Bill. 'When was the last time you saw any hills through the clouds? It's always pissing down there. Sheep all over the place, and as for quiet country pubs nestled in villages, where's the nightlife? There's nothing to do unless you're over seventy.'

'You're not far off that!'

'Bloody cheek! I'm a very young looking mid to late fifty... possibly, sixty something. Anyway, that's not the point. Having lived here for a good part of my life, I will defend my adopted Essexites from the scourge of you Northern marauders.

'I'd like to see you try.'

'Well for starters, the people are friendly.'

'Hmm...'

'Granted, "Sod off you Gay Bastards" can sound quite aggressive with the Essex inflection, but it's not a pleasant term in any dialect. At least you can understand it here.'

'True. I'll give you that one. What else?'

'Well, from Essex, you can get to London within the hour. International travel, too, is on your doorstep. You can be in Torremolinos inside half a day.'

'Why would I want to be in Torremolinos within half a day? I know it was where we met but, having spent half my time there dodging the piles of sick from the mouths of all those Essex boys you're so fond of on various stag weekends, I can't think of anywhere worse.'

Maggie inwardly cringed at the last comment; she knew the honeymoon arrangements had been left to Bill to sort out as a surprise. Judging by Ben's reaction, it was not going to be the trip down memory lane Bill hoped for.

Still, she had to smile as their bickering continued; it was all in good heart. Carlos put the radio on.

'I'd rather they didn't hear us talk,' he said. Lady Gaga played out from the speakers.

'I'm not sure about something. The...' he began, then stopped. 'Are you singing, Maggie?'

'Pardon?' she said, mid-hum.

'Maggie, are you listening to me?'

'Yes... sort of. Poker Face… oh, I do love this song. Lady Goo Ga.' Maggie had started to move her hands from side to side in time to the music, doing what she liked to call the 'Saggy Bums on Seats Jig', the one that old folk do at weddings when they are sitting waiting for the buffet and the DJ has just put on "High Ho, Silver Lining".

'Muh, muh, muh, muh... my...'

'Maggie!' Carlos turned the radio right down. 'I was trying to speak to you.'

'If you want to speak to me then don't turn the radio on. You can't expect me to hear you with that blaring out. Besides, I just love to sing!'

He turned it off. 'Is that better?'

'Okay, I can hear you now,' she said. 'You have my full attention.'

'I was trying to tell you that I'm having second thoughts about seeing Joshua. The blackmailers insisted that I shouldn't get the authorities involved if I wanted to see my kids again. I think I've messed up again, Maggie.'

'Are you prepared to tell me who these blackmailers are yet?'

'Er... no. I can't.'

'Look, I understand you're scared, but if you won't tell me, how can I help you?'

'I don't know if anyone can help now. That's what I'm concerned about.'

'Well, speak to Joshua anyway and tell him whatever you can. He'll know what to do. Now, Joshua said to meet in the old town, near the Duke pub, just outside the R.N.L.I. museum. I like that place. Shame the shop won't be open at this time of evening. They do all sorts of stuff. Mind you, I love any charity shop. I like the coasters they do here. If I had a bigger place I would make sure I had lots of surfaces you could put coasters on. You can't beat a good coaster. That and tea cosies. Best insulator is wool. Sheep seem to think so anyway.'

She stopped, annoyed with herself for slipping into 'prattling-on mode'. She did it when she was anxious or nervous about something, increasingly so these days. Was she nervous? Possibly; a little excited, at the very least.

She looked in the wing mirror and realised the car that had pulled in behind them when they joined the main road at Frampton-on-Sea was still on their tail, despite Carlos's modest speed and plenty of opportunities on the dual carriageway to overtake. It was too dark to make out any features of the figure driving it, but she was pretty sure, in the twilight's gloominess, that there was just the one person.

'Oh crikey, there's you all worried about everything, and I'm going on about coasters and tea cosies. Not far now, dear. When we hit the old town, just keep going straight on towards the quay. Turn right before we hit the sea, and we can pull in somewhere along there. We've made good time, haven't we?'

They arrived soon after, and Carlos found a parking spot. As Maggie got out, she took a deep breath. The evening was fresh but pleasant with a small breeze ensuring the saltiness brought off the sea was well circulated around the old part of the town. It was not quite warm enough to encourage the locals to be out and about, though. The lights on in the downstairs rooms of the terraced houses along the quayside added a feeling of cosiness to the twinkles of the nearby port. Three seagulls were fighting over a piece of stale bread that had fallen out of a bin, their agitated squawks piercing the silence of the place.

They doubled back on themselves along the promenade, and it was then that Maggie again spotted the car that had been following them. As it continued along past them, she tried to catch a better look at the driver, but all she could make out was that he, or she, seemed quite small, the head barely above the steering wheel. The person had turned their face away as they drove past, a deliberate act, no doubt.

'Do you recognise that car, Carlos, that BMX that's just gone past?'

'Do you mean BMW? No, why? Are we being followed? You're making me more nervous than ever, Maggie.'

'Of course we're being followed. I wouldn't expect anything less. This is what spies do. Follow each other. Exciting, isn't it?'

'It could be one of my contacts, I guess, but I don't recognise the car.'

Maggie nodded thoughtfully, and they continued on for a while. Before long, she pointed at someone ahead, crossing the road. 'Ah, that must be Joshua. I'll let the boys know they can go back home now.' She turned round to address the pair, but as she did so, she stumbled on a piece of broken paving and fell forward.

Maggie was used to falling over; it was one of the risks of being old. But she had learnt to use the skills she had acquired in the Service to reduce the chance of serious injury. Too many of her peers had ended up in hospital with broken hips or worse because they had tripped over something innocuous, just as she had done now. On her way down, she deftly twisted, tucked her head to one side and executed a forward roll over her shoulder so that her upper back took the impact, rather than an arm or hip. She took a few deep breaths from her now seated position on the ground close to a post box.

Carlos was quickly at her side. 'I'm ok. I'm ok. Help me up will you?'

It was then that she became aware of a groaning sound behind her. She turned to see Bill was slumped against a car, his left hand holding his bloodied right shoulder. Ben was next to him. 'I think he's been shot!' he said incredulously.

Maggie swivelled around in an attempt to see where the shot had come from. It was hard to see anything in the dimming light.

'Maggie!' Joshua suddenly appeared from the shadows nearby, a gun in his hand pointed towards where Maggie was looking. She was convinced she saw someone running away in the other direction. Judging by the gait, she was almost certainly a woman.

'Looks like they've gone,' Joshua said. 'His phone bleeped and he checked it hurriedly. 'Okay. That's confirmed. Two of my colleagues are in pursuit of the shooter. Good job you fell when you did. The shot must have gone right over you.'

Carlos helped her to her feet, and they hurried the few paces back to Bill.

'But it hit him,' said Maggie. 'God...'

'I'm alright,' Bill said. 'Really, it's not serious.'

'Not serious?' said Ben. 'You've been shot. Of course it's serious. What is going on here?'

Joshua checked the wound. 'It's a graze I think, top of the shoulder, but I'll make a better assessment when we get to safety. In the meantime, we best get out of here, in case there are others around.'

'Others?' said Ben. 'Other what?'

'My car's just there.' He pointed. 'Help him over to it.' Maggie could just about make out through the gloom what looked like a Fiat 500 squeezed onto the pavement across the road between a waste paper bin and a road sign.

Ben seemed too shocked to respond to Joshua's command at first, but after a nudge from Maggie, he and Carlos supported Bill over to the car where Joshua was now waiting with the door open.

'Get in,' Joshua said, pulling the front seat forward.

Perplexed, Maggie scrutinised the car. 'This needs a bit of thought, Joshua. This matchbox on wheels is going to be a squeeze. The words "quart, pint pot" and "My fat bottom is much too big to fit in there" spring to mind. Why don't we use Carlos's car?'

'Too risky to head back that way,' he said, supporting Bill on his uninjured side. 'I'll help him get in the front where there's a bit more space. The rest of you will have to squeeze in the back.'

As Ben clambered in, he said, 'We're going straight to a hospital, right?'

'No time,' said Joshua.

'I'll be okay, Darren,' said Bill. 'It's nothing. Do as he says.'

Maggie got in after Carlos and Ben who had shuffled along behind the driver's seat. Both sets of their knees were unnaturally close to their respective ears. Joshua shut the passenger door after making sure Bill was in, before going round and climbing into the driver's side. Maggie ended up sprawled across Carlos and Ben as Joshua encouraged the car's tiny engine to reverse off the pavement and then away from the quay.

'Where are we going?' Carlos asked.

'We've got a ferry to the Hook of Holland to catch.'

'What all of us?' said Ben.

'Not ideal, but probably best in the circumstances. Quicker and safer. I'll book a cabin and we can get sorted there.'

Carlos spoke up. 'Whoever that was might have been shooting at me.' Maggie sensed the strain in Carlos' voice. Her sympathy doubled as she suddenly realised the strain might not be totally emotion based; she had no real idea where her left elbow currently was.

'That's possible,' said Joshua, 'Or at Maggie.'

'At me?'

'Yes. We need to get you on the boat, Maggie, in any case. We'll talk more then. Okay?'

Carlos was not the only one who was worried. Maggie heard a

quiet sob.

'Don't worry; it's going to be okay, Ben love. By the way, is that your phone digging into me, or have my comely female ways, fancy perfume and close proximity finally managed to turn you?'

She heard a half chuckle from the front and Bill spoke. 'Don't tease him, Maggie. Look, Ben, the bullet only scratched me. Must have deflected off my bus pass in my top pocket.'

'That's not even funny,' said Ben.

Maggie tried her best to sound serious for a moment. 'Are you sure this is the right thing to bring Bill and Ben along too, Joshua? Maybe Ben's right. We ought to get him to a hospital. You and I can go with Carlos.'

'That won't work,' said Bill.

'Why not?'

There was no immediate answer. Maggie found herself suddenly jerked over as Joshua negotiated the last roundabout before the ferry port entrance.

Eventually Bill spoke. 'I can't keep up the pretence any longer.'

'This is not what we agreed,' said Joshua. 'It's too soon.'

'I think now is as good a time as any, Agent Harley.'

'Bill, did you just say, "Agent Harley"? How does he know your name, Joshua?' *Another twist, Maggs.* 'You know each other?'

'Are you sure?' said Joshua to Bill.

'She's got to find out sooner or later. She may as well know now.'

'It's your call.'

'Know what exactly?' Maggie asked.

'Yes, what exactly?' Ben echoed.

'I'd quite like to know what's going on too,' said Carlos, his voice muffled by... well Maggie was not quite sure what part of her was causing it to sound so muffled now.

From her unusual vantage point, she could just make out Bill twisting his neck to look behind him. 'I'm sorry about this, Darren, but it doesn't affect our relationship, nor the way I feel about you.'

'What are you talking about? What doesn't affect our relationship?'

'Maggie... Darren,' he said quietly. 'There's something both of you ought to know.'

*   *   *   *

Chapter 11

After driving onto the ferry, Maggie and Ben, both in somewhat of a daze after Bill's revelation, had followed Joshua up to the main deck to the bursar's office where he hoped to secure a cabin for them. Bill suggested they left Carlos with him a few decks below. He was feeling okay now, he had said, and it made sense for not all of them to be wandering around.

The ferry was full of football fans travelling over to Amsterdam for Arsenal's away leg in the Europa cup, so the three of them were now surrounded by fans in red and white scarves, singing and shouting, and generally having a great time. There was no sign of trouble, but the noise was incessant, and the carpet was already covered in beer outside the bar adjacent to where they were now standing. Any seats that were not taken by an irate business person or a cowering holiday maker who had, without checking the European fixture list, booked a "relaxing and enjoyable one night cruise onboard our luxury flagship liner" had a fan standing on it, joining in whichever chant or song was closest to them. One supporter, somewhat worse for wear, swung by with a tray of beer and stumbled, just catching himself before the whole lot ended up on the floor.

Ben winced, clearly uncomfortable with the situation. But he was also clearly preoccupied, and who could blame him? He had not said a thing since his long term partner, and future husband, had disclosed that he was an agent in the Secret Service, and was currently on an important mission. The further news that the little old lady they had shared tea, pasta and Chianti with for many years was also a spy – as was the young man driving them onto the ferry – probably made Carlos' role as a failed gun-toting kidnapper seem comparatively insignificant.

Maggie had been rocked back too, she had to admit. She thought she had seen so much of life that there was nothing left that could surprise her. But Bill's confession had thrown her, for two reasons:

One – she had had absolutely no inkling that Bill had been working undercover. She had known the pair since they moved to Frampton two years previously and, although they only really saw each other at the restaurant, she considered them her friends. There had been nothing about his demeanour, back story or behaviour which had given her any idea whatsoever. *Think about it, Maggs. He wouldn't be much of a spy if there had been.* Point taken... but she was peeved that she had not spotted the signs. After all, that used to be part of what she did.

Two – it was another twist to an already complicated situation. Bill had said he had been placed undercover to protect her. That meant this case had been ongoing for at least the two years Bill and Ben had been in Frampton, and she had been an unwitting player until only very recently. She thought back to Joshua's briefing at the café in London. They wanted her to play the part of Voigt's mother, to infiltrate his organisation and help destroy it. So why had she needed protection before she was even recruited? Was it a plan that had been in the making for all that time? And who, exactly, was she being protected from?

There was a lot to mull over, but she was struggling to think in the noise. As difficult as it might be to be heard, she decided to attempt some conversation with Ben.

'They really ought to practise their songs before they come away on a trip like this,' she shouted. 'It could be really nice if they tried to sing the same song for starters. Who's in charge of deciding what to sing?'

'I don't think there's anything as sophisticated as that,' Ben shouted back, arching his back in an attempt to protect Maggie from some of the good-humoured pushing and shoving going on all around them. 'I know they used to have ringleaders on the terraces, but it seems to be a free-for-all here.'

'I'm all for artistic expression, but it really could do with a bit more organisation. Perhaps I could speak to someone to suggest it?'

She was momentarily taken off her feet as the crowd suddenly surged forward towards the bar. Ben grabbed her arm and hauled her out and back to the side of the desk where Joshua was in animated discussions about the cabin. They found a slightly quieter spot where they could speak fairly normally.

'Thanks, Ben,' Maggie said brushing down her skirt, 'but I can look after myself. Don't forget, as you now know, I'm a Ninja spy.' She lowered her glasses and winked.

'Hmm... and not the only one round here!'

'We may not understand it yet, but there will be reasons for Bill's little deceit.'

'It's hardly a *little* deceit revealing that he's been working for the government's Secret Service for the last thirty odd years. I had no idea! We set up that nail bar together. It was going to be our pension fund for when he retires.'

'And so it still will be. It just means you will have a nice civil service pension to supplement it.'

Ben stood on tiptoes and looked around the bar and foyer area. 'How do we know it's safe amongst this lot? That assassin who shot at us could be on board.'

'Even if they are, they're hardly likely to try anything with so many people around. Anyway, I have some protection.' She pointed to her handbag which still had Carlos' gun inside.

'Swinging around a handbag is hardly likely to help much, is it?'

'Not the handbag...'

They were interrupted by Joshua who returned with keys to a cabin. 'Okay, that's all sorted, kind of. I couldn't get two cabins so we're all in together. It's a cabin for four, but I'll sleep on the floor. I had hoped we could grab a bite to eat while we were up here and take some down for the other two, but the canteen looks packed. Let's go back down first and decide what to do from there.'

Ben took up the rear behind Maggie, as Joshua forged a path through the throng to the stairwell. The stairs were steep and Maggie could feel it in her knees. Her doctor had recently suggested she consider using a stick when she went out. She had flatly refused, saying that she would only use one when she was old. She was regretting it now as she teetered down the stairs. With her handbag over her shoulder and a hand clinging firmly to the banister, she spoke to Ben over her shoulder.

'Carlos, Joshua and I had our passports already. It was lucky you and Bill have those false Dutch I.D cards. Why do you have them, by the way?'

Ben's reply sounded a little embarrassed. 'Let's just say we have good cause to visit Amsterdam on quite a regular basis.'

She stopped on the landing and looked at him. 'What on Earth for? Are you fans of the Rijksmuseum?'

'Well… yes. We are partial to a bit of art, but there's also other stuff there we are interested in. Pretending to be Dutch gets us into certain places where we can enjoy… ahem…'

Maggie slapped her hand to her forehead. 'Of course,' she said at the top of her voice. 'It's for the weed!'

'Shush! Not so loud, Maggie. Anyway, it's medicinal. Mainly…' He paused as some passengers navigated their way past on their way up from the car decks. 'It's all making sense now,' he continued. 'I wondered how Nigel had got hold of those cards so easily. It's who you know, I guess. And who you know isn't always who you think it is you know.'

Maggie spotted the flicker of hurt in his expression. She reached up to give a consoling pat on the shoulder. 'He's still good old Bill…'

'His name is Nigel.' He sounded irritated.

'Nigel. Yes, Sukie did mention his name was Nigel.'

'Come on you two.' Joshua called up to them from halfway down the next staircase.

'We're coming.' She turned back to Ben. 'You do know Bill loves you still, Ben, don't you?'

'I'm Darren.'

'Sorry... Darren. Really he does, though. I can see it in his eyes, Ben love.'

They set off again to negotiate the last set of stairs until they reached Deck C where Bill and Carlos were waiting.

'Ah, there they are! You're looking a bit better, Bill. Do you feel it?'

Bill looked sheepishly at Ben before answering. 'Quite a bit, thanks Maggie. It's nothing really. I've had a lot worse.'

'Worse?' said Ben sarcastically. 'How could there be anything worse than getting shot?'

'Look… Darren… I've got a lot of explaining to do. Please don't judge me. There's a lot to understand.'

Ben found a spot on the floor to stare at. Maggie touched Bill's hand. 'Give him time, Bill. Now, where's this cabin, Joshua?'

'It's just down here and on the right.'

Inside the cabin, Maggie sat at the end of one of the bunks while Joshua tended to Bill's wound using the first aid kit from his car. Ben had gone off, apparently in a huff, but ostensibly to get some food for all except Maggie who had insisted she did not want anything. Carlos stretched out on one of the top bunks with his hands behind his head and stared up at the ceiling. He had been suspiciously quiet for some time.

'Definitely just a graze,' declared Joshua. 'The potential assassin must have been going for a head shot on Maggie for it to have hit you there.'

'How lovely!' Maggie commented brightly, her sarcasm hiding her deep concern that it could have been a lot worse... for either one of them.

'I'll patch him up, and then we'll get out of your way, Maggie. I'm sure you need to get changed ready for bed.'

'Where will you go?'

'There's a small quiet lounge further down the corridor for 'exclusive' members. I've paid a bit extra. We can eat in there when Ben brings the food back. You look whacked. Get some sleep.'

'If you're sure?'

Carlos clambered back down from the bunk and they left her with strict instructions from Joshua not to leave the cabin. She began mulling over which bunk to take, although, practically, there was only a choice of two. She dreaded to think how she would have managed the climb up the tiny ladder to a top bunk. And she did not trust herself to be able to stay in it either, even if she got up there, what with the narrowness and potential swell of the ship. At least with a lower one, she only had a couple of feet to fall to the floor.

She checked her handbag, relieved that she had bought a few basic toiletries at the shop in the terminal before they boarded (her suitcase was still sitting in the boot of Carlos' car in Harwich). They would supplement the underwear she already had in her handbag. Frankie had always teased her about always carrying spare knickers and tights around with her, but there had been times when she had been called away on a job and been grateful for her idiosyncratic ways. She had continued to carry spares around, ever since her Service days. The habit had not changed, but the size of the bag needed had, proportional to the knickers.

She pulled her things out of her bag, and allowed herself a smile. The action reminded her of the film Mary Poppins where Mary extracts a raft of items from her holdall to the astonishment of Michael and Jane. She remembered her and Frankie watching Sharon at her junior school's production of the film, a rare chance to prove that they were 'normal' parents doing 'normal' things. That magical scene had particularly struck her, and she had proudly recreated her own version of it in front of Frankie and Sharon when they got home, using an old battered suitcase and some hastily packed goodies from around the house, much to her daughter's amazement and laughter.

Such memories, Maggs. She sighed as she arranged her things, then grabbed her handbag and left the cabin to make her way back up to the bar where all the action was.

Time to create some more.

* * * *

Chapter 12

'Joshua! What are you doing here? I thought you'd be in bed by now.'

'Can you get down from that table please, Maggie?' Joshua shouted.

Maggie continued to wave her hands around in time to the music, keeping the beat as the packed bar bellowed out, 'We All Follow the Arsenal.'

'If I stop now, this lot will go to rack and ruin! It's taken me this long to get most of them singing the same song at the same time.'

'Is that a knitting needle you are using as a baton?'

'Yes! It's perfect, isn't it? Multifunctional!' Maggie swayed from side to side, making the table rock rather disturbingly.

'We need to talk, Maggie. Tell them you're on a break, please.'

'Alright then. I must admit I'm a bit pooped, but I'm having so much fun.' She waited until the end of the verse before shouting across the bar, 'Bazza and Dano! Let's take five. I'll be back soon.'

'Hear what the lady said, everyone?' called out Bazza. 'Take five.'

'What, five pints?' chuckled Dano, followed by a loud 'Oi, oi!' from those around them.

The two men came over, unceremoniously shoving fellow fans out of the way, and stood either side of the table where Maggie had been holding court. She beamed as they held out their hands, ready to help her down.

Both men were built like what her Frankie would have described in his mock posh voice as, 'a rather large and sturdy brick establishment in which a gentleman could conduct a movement of the bowels'. Bazza had scars all over his face, an impressive array to rival a bevy of pirates on a wild weekend in Magaluf. Dano had a nose that looked like… well, Maggie had thought long and hard what it reminded her of. In the end, she decided that it had been surgically removed, pummelled by an enthusiastic five year old boy who had mistaken it for play-dough, before it was thrown back in the general direction of Dano's face. They certainly did not present as individuals most people would choose to spend time with. Then again, Maggie had always prided herself as not being 'most people.'

'It took me ages to work out what that last tune was supposed to be, but now I've got them a bit better organised, with help from Bazza and Dano here, you can recognise the original at least – *Land of Hope and Glory*. One of my favourites! There's some hidden talent here too. I've spotted some lovely voices and, in particular, I want to get those over there to work on harmonising.' She pointed to a group of five men and one woman at the bar who seemed more concerned about harmonising with the twelve shots of Tequila being passed round on a tray.

'Thank you boys, that's very good mannered of you,' she added, handing Joshua her knitting needle and placing her hands into those of her two helpers.

'No problem, Maggie. Is this your grandson you were talking about?' asked Dano.

Maggie tried to look as graceful as she could as she stepped down first onto a bar stool, and then to the floor. The final flourish of having to hitch up her knickers afterwards rather ruined the illusion of grandeur. Nevertheless, she had a big smile on her face as she replied, 'Great grandson, but yes, this is Joshua.'

'I hope you're looking after her well, mate. You've got a good'un here.' Bazza gave Maggie an affectionate squeeze round the shoulders, squatting down to her height as he did so. 'Is it okay if some of us have a quiet practice in the corner, Maggie? Seasick Simon's timing is awry on the second verse, and I don't know what the fuck Phil the Flamingo is doing during the climax at the end. Excuse the language. I think that he's so wrapped up in the emotion of the moment that his voice goes to shit on the high notes.'

They barged their way back to the bar to meet up with the others, leaving Joshua staring at Maggie with a quizzical look on his face. 'I get "Seasick Simon" but "Phil the Flamingo"... where does that come from?'

'Apparently, Phil the Flamingo goes pink when he drinks too much, and has a habit of standing on one leg because he gets gout in his big toe. I've had that: it's a bugger. There's a logic to all their nicknames: "Not So Steady Eddie"; "Gift Horse Harry" because he never refuses a free drink; "Tawny Al" – a bird lover who likes a drop of port.'

'Nice one. Owls are partial to a drop of Cockburn's, I heard.'

'Good for their eyesight. I'll have to warn him about gout, or he'll end up like Phil the Flamingo. And a bloke they call "Enid" because he once admitted that his auntie bought him one of the "Famous Five" books when he was younger. There's one I don't quite get though: "Billy the Banker". Apparently, he doesn't even work in a bank. Bazza did mention that he spends a lot of time in his room at home with the door shut and gets through a lot of tissues. Can't quite see why either of those things is relevant to anything.'

Joshua smiled. 'Bazza and Dano seem like genuine guys.'

'They are. Hearts of gold. You should never judge people by their appearances. Don't be fooled by all the tattoos and studs. I once spent a month on a case in the depths of the Amazon and most the tribe there were covered in tattoos, head to toe, with studs and rings coming out of parts of the body I didn't even know existed! They scared the life out of me when I first met them, but they couldn't be a nicer group of people.

Now you've dragged me away from my new friends, what is it you want to see me about?'

'Well, if you've quite finished carrying out your auditions for your own version of "The Great British Choir", can you tell me why you ignored my explicit instructions to stay in your cabin? It wasn't that long ago that you were shot at.'

'The shooter, she was definitely aiming for me?'

'We think so. Fortunately for us all, our agents managed to take her into custody soon after the incident. She's being interrogated back at Harwich.'

'Why didn't you tell me?'

'Because I wanted you to stay in your cabin where you would be safe. You've been out hunting for her, haven't you?'

'Quite possibly, amongst other things. I got a bit distracted.'

'Listen; there could be other players around, Maggie, people that want to hurt you.'

She could see from his face that he was genuinely worried. His concern touched her. 'That's sweet, Joshua, but as you can see, I am fine. Mind you, if you had kept me in the loop, I wouldn't have left in the first place to go looking for her. I probably need to brush up on my surveillance techniques, though.'

'You're telling me! Standing up on a table in the middle of a bar waving a knitting needle around is hardly inconspicuous.'

'You only live once, don't you?'

'Well, now I know you're safe, can we go somewhere a bit less noisy to talk? Everywhere is packed, but I think there's a quiet room come prayer room which we could go to.'

The room was near the prow, and it took a couple of minutes to get there. Maggie noticed one or two annoyed looks from exhausted passengers as they passed; people who may have been into the bar in an attempt to plead for peace, seen a pensioner on a table orchestrating a mass of exuberant fans, and then thought better of it. Maggie sympathised; there would have been a time when she might have been one of those passengers, but losing people close to her had changed her perspective on life, and encouraged her to make the most of the time she had left. Still, they deserved their rest. It was probably time to quieten things down.

The room was unlocked and empty. Joshua and Maggie sat down next to each other on a couple of chairs at the front, facing the vase of fake flowers that had been placed on a small table. On the wall next to the flowers was a sign explaining that all were welcome to use the room as a space for "contemplative thought and respite, a haven in an otherwise busy and demanding world". The words and atmosphere had a calming effect on her, and she realised that she was indeed 'pooped'. It had been a busy day.

What had started as a visit to her favourite restaurant had ended up with her leading a singsong with dozens of Arsenal fans on a ferry to Holland, via an attempted kidnapping, an attempt to shoot her outside the Royal National Lifeboat Institute shop in Harwich, and a game of sardines in a Fiat 500 with four men. Had she had stranger days? *Quite probably, Maggs.*

She was eased out of her reverie by Joshua's soft voice. 'I'm going to take you back to our cabin shortly, and you're going to stay there. I shouldn't even have left you. If I'd known you would go straight out…'

She interrupted him. 'Tell me more about the shooter.'

'Well, like I said, we have her. She's being interrogated at the Military Police HQ in Colchester.' He explained that they soon hoped to have a handle on what her motives were, if they could get her to talk. Word was that she was proving a tough nut to crack. The suspicion was that she was Russian, but they had no proof and no record of her on their files. He had been told that her understanding of English was poor, or at least she had given that impression, but the likelihood was that she was the same girl that had been in the restaurant before the car crashed into it. She looked like it from the photo that had been texted to him.

'She could have killed me at the restaurant.'

'Yes. I don't know why she didn't try. Perhaps because circumstances have changed.'

'What circumstances?'

'Look, nothing really. The situation is fluid.'

'You sound like Sheldon. She speaks like that.'

'Sorry.' He tried to stifle a yawn, but Maggie spotted it.

'You need your sleep, Joshua.'

'Maggie, I may not look that old, but remember that I'm a fully trained agent, used to sleep deprivation. I can handle it. You, however, definitely do need your sleep. You are crucial to the success of this mission. Without you, we have no real chance of stopping Voigt and his organisation.'

His words struck a chord. She was rapidly realising just how important she appeared to be in all this, although she was yet to fathom out exactly what everyone – Carlos, the girl, the driver of the car and now the Service, apparently, judging by Bill's protection role for the last two years – thought she had that was so important. Was it this illusive data chip that Carlos referred to? Possibly, but if she did have it, she was certainly unaware of it.

Something was stopping her asking Joshua outright at the moment. Was it a trust issue, still? Was it because she did not want to put him in too compromising a situation? *Just ask him, Maggs. You don't normally hold back on such things.*

No, she decided to play it cool for now and concentrate on what Joshua had originally recruited her for: to infiltrate Voigt's organisation, posing as his mother.

'What's the plan, then? I thought we were off to Vienna originally?'

'That's changed. After your temporary withdrawal from the Service, the centre of the operation seems to have moved to Bruges. When we spoke on the phone, I had to make a quick decision. Meeting you in Harwich made sense to get you over to Holland as quickly as possible. We have people in Amsterdam who can help with changes to your persona so that you look and act more like Voigt's mother. From there, we will get you to Bruges. It's not far, as you probably know. If he moves again, we will have to follow. That's part of what he does to throw people off the trail.'

'What about Carlos and Bill and Ben? Are they coming?'

'Bill, yes. He's a very capable agent, one of our best. He will want to see out his protection role over you. Carlos I want to keep close to us, partly for his own good and partly because I need to pump him for information.'

'And Ben?'

'I'd rather he wasn't here. He has no real role to play, but he got dragged into this. I'll explain to Bill that Ben's his responsibility. Ben did say that he got a look at the woman who shot at you. That might be useful for identification purposes By the way, you do know that they're not really called Bill and Ben, don't you?'

'Ah, but it suits them, doesn't it? Even you can't help calling them that.'

He shook his head, but his expression told her he agreed. He continued, 'So, back to plan A, albeit an adapted one. We arrive at The Hook, hire a car to take us to Amsterdam, meet my contacts to get you fully in disguise as Voigt's mother and then off to Bruges. I feel reasonably good now that you're in safer hands, providing you do what you're told.' He wagged his finger at her in a mock telling off. 'Okay?'

'Okay.'

'Now, let's get you back to your cabin, Maggie.'

Gently, he held her elbow as she stood up. Her back felt stiff and the arthritis was playing havoc in her knees again. She limped along towards the door until she felt able to extend her back a bit more and straighten up. 'I'm alright once I get going.'

'Now, will you promise to get a good night's rest?'

She adjusted her glasses, gave him a serious look and then nodded slowly. 'Yes, Joshua. I promise… Just as soon as I've had a couple more songs in the bar with the lads.'

Chapter 13

It was just before midnight, when, on Maggie's instructions, the party-goers in the bar headed to their respective places of rest, which, for many, was just a metre or two lower than where they had been standing, on the bar floor.

Her roommates were already asleep and, with Joshua waiting outside the door, she had to fumble around in the half-light of a nightlight to try and get ready for bed. She was well and truly exhausted, and now regretted joining Bazza and Dano in one of many 'one last' Tia-Marias. On the plus-side, she was relieved she no longer had to spend time cleaning her teeth, as she popped a Steradent tablet into a plastic cup, extracted her dentures and dropped them, in before tucking them under her bed. She had the presence of mind to put the cup into one of her shoes first to counteract any movement of the boat. She draped her coat on the end of the bed before getting in otherwise fully clothed. The spontaneity and audacity of it took her back to a time when she had been forced to sleep when and where she could on missions under far rougher conditions than this. Although, back in those days, her teeth tended to stay in much closer proximity to her gums.

Within seconds, with those happy thoughts, she was fast asleep.

It took a moment to work out that the deep breathing she could hear was real and not a dream. She slowly moved her eyes to the left to find Ben staring at her with an expression of horror. There was also a very alert and worried looking Joshua standing behind him, with two more concerned faces peering down at her from their bunks.

'My God,' said Ben. 'We thought you were dead!'

It took a moment for Maggie to make out where she was. All the lights in the cabin were on, a cue for the kettle drummer to wake up too and begin pounding out a rhythmic beat from the back of her head.

'Ben, Joshua?' she croaked. 'What's happening?' She tried to sit up, but that only encouraged the rest of the percussion section to join in, so she lay back in the hope they would get bored and go home. They did not; they were having a lovely time. It was a while since she had suffered a hangover, and she vowed now that it would be the last time.

'It's okay, Maggie,' said Joshua. 'Nothing's happening. We were worried about you.'

She put her hand over her eyes. 'Did you say you thought I was dead?'

'Yes! You scared the life out of me,' Ben said. 'I turned my little light on and there you were, like that.'

'Like what? What made you think I was dead?'

'To be fair,' Joshua said, 'I can see why anyone would be shocked. You were flat on your back, unmoving, pale, eyes shut and mouth wide open, clutching your handbag over your chest. Where are your teeth, Maggie?'

'In my shoes, under the bed.' She groaned as she rolled over to check they were still there. They were, but they seemed a million miles away, something that bothered the brass section who were never ones to play second fiddle to the second fiddle, let alone to the upstarts at the back who just banged on things. 'Help me,' she pleaded as the whole orchestra joined in.

Joshua reached down and handed Maggie the glass and dentures. She sat up on her side and, as discretely as she could, waggled her teeth into position, before collapsing back onto the bed and shutting her eyes again.

'We're going to dock in about an hour, Maggie. How long do you need to get ready?'

She opened one eye. 'Depends on how fussy you are. If you want me to look like Liz Taylor, I may be some considerable time. Daughter of Frankenstein I can do in five minutes.'

'I'll take the latter. Hopefully, we can get a bit of breakfast in the canteen before it gets too busy. That should help you feel a bit better.'

Surprising herself, Maggie was outside with her bag and coat on in about ten minutes, allowing the others back in to get themselves ready. Joshua stayed with her. The severe headache had subsided after several cups of water, leaving her with an occasional mild throb, a calling card from Tia Maria who always did this to her.

'You know what I could do with now?' she said as the others came out to join her.

'I think we can guess,' said Bill. 'Does it involve the words, cup, nice, tea, a, of?'

'Spot on! How are you feeling now, Bill?'

'All good. As I said, it was just a graze. I was lucky. A big plaster, quick rinse of my shirt, and I'm as good as new. Ben and I have had a good chat too and think we've come to an understanding.'

'You're a sly one, you are, Bill,' said Maggie. 'I would never have guessed you were one of us.'

'Spent most my school days being called, "One of Them" so it's a refreshing change.' He lessened the impact of self derision with an awkward smile, but Maggie had had enough conversations with her two friends to know that humour was part of a self-defence mechanism, born out of bitter experience of prejudice over many years. 'I don't know if Darren is more shocked about me being in the Service, or the fact that you are too, Maggie.'

Carlos broke his silence, not with a question about spying, kidnappers or guns, but something more mundane. 'I'm getting quite confused,' he said to Ben. 'Are you Darren or Ben?'

Maggie held off from a reply this time. Ben looked at her and sighed. 'Ben. Call me Ben. It will be easier.'

When they arrived in the canteen, they found it busy, but not overly so. Maggie was greeted with glee by many of the football supporters, most of who were tucking into various combinations of greasy objects arranged on their plates. Maggie looked out for Bazza and Dano, but there was no sign. She had left them last night, each insisting they carried the other to the front of the ship in search of spare seats.

They picked a quiet table far enough away from most of the other eaters. Carlos volunteered to go up with Joshua to get the food, returning shortly afterwards with trays of food and mugs of steaming hot teas and coffees. They had all gone for the continental option of croissants, butter and jam, all except Carlos who opted for the full English. As he ate, Maggie thought back to when she had first seen him in Sukuel's, and how he had waved the sausage around before placing it haphazardly in his mouth. He had sauce in the corner of his lips again, and she had her napkin poised. *Resist, Maggs, resist!* She clenched her fist to stop herself from wiping it off, then used the napkin to brush away croissant crumbs from her lap, inadvertently knocking them onto Ben's.

'Carlos,' she said thoughtfully, oblivious to Ben who was now busy knocking the crumbs back onto her lap, 'I want to ask you something.'

He looked up, but carried on cutting his sausage and bacon, in the process making a complete mess of the beans which were now falling off the plate. For a moment, she considered abandoning her original question, which was an important one to do with the timing of the text he had received in Sukuel's, and instead ask him why he had been brought up with no table manners. *Focus, Maggs. You're a spy, remember?*

'Carlos, you told me that you didn't know the girl in the restaurant.'

A slither of bacon disappeared into his mouth before reappearing again as he spoke. 'That's right. I don't know who she was.'

Sod it. If I carry on letting him eat like this, he will never learn. 'It would be so much more pleasant for all of us here if you waited until you finished your mouthful next time before replying.'

Maggie had an ability that only a few people have of being able to raise quite sensitive matters without the other person taking massive offence. She was particularly adept at encouraging parents to do something to stop unruly young children running around screaming at the top of their voices in cinemas and during solemn moments at weddings and christenings. The use of her posh, but firm, voice was the most effective. Comments and questions to the offending parents starting with, 'Isn't this all so lovely?' followed by, 'It's so important that everyone respects the importance of the occasion, don't you agree?' Or 'Children can be so well behaved with the right guidance, can't they?' accompanied by a broad smile usually did the trick. Failing that, the more colloquial, 'For Pete's sake: get a grip of your kid, will you, and stop bloody ruining it for the rest of us,' brought about the desired result.

Carlos swallowed hard before answering. 'Sorry, Maggie. No, I'd never seen her before.'

'Hmm, are you sure about that?' She had the attention of the other three by now who had all leant in to listen. 'Leave your egg for the moment, Carlos, and think carefully. How you answer this next question might well affect the amount of support the Service can give you.' She had no idea if that was the case or not, but it had always been one of her favourite lines when trying to persuade informants. She looked at Joshua who gave her a nod of encouragement. 'Seeing you eat your breakfast has brought back a few more memories of that day at the restaurant. Now I've had time to reflect on the order of events a little more, I think I've worked out one or two things. You slammed your phone down…'

He put down his knife and fork. 'I already explained why. It was because I was annoyed at what the people who were blackmailing me wanted me to do.'

'… and I could have sworn that girl jumped up into her karate pose as the car came crashing through.'

'That's possible. I was too busy dodging out the way of the car. I couldn't say.'

'Right. So neither you or the girl were expecting the crash?'

'I can't speak for her, but I certainly wasn't.'

'So was it the car that made her jump up, then?' *Stupid, Maggs. It's been staring you in the face.* For some reason, she had always thought the girl's reaction had been to the car crashing through. It all happened very quickly, so she had assumed it was a defensive reflex. But now she suspected that was not the case.

'I don't know. I expect so. I told you, I don't know anything about the girl or what she did. Avoiding being killed was high on my priority list.'

She very slowly and deliberately stood up. With four sets of eyes on her, she pulled back her sleeves and said simply: 'Watch.'

There was a pause, and then a quiet, 'Beep, beep,' mimicking a phone ring tone. It contrasted with a sudden loud bang as she slammed her hand on the table. Then, her eyes staring above their heads, she thrust out her left hand – fist clenched and rotated, palm facing up – and tucked her right next to her hip with her fist in a similar rotation. It was the classic 'ready for fighting' position in karate. Maggie held that position for a few seconds before finishing up with an extravagant outward movement of her arms and shouting the word, 'KABOOM!' at the top of her voice. It got the attention of the restaurant, but it was only the non-Arsenal fans who seemed perplexed. The others, having seen her performance in the bar the previous evening, gave a thumbs up or called out a 'Morning, Maggie' and carried on eating their breakfasts. She acknowledged a few with a wave, and sat back down again.

Carlos stared at her open-mouthed. She stared back, convinced that, had he had a piece of sausage on his fork, he would have been waving it around again in front of his mouth. He had not (he was actually sitting on his hands now, after her telling off).

'What was that?' Carlos said eventually.

'That, young Carlos, was a re-creation of a famous restaurant scene, but not the one involving Meg Ryan, Billy Crystal and a fake climax. I save doing that one for W.I. tea parties.'

'What do you mean a re-creation?' The others were still listening attentively; Joshua in particular.

'That was the exact order of events the day the of the car crash. Would you like me to show you again?'

She was answered by vigorous headshaking.

'There was a definite order: a text which you reacted to by slamming your phone down. The girl then got into the karate stance. After that, the car crash. She did what she did in response to your text, not to the car as I first thought. That means she was reacting to you, and not the car.'

'So? Maybe she was distracted by the sound my phone makes when I receive a text.'

'A rather extreme reaction to a text, don't you think? I don't text, as you have probably gathered, but I imagine some of these people in the canteen are receiving texts at this moment. None of them are up on the tables doing Kung-Fu Panda impressions. And before you mention anything about anyone getting up onto tables, Joshua, I was on the table last night for a very specific reason, not phone related.'

Joshua mimicked zipping his mouth closed.

Bill chipped in. 'What are you suggesting here, Maggie?'

Maggie studied Carlos for a reaction, but his face remained inscrutable. 'The girl knew the text Carlos received was important. That's why she reacted as she did. When it went off, she took it as a signal that something was going to happen. She was half expecting it. Maybe it was the warning that the car was about to come through, telling her to be ready to get out of the way.'

Bill had his eyes fixed firmly on Carlos as he spoke. 'Which means Carlos here got the same warning.'

'That's nonsense. If I was being warned that a car was about to come crashing through, why would I slam my phone down? Surely I would just get straight out of there?'

'That's fair,' said Maggie. 'But my point is that the girl, who we think tried to kill me last night and was in the restaurant that day, knew that you were being contacted by someone important. She took the text as a signal to take cover or to be ready to take some sort of action in response to a direct threat. It may or not be true when you say you have no connection to her, but she certainly knows quite a lot about what's going on.'

'Maybe we should arrange to take Carlos in for more questioning, Joshua,' suggested Bill.

Joshua took a sip of his coffee before answering. 'Possibly. Maggie has made a very good point, but I think we can find out more by keeping him with us. I certainly want to keep a close eye on you, Carlos. And if you have any ideas about running off, don't. We can find you again quite easily. And if that isn't a big enough incentive, remember that it's illegal to kidnap old ladies.'

'Any ladies, in fact,' Ben pointed out. 'Or anyone else.'

'Indeed,' said Joshua. 'We'll come back to this, no doubt, but now we need to get ready to get off the ferry and arrange our transport to Amsterdam. Bill, stay here with the others, please, while I enquire at the desk about car hire.'

Maggie had gone quiet while she processed the conversation that had just gone on. Had she been right to raise her concerns in front of all the others? Maybe not, but it had resulted in some interesting, if not so much facts, then theories, at least. It had clarified one or two things in her mind, specifically the timing of things happening in the restaurant. It had also raised more questions, the most pressing of which was one she deliberately had not voiced. Namely that, if indeed the girl had reacted to Carlos's text, then surely that had been the stimulus for the boy with the gun to be next to her as the car came through, that boy being Joshua of course. Which meant there was a possibility that Joshua knew what that text meant too.

What made it even more interesting was that if she knew that he knew what the text meant, then he knew that she knew he knew what that text meant. A classic spy dilemma. *And right up your street, Maggs!*

*   *   *   *

Chapter 14

By the time they were on the motorway, Maggie had already decided that travelling vertically in the front of a spacious Ford Mondeo was infinitely more preferable to travelling horizontally in the back of a Fiat 500. Ben had taken the wheel, and Carlos was sandwiched between Bill and Joshua in the back which, following Maggie's sharing of her theories in the canteen, might have been seen as a sign of a new distrust the group felt towards him. She hoped not. Had he wanted to, there had been ample opportunity for him to escape, for example, as they went through border control. She was convinced he had no reason to do so. He was reliant on her and the Service to help him out, and, besides, would he have the necessary knowhow to just go off on his own and act independently? *Judging by his poor kidnapping skills, no.*

Joshua had explained that Maggie's transformation to Mamma Neumann / Voigt would need time today, plus part of the following the day, then they could move on to Bruges. He had booked a room at a hotel in the centre of Amsterdam, not far from Dam Square. It was an expensive option, and there were currently not enough beds to accommodate them all, but it was all that remained because of the football match. The hope was that they would turn up and take a cancellation if one room, two ideally, became available.

The male receptionist's English, when they arrived, was impeccable. 'Good morning, Madam and Sirs. Welcome to the Koning Hotel. How may I be of assistance today?'

Maggie had had to manage in several languages as part of her work, but Dutch was not one she had got the hang of at all, despite having spent time previously in the Dutch capital. Her experience had been that everyone there seemed to speak English, and to a much higher standard than she could attain in Dutch. She had rarely had the opportunity to use any of the languages she did get by in since she had retired and, like many of her English words these days, much of the vocabulary had disappeared into the recesses of her mind and fallen out the back. But she liked to put the effort in, so those words that did remain she enjoyed putting together to form a totally new language of its own, one to rival Esperanto.

'Guten Tag. Wir haben déjà un chambre mais wir wollen encore dos. Dank u.'

The receptionist, no doubt used to humouring attempts by English people to try out their O-levels in French, German or Spanish, did not bat any eyelid and nodded encouragingly.

'Ce soir, merci,' Maggie added in case there was any doubt that they wanted it for that evening.

'We are fully booked, Madam, but I can put you on our list in case we get any cancellations during the day. In what name is your existing booking?'

She turned to Joshua who was standing patiently beside her, and squeezed her eyes tight shut as she recalled the words she needed. 'Joshua, quel nom pour le zimmer?'

'Maggie. He speaks perfect English, I speak it, and so do you. Why don't we just talk to him in English?'

She folded her arms. 'It's that kind of attitude which is the reason why we're leaving the Common Market. A bit more effort from some people and we might have got on a lot better with our friends on the continent. Mind you, I do accept not everyone has the same attitude as me. Eric, two flats along, has given up eating bacon because he says it's all Danish and the Danes have no idea how to keep pigs. He said he read it in a book somewhere about Vikings. God knows which book. Eleanor from upstairs refuses to travel anywhere outside England. She said that she went abroad once and didn't like it. Turned out it was one of those booze cruises to a Calais supermarket. She couldn't cope with the fact that everything was written in foreign. Not even the cheap fags and fifty pence litres of wine could tempt her to go back or try somewhere else. Little England mentality. I just don't get it.'

'Sir, Madam. What name for your existing reservation, if you please?'

'Tilson. Paul Tilson,' Joshua said, handing over what Maggie assumed must have been a false passport. 'It should be a twin with an extra bed, but ideally we want three rooms now. How long is the reserve list?'

'There are only two potential reservations ahead of you at the moment. I would rate your chances as being good for getting at least one extra room to your booking. Just to confirm, was it dos more zimmers vous wanted?' He looked up from his screen and gave a warm smile to Maggie who immediately decided she liked this man very much.

'As a matter of interest, how many languages do you speak?' she asked while he checked his screen.

'Six, including my native Dutch: French, English, German, Spanish and Italian. Seven if you include Cockney. I like to try it now and again. Ahem… would you like one of our porters to take your crowded spaces to your bride and groom?'

'Very clever Mr....' she peered over her glasses to check his name badge, '... de Haas. Strictly, bride and groom is a living room, but I'll give you that one, and yes, thank y ...'

'... But we have no need for you to take our suitcases or crowded spaces as you quaintly called them,' interrupted Joshua, pulling Maggie to one side. 'Maggie,' he hissed. 'We don't have any luggage. In any case, don't you think we might be drawing a little too much attention to ourselves here? We're supposed to be undercover spies.'

'Nonsense, Joshua. Mr. de Haas is very discreet, I'm sure. Receptionists have to be.' She turned back towards the desk. Before she could engage with him again, Joshua jumped in.

'I'll check in, but leave the key behind the desk for now, please. Will you ring me if the other rooms become available?'

'Of course, Sir.'

'On the old dog and bone?' added Maggie who was mightily entertained by the thought of a Dutchman using cockney rhyming slang.

'Naturally, Madam.'

They made their way over to the lounge area. Carlos looked twitchy, which Maggie put down to general nerves and worry. Again, he had been silent on the journey from the port to the city, apart from a quick word with Bill as they went through passport control which, if she did not trust Bill so implicitly, would have looked suspicious. She decided it was high time he opened up a little more to her. Maybe his tongue needed loosening a little.

'It's already eleven. Does anyone fancy a quick drink?' she ventured.

'Not a good idea at this stage,' said Joshua. 'We are due to meet my contact about two to get you kitted out as Signora Neumann. We need to eat before then, and I could do with buying a change of shirt and underwear, to be honest, having spent the night in these same clothes. I'm sure you boys could do with the same. Maggie, you'll have a complete new wardrobe provided by my contact. Signora Neumann was very particular with the types of clothes she wore, colours in particular. We put it down to her Italian heritage.'

'Sounds good to me. Italians always look amazing in clothes. So stylish. As long as there are flat shoes. I can't handle anything with a big heel on it these days. The height makes me dizzy.'

'We'll see. Anyway, we all need to be on it from now on. Utmost concentration is needed and I'm going to say "no" to having a drink. We can't risk alcohol at this stage. Right, follow me.'

'Understood, young Joshua. Very sensible approach. Just the one then,' said Maggs who was already heading in the opposite direction towards the bar.

Much to Maggie's disappointment, it was just the one drink, although the time in the hotel bar did not pass by without incident.

They had all followed her in, and she and Bill had volunteered to get a round. On the way to the bar, she accidently bumped into a very drunk man in a suit who looked as if he had spent the whole night and following morning, if not drowning his sorrows, then certainly lubricating his tonsils in preparation for tackling deep issues. She was nearly bowled over by the stench of brandy and stale smoke.

'Oi , you stupid cow,' he slurred. 'You've spilt my drink. You should look where you're going.' He stepped even closer towards her before wobbling sideways and spluttering into her face, 'You stupid f-ing bitch.'

Maggie was very tolerant of people when they were drunk – empathy was a strong point of hers, particularly if she had spent the whole night 'empathising' with the person concerned. But there was something in the man's tone that wound her up. Still, she kept her composure.

'I am so sorry for the accident. I do hope that now I've apologised to you, you might be able to apologise for your abuse towards me, despite your inebriated state.'

'I am not inebreestated… inde…inberated. Anyway, as Winston Churchill said: You are sober, but tomorrow, you shall… no… I shall be ugly and you will still be sober. No, that's not right.'

She heard Bill's quiet words behind her. 'Best leave it, Maggie. He looks past it. Come on; let's get the drinks.'

Maggie looked at the man who was swaying from side to side, a glazed look in his eyes. 'You're probably right, Bill. He's harmless enough… I forgive you, young man.' She squeezed past him and started towards the bar.

And that is how the incident might have concluded, had Maggie not been distracted by a broader version of the same man – similar jacket with stains on, drunk as a skunk – who pushed past her and confronted Bill.

'You f-ing poofta. Yes, I said, "poofta". I saw you touching hands with your boyfriend earlier. You and this hag here have spilt my friend's drink. What are you going to do about it? Hey?' The man jabbed him in the chest twice before repeating, 'Hey? Hey?'

Bill caught Maggie's eye and held his hand up in reassurance, as he addressed the man.

'We don't want any trouble. Look, as a gesture of goodwill, I'll leave some Euros behind the bar and, if you're still here tomorrow, have a drink on me.'

'We'll have that drink now, matey, unless you're suggesting we can't hold our alcohol? What, do you think we are queer, like you?' He laughed and jabbed him again, several times, each one with more effort.

It drew a chortle from the smaller man who, encouraged by his friend's bravado, had joined in the abuse. 'Yes,' he said. 'Queero.'

'I appreciate the feedback, gentlemen.' Maggie saw an ominous shift in attitude in Bill. 'Since you are being so honest and frank with me,' he said calmly, 'I will be honest and frank with you, and give you two options. Make sure you consider these carefully. Option one: both of you will step aside now, quietly make your way back to your rooms to sober up, and we'll say no more about this little encounter.'

There was a confused look, followed by a nervous laugh from the larger man before he recovered sufficiently to try to put a touch of menace into his voice. 'And what would option two be, Queero?'

'Option two would involve your friend's empty glass, and your current half full one, being placed firmly up your respective backsides. His brandy glass is a tricky shape, but I'm sure it can be done. In fact…' He paused. '… I know it can be done. As for your tankard with the handle, well…'

Bill left the sentence dangling, as he held the gaze of the man who was a good three inches taller than him. Maggie had never seen this side of Bill before, but she liked it. He stood his ground, cocked his head to one side, and widened his eyes slightly, before returning his head and eyes to their normal position. It was followed up with a smile. *Good lad, Bill. Nice touch.* 'Option one or two, gentlemen? You choose.'

There was a very short moment where Maggie could have sworn both men shrunk by half a foot, before they slinked away. Bill joined Maggie at the bar. She beamed, 'Impressive, young Bill. I couldn't have done any better myself.'

'Thanks, Maggie. You've either got it or you haven't, I guess. You okay?'

'I'm fine. This sort of thing seems to happen to me quite a lot. I must attract trouble. Now, what can I get you? A brandy? Or a pint maybe? They've got some nice tankards here to choose from.'

*　*　*　*

Maggie had to be bribed with the promise of raw herrings at the fish stall in the corner of the square, just to distract her from that second drink. She chatted excitedly as they made their way over. While they were waiting to cross the busy road, Ben admitted to her he would have seen the idea of eating raw herrings more of a threat than a bribe.

'Nonsense! They're lovely. Reminds me of Tubby Isaacs' stall in Aldgate. I used to go up there with my Nan for a treat. It was famous for all types of seafood, but mainly jellied eels. It's closed now, I think. Not quite so popular with the City types.'

'I'm with them. Disgusting!' said Ben. 'Was Sukie serious about selling eels with pasta, do you think?'

'Not my ideal way of eating them, but I enjoyed them as a kid.

We all did. Raw herrings are different though: a speciality here. You should try them.'

Ben's obvious distaste for them could not deter Maggie. She was feeling very much alive at that moment and wanting to make the most of every experience. Eating a smelly raw fish was just one of those experiences, an essential one, as far as she was concerned.

She had been to Amsterdam before, on several occasions, the first time was her maiden solo undercover operation. She had been young and naïve back then, taken aback by the brazenness of the sex shops in the red-light district, but keen not to show any sort of prudishness in case her handler saw it as a sign of weakness. Somehow, she had got through that mission unscathed, mentally at least, if not physically. It was a difficult mission, for lots of reasons, and the whole episode had stuck with her. It had taught her to always expect the unexpected and, more importantly, not to be too quick to make assumptions about others because of what they did or the way they looked. She had met some wonderful people from all walks of life. Her early, rather sheltered life in the East End had not exposed her much to the adult world and she, like many, had grown up with a low opinion of prostitutes. Amsterdam changed that.

One of the sex workers she had met, Marijke, had taken her under her wing to show her around the city. They became firm friends, but it had been difficult to maintain contact because of the nature of Maggie's job. Maggie had tried looking up Marijke on subsequent visits, but to no avail. When Joshua told them they were heading for Amsterdam, she had been tempted to try again, but feared that, as with so many of her other friends, it would only end up in her learning of yet another loss to someone of her generation. She brushed that thought to one side now; it did not do to dwell on such things.

The five of them found a bench in the square to sit down to eat their respective lunches. Bill had joined Maggie in eating the herrings, while the others, having turned their noses up at the delicacy, opted for cones of chips. Carlos, predictably, went for tomato sauce with his. Ben and Joshua chose the more traditional Dutch accompaniment: mayonnaise. The place was busy, mainly tourists, with some locals, including the inevitable cyclists taking shortcuts across the square. There were very few football fans around, just a few in Ajax shirts enjoying the autumnal sun. Most other supporters had, no doubt, headed for the bars to await the evening kick off. Despite the pressures and worries, it was a pleasant place to be right now, Maggie concluded.

Maggie could see that Bill could not quite relax, though. He remained standing, scanning the area as he nervously picked at his herrings.

'Come and sit down, Bill. You don't need to protect me all the time. Joshua said that my would-be assassin is in custody.'

'It's not just her I'm worried about,' Bill replied. 'Don't forget the driver of the car that crashed into Sukuel's was out to get you too. He or she is still on the loose.'

'And has had ample time and opportunity to kill me. They would have done it by now.'

'Bill's right, Maggie,' said Joshua. 'We have to stay on the alert, but, similarly, I don't think there is a direct threat at the moment. Perhaps your cunning disguise as an elderly Gareth Malone in drag, fine tuning the choral skills of two hundred football fans, fooled the assassin.'

'Sarcasm doesn't suit you, Joshua. Besides, if you wanted someone to blend into the background then you picked the wrong person.'

'Isn't that what spies are supposed to do?' asked Ben. 'Blend in.'

'There's ways and means. Spying isn't about hiding away without being seen.'

'Surely it is,' said Carlos who had perked up a touch after sampling his chips.

'I was opting for a subtle, more refined approach.'

Joshua's tone was gentle, but it was clear he was making a point. 'The approach which says, "Here I am on a table waving around a knitting needle, come and get me"? You're right. Definitely very subtle, Maggie.'

'Ah, but they didn't come and get me, did they? I was so obvious, they wouldn't dare. Sometimes, slinking around trying to avoid being got, only means that that's exactly what happens. Anyway, I'm too old to worry too much. If I'm going to pop my clogs, excuse the pun in this location, I might as well do it in the middle of a singsong with a load of mates.' She handed out her plate of fish. 'These herrings are really rather good. Are you sure you don't want one, Carlos or Ben? Joshua?'

There were firm shakes of the head from Ben and Joshua, but Carlos remained motionless, staring out at something in the distance. Maggie noticed first.

'Carlos, you alright, love? What have you seen?' She tried to follow his line of sight, peering into the distance to see if she could work out what had caught his attention. She nudged herself along the bench to get as good a view as possible, easing her shoulder into his. It was only after another nudge which forced the chips out of his hand and he fell off the end of the bench, that they realised something was seriously wrong.

On closer examination, ‘seriously wrong’ did not do justice to Carlos’s status.

‘Dead’ was a more apt description.

*   *   *   *

Chapter 15

Maggie knew from bitter experience that getting rid of a dead body anywhere, but especially in a foreign country, was a difficult challenge. As Joshua made some phone calls, she pondered briefly whether specific bi-lateral agreements between authorities for dodgy body disposals would be needed post-Brexit, or whether it would just come under the auspices of an international trade agreement. Part of her felt bad thinking in such a light-hearted way, but she had learnt early in the Service that tragedies came with the job. Putting a spin on upsetting incidences helped deal with them.

At first, they had thought Carlos's dramatic fall to the pavement was as a result of joking around. But Bill, after checking his pulse and breathing, confirmed the bad news. The pupils in his eyes were actually up behind his top eyelids, and his lips had turned very blue. There was no outward sign of injury. Aware that Carlos being on the floor might draw unwanted attention, they propped him back up on the bench in a sitting position, and waited for Joshua to tell them what to do next.

Maggie did her best to stay strong. She shrugged off a consoling arm from Ben, then immediately regretted it. *Don't be dismissive, Maggs. Think what he's been through.* His unwitting foray into the world of espionage had so far involved being shot at, a startling revelation about the past of his fiancé, and now, someone he had only recently met, had collapsed and died in the middle of Dam Square. Added to that, as soon as Maggie and Bill had started eating the herrings, he had made it clear that the smell had made him feel queasy. He had good reason to look so pale, so she patted his hand, gave him a consoling smile and concentrated on trying to work out what – and who – had killed Carlos.

Her thoughts were soon interrupted as Joshua came off the phone. 'A white van will be here within ten minutes to take him away. Until then, we are to act as if nothing has happened. I'm sorry to be so clinical about it, but it's the best way to deal with a situation like this.'

Maggie knew that he was right, but that did not stop her feeling guilty. She had encouraged Carlos to come with her to meet Joshua. If she had not done that, then he would still be alive now. She had wanted to protect him, help him resolve his difficulties with those who were blackmailing him. Help him to see his family too. Now he was dead, and his children would be fatherless. It was just dreadful.

She had not managed to get any useful information out of him that might help answer some wider questions. Her challenge to him about the timing of events before the car crash had left a tension between them which she had hoped to resolve by pulling him to one side again for a quiet chat. That obviously was not going to happen now. He could well have died resenting her interference. *He did try to kidnap you though, Maggs*, she tried telling herself, but the guilt remained. *Bloody conscience.*

'It looks like poisoning,' said Joshua. 'That's the only possible explanation. A powerful, fast acting one too.'

Maggie had to agree. She had heard of similar cases before, and seen pictures of dead agents who looked exactly as Carlos did now. The eyes and the lips, along with the dramatic suddenness of it all, were a giveaway.

'Where from?' Ben asked nervously. 'The poison, where has it come from?'

There was only one possible source. 'All three of you had chips,' said Maggie. She pointed to the empty space where the chip stall had been. 'Are you two okay?'

'I'm fine,' said Joshua. 'What about you?' he asked Ben whose paleness had suddenly got even worse.

'I'm wobbly because of what's happened, but I don't feel there's anything bad going on inside.' His look of panic was plain to see.

Bill stretched out a hand to him. 'You would have felt it by now if you'd eaten the same thing. It's not the chips... but it could be the sauce.'

Maggie got up and examined the cones he and Joshua had discarded on the floor. They were smothered in white mayonnaise; the one Carlos had dropped was still lathered in red. She looked at Carlos, and had to smile a sad but ironic smile as she spotted a blob of ketchup nestled in the corner of his lips.

The Dutch agents were efficient when they arrived. Carlos was taken away, along with the remnants of the food they had bought, with the promise that tests and a post-mortem would be done quickly and the results fed back. Two agents remained to question the other stall holders about whether they had any information on the mysterious chip seller. They said they would let Joshua know if anything came to light.

Maggie's appetite for the mission had considerably lessened. She tried to force herself to be positive again, but the lack of decent sleep was not helping. She had experienced setbacks before, many times, and had gained a reputation as an agent who could bounce back quickly. And be the stronger for it. Still, she was finding this hard.

The personal responsibility she felt for Carlos' death sat heavily, as did the injustice. She was also struggling to find a motive. Surely, she was the target, not him. And why had the perpetrators waited until now, and used this method? Planting poison into tomato sauce was a convoluted way of killing someone, with risks of failure. Why had he not simply been shot or an accident arranged? The more she thought about it, the stranger it seemed. The proportion of new questions to unanswered ones was ratcheting up to the point where she was feeling very uncomfortable about it, almost overwhelmed. Then there were his children... *Oh God! Poor things!*

Once they had the nod from the Dutch agents that they could leave, they walked back to the hotel and sat in the lounge once more. The receptionist bustled over as soon as they arrived, possibly keen to try out a new slang term, but quickly retreated to his desk. It did not surprise Maggie; the group's mood had changed dramatically compared to earlier.

'I hoped he was coming to tell us we have that extra room available,' said Joshua. 'We won't need two more now.' He turned to address Ben directly. 'This is getting too dangerous for civilians. You should get on the next flight out. Our Dutch colleagues have arranged for us to be tailed while we're here, in case we need additional support. They'll post someone outside our rooms overnight. Thank God they're on board with this operation.'

'I want to stay,' said Ben.

'No,' said Joshua firmly.

'Joshua's right,' said Bill. 'Go home, Ben.'

'Ben?'

'Sorry, Darren. That's Maggie making me say that.'

'Making you say what, Bill?' said Maggie, only half-listening.

A little flustered, Bill continued. 'I thought it was fine you tagging along, but that was reckless of me. I should never have let you come on the ferry to start with. It was the excitement and momentum, I guess. You need to go, please. You're too precious to me to risk you getting harmed.'

Ben had recovered some colour and with it some new determination, Maggie was pleased to note. She wished she could do the same; her eyes were drooping.

'I'm not going anywhere. I have the right to do what I want. Just like you think you had the right to spend the last six years I've known you hiding a secret from me.'

'Ouch. That's a bit close to the knuckle.'

'It's a fact. No more secrets. We're in this together.' They all looked across at Joshua in expectation. Joshua hesitated.

'Come on, Joshua,' said Ben. 'The killers have seen me with you. I could be picked off. The fact is that I'm safer here with three agents than at home on my own.'

'I didn't think of that,' said Bill.

'Well... okay, but only for now,' said Joshua. 'As mission leader, I get to change my mind, if I so choose. At short notice too.'

'Good, that's settled then,' Ben said. 'It's a good job I'm staying. I've seen the way these two flirt with each other.'

Maggie, whose eyes had given up the fight to stay open, imagined she was sitting bolt upright, and she and Bill were smiling back in response to Ben's teasing. In reality, her upper body was in danger of following her nose and chin to check out what was so interesting about her knees.

She felt a hand shaking her shoulder. 'So, what next, Joshua?' said the hand belonging to Bill.

'Quick shop for a change of clothes, for those that need it.'

'Shopping?' Maggie's eyes snapped open.

'For essentials only, Maggie, and then off to see my contact to transform you into a proper Italian woman. It's a twenty minute ride from where we left the car. We can go to the shopping mall on the way to get a few things.'

'Who is your contact? Anyone I might know?' asked Bill.

'Doubt it. She's contracted to us as and when we need help with identity changes. She's an expert on clothing, wigs and make up, and since we needed something a little more solid regarding Maggie's nose, she put us in touch with someone who can provide expert advice in that department. That's why I've allowed an extra morning here tomorrow. Don't worry, Maggie. Nothing too painful, and it's all reversible.'

Maggie took a moment to look at Joshua as he talked. The way he spoke and behaved, the quick decisions he seemed capable of making, and his general confidence, belied his very young looking years. He definitely had the characteristics of his great granddad in that regard. Frankie also always managed to command the respect of much older people around him. She had noticed Joshua's poise when he spoke to the Dutch agents earlier. Even the way he handled other people, like the receptionist and the bursar on the boat, seemed like he had been an agent, travelling and staying in hotels for years. That just did not seem possible based on his apparent youth. It was comforting. So comforting that she felt her head begin to nod again and she closed one eye, as sleep threatened to envelop her once more.

She became fully alert, however, when Joshua told them the name of the contact they were going to see that afternoon.

* * * *

Chapter 16

Marijke had barely changed since Maggie had last seen her nearly sixty years ago. Her warm smile as they embraced at her doorway was exactly the same, as was her voice, the distinctive huskiness exacerbated by a lifetime of smoking. The smell of her, a mixture of a floral perfume with the distinctive Gaulloise she was still apparently hooked on, took Maggie straight back to the times they had spent together at her apartment, and around the cafés and bars by the canals. These days Maggie baulked at the merest whiff of cigarette smoke, but, as they greeted each other excitedly, the smell sat comfortably on her friend, a remnant of happy times in difficult circumstances.

Now, that had been a very tricky case, one Maggie would never forget, even accounting for her memory lapses. Not only was it her first solo one without Frankie, or any other partner, it very nearly became her last case; in fact, her last anything. Her handler had largely left her to her own devices, stating only that she was to infiltrate the Amsterdam sex scene to monitor the movements of Kiril Dimitrov, a stocky Major in the Bulgarian army. He was suspected of reneging on his double agent status and passing back British secrets to Russian contacts. Dimitrov was a regular visitor to the brothels and, judging by past experiences, could be very talkative, particularly once he was fully relaxed. Maggie's cover that she had run away from a violent relationship in England helped Marijke convince her Madame that she should feel sorry for

Maggie. She gave her a job on the front desk at her brothel. From there she was in an excellent position to pick up on any of verbal indiscretions, English being the usual language of choice for the international clients.

It had started well enough with Maggie gradually getting to know Dimitrov a little as his visits increased. However, it soon became clear that he was interested in her not just because she was a receptionist. She had had to be quite firm to hold off his advances and constant demands to the Madam to use her in a more 'proactive' role. Nevertheless, his propensity to be part-inebriated when at the brothel did result in some nuggets of information that Maggie was able to pass on to her handler. All that stopped one cold and wet March evening.

Dimitrov had waited for Maggie to come off her shift and then taken the opportunity to make his intentions violently clear in one of the many dark alleys that ran through the district. Maggie had come out of the encounter with two cracked ribs, a black eye and one less stiletto. Dimitrov came out of it with a broken jaw, a damaged kidney and one more stiletto. Maggie heard later that it had taken a very delicate operation at the hospital to remove her shoe's heel from the centre of his foot.

It was a chastening experience and she was badly shaken. More so when her handler said she should have been more flexible in her dealings with Dimitrov, implying that, as a girl, she should have succumbed to his needs in the interests of national security. 'Lie back and think of England, you mean?' she had said. 'No bloody chance.' Frankie had been furious and was all for both of them resigning from the Service on principle. For Maggie though, once her own anger had abated, it was all part of the learning experience. As with many things in her life, she used it to make her stronger and more determined. *Live and learn, Maggs. Live and learn.*

Marijke's broad smile and friendship had been a beacon of light through some of those darker days. As were her choice of clothes.

'I see you still wear garish pantaloon trousers and hippy tops,' Maggie joked now, holding Marijke at arms' length to examine her, before pulling her back in again for a hug. 'And those round rimmed glasses. Red really suits you.'

'It matches the dyed hair, at the moment, but I am … how you say… fussy, and keep changing colours. It depends how I am feeling. Tomorrow both could be blue.' Her accent was thick, but she had maintained her good standard of English over the years. 'And you, my Maggs. What about you? I see you have been working out in the gym!'

They both laughed. 'It's all muscle, especially around the hips and stomach. I have several six packs underneath all these clothes. Unlike me, you look great, Marijke. So young and vibrant. So colourful! I'm jealous. I don't know when it happened, but now I buy all my clothes from Marks and Sparks, literally all of them. I never used to go there when I was younger. It must be the old person's gene that kicks in at the age of sixty and pulls us in.' She opened up her beige coat and showed off the blue cardigan underneath. 'Why on Earth did I buy this saggy thing? What on Earth possessed me?'

'It is fine, Maggs. You look good.'

'I'm looking forward to being transformed into this Italian Diva that Joshua's talking about. Sophia Loren had better watch out!'

'Hmm… that's not the description I've been given, but anyway, we will see what we can do. Joshua…' She let go of Maggie and moved forward to kiss Joshua on both cheeks. 'It's good to see you again. I hope you are well. How is the basketball going?'

Once again Maggie marvelled at Joshua's ability to be so comfortable in a variety of situations, both social and professional. How and when had such a young man been able to find the time to become on such familiar terms with an eighty year old ex-prostitute (she assumed it was 'ex' anyway) from Amsterdam?

'All good thanks, Marijke. Last time I was here,' he explained to the others, 'Marijke was trying to persuade me to set up a korfball league as a alternative to the basketball league I'm involved in. Nothing doing round our way, though, I'm afraid. People are too set in their ways to try anything new.' He stepped aside to introduce Bill and Ben who seemed, by now, resigned to accepting their 'Maggie-given' names.

'Hello, Bill and Ben,' said Marijke warmly. 'Come through to the lounge all of you. I have all the clothes out ready to go. But first, coffee?'

'A quick one only, please, Marijke,' said Joshua. 'We have to get on.'

'Come now. There's always time for coffee, although tea for you, Maggs, at this time of day I am guessing.'

They followed her through to the back of the house which overlooked a pleasant and well kept garden. Marijke lived on the outskirts of the city in a very nice suburb. The immaculate streets were made up of brick houses with clean, straight lines, so typical of Dutch architecture, and apartment blocks presenting balconies strewn with well kept window boxes. Cycle paths weaved in and out of the roads. Maggie lost count of the cyclists on the way to

Marijke's house, all of them effortlessly meandering along on upright bikes which seemed to float across the tarmac. The last time Maggie had been on a bike was at Center Parcs with some friends about ten years previously. She had ended up in a sweaty heap outside the entrance to the mini-golf, convinced the saddle was some sort of instrument on loan from the Tower of London Torture Chamber.

Everyone they had passed here seemed to have an aura surrounding them, possibly a slightly forced contentment, it seemed to Maggie. *Reminds me of 'The Stepford Wives'.* Marijke's modern and clean apartment was a stark contrast to the hovel she used to ply her trade in years ago and, unsurprisingly, lacked the grittiness and variety of life in the Red Light District. *That isn't necessarily a bad thing,* she told herself.

Marijke left them in the lounge while she made her way into the kitchen. She was gone a few minutes before she came back with a tray holding a pot of tea and a jug of coffee, along with a plate of biscuits which she offered around.

'I love these,' said Maggie. 'I remember you used to go out specially to get them when I was here, and we used to stuff our faces. What are they called again?'

'Speculaas. It's a bit early to have them before Christmas, but when Joshua told me you were coming, I had to go and get some. Take a few.'

Maggie needed no further invitation. She still had the sour taste of the herring from earlier at the back of her throat, and was pleased to replace it with something sweeter. She munched away contentedly while Marijke made small talk with Bill and Ben about life in the suburbs and her obsession with cultivating geraniums.

Bill, it turned out, was an enthusiastic horticulturist, and the conversation began to get quite technical. After the excitement of the day, she quite liked this feeling of the mundane, but she could see Joshua was keen to get on.

Before he could jump in, she asked, 'So when did you give up life on the Game, Marijke?'

'To the point, as ever, Maggs,' she laughed. 'Who said I have? They don't call me the "Hooker of Holland" for nothing.' Ben spluttered into his coffee cup. 'In truth, I stopped many years ago. It became too dangerous. Some of the customers were not nice, and then hard criminals got involved. Gangs. I moved away and tried to make a living at it in other places like Antwerp and even Paris. But it is all the same. I then moved to Maastricht, met a very good man and we had a family. He died fifteen years ago.'

'I'm sorry,' said Maggie.

'It is okay. What about Frankie?'

'I lost him nine years ago.'

'I'm sorry too.' Maggie was quite relieved Marijke carried straight on. Now was not the time to dwell. 'I had already retrained in dress making and made a good living. Then I helped out at the local theatre doing costumes and make up. I was good at it, if that's not too…too…'

'Boastful?' Bill interjected helpfully.

'Boatful, as in full in a boat?'

'No, boastful. With an s.'

'Ah, excuse me. I often get my mixes worded up.' She threw a broad grin at Maggie who returned it with relish. Marijke's creative use of English used to be a longstanding joke between them. Maggie had never been too sure whether her mistakes were feigned, or were genuine misunderstandings of the language. Maggie had concluded it was probably a combination of both. She loved her for it.

Marijke went on, 'I decided to come back to Amsterdam. I was going to retire here, but I got bored. I met a guy called Max at the Sex Club who had connections and said my skills could be very useful. Here I am, working now and again for the Secret Service. I still do the theatre work too, which is very fun.'

'Did you say you met Max in a sex club?' asked Ben.

'Did I say, "Sex club"? I meant to say, "Origami" club. Oh, my memory is so bad!'

Maggie could tell from Ben's face that he was not sure whether she was joking or not. Marijke gave her a look and a raise of one of her eyebrow that suggested it definitely was not an origami club.

'Well, we're pleased you did specialise in a new trade,' said Joshua. 'I'm sure you and Maggie have a lot to catch up on, but can I suggest you do so while you get Maggie ready. I want her in her new role as soon as possible so she has time to adjust. You've seen the pictures we sent you of Voigt's mother, Marijke?'

'Yes, Joshua. I think I can get her looking like her. They are very similar, no?'

'Like peas in a pod. Marijke will be able to give you advice about behavioural quirks too, Maggie.'

'Quirks? What is this, quirks?' said Marijke.

'Little tips on movements and mannerisms, Marijke. We don't have that much on Mamma Voigt, but we have come up with a plan which would excuse any small behavioural anomalies Voigt might be suspicious of. Remember, it's a long, long time since he has seen her, but she's still his mother. He will obviously have strong memories of her. You are the right height, Maggie, and, as I told you before, there is a good resemblance to her. We need to make this as convincing as we can to get you into his inner circle. We'll see how you look after Marijke has got to work on you before deciding if we need any further facial work. I want a quick word with the Dutch Secret Service protection guys who are outside. Come on you two. I suggest you adjourn to the kitchen while we let these two ladies get on.'

'We'll check out your wonderful garden if that's okay, Marijke?' said Bill.

Ben rolled his eyes. 'A stroll round the garden? You secret agents certainly know how to live dangerously, don't you? Or does free membership of the Gardening Club come as one of the perks after a certain number of years service?' His tone suggested he still was not letting Bill totally off the hook for his deceit.

Marijke directed Maggie to a small room off the lounge which was filled with several rails of outfits of all types. Maggie was impressed with the choice. 'I'm looking forward to getting out of these drab clothes and into something more enticing. What have you got for me?' She ran her hands along the rail. 'I quite like this two-piece set. It's a long time since I wore a trouser suit, but I think I can carry it off still. The jacket should cover my wide hips. I quite like the idea of mooching around Bruges and other European cities sporting a bright 1950s or 1960s Italian chic number.'

Marijke's 'Hmm…' in response did not fill her with confidence. Very soon, she found out why.

Ben's hand did not conceal his snigger when Marijke presented Maggie's new image to the three of them. She could see Bill was also trying to hold it together. Joshua looked more serious.

Maggie muttered under her breath as she did a slow twirl round.

'You look very convincing, Maggie,' said Joshua encouragingly. 'The hair, makeup, everything is perfect. It's just your nose that might need an enhancement. You've done a great job, Marijke. Thank you so much.'

'It is fine, Joshua. It was quite easy. I am happy with it. Maggie is not, I think.'

'This is not what I had in mind at all,' said Maggie. 'All black: black top, black skirt, black stockings, black cardigan. Hair done up in a bun. Makeup like I've seen a ghost.'

'The makeup I have put in is supple,' said Marijke.

'It can move around a lot?' said Ben, sounding confused.

'I think Marijke means subtle,' explained Joshua.

'Yes, I think so. Sorry again for my English. I like to try long words, but I'm not always sexsexful.'

Maggie shot a glance across at Ben to see whether he would correct her English. His broad smile, though, suggested he was getting used to Marijke's pronunciation, and indeed probably much preferred it.

Marijke continued, 'It pulls out some of the lady's features, I think. You can do the makeup yourself now I've shown you, Maggie. Lots of white powder.'

'You look fine, Maggie,' said Bill. 'Very respectful… the peasant look is in this year, I'm told.'

'Did you have to dress me up like I've just come out of a funeral?'

'That's the idea exactly,' said Joshua. 'It's a big tradition in the Italian countryside and in many towns for women of a certain generation to continue to wear black for many years after the death of their spouse. We do know her husband, Voigt's father, died a long time ago, before she and Voigt lost contact. Almost certainly, she would have worn black then and it's very possible she could decide to do so again. If he questions you, just say that as you near your own death, it's brought back memories of him.'

'Nearing my own death? Thanks very much! I don't need any reminders. What if he asks more about his father?'

'You can make something up. He left the family home when Voigt was still young.' Maggie's shoulders slumped as she studied herself in a mirror. 'That look is good! Kind of hangdog, sad old mother.'

'Charming!'

'You can brighten up a little bit once you get to know him. But if you tone down things from the start, you will be less conspicuous. They might leave you to your own devices because they won't see you as a threat. Remember, it's not just Voigt you need to convince; he will have others there who may be suspicious of you turning up. The fact you have started mourning the loss of your husband from years ago again shows that maybe your mental faculties aren't all there. If you're caught nosing around in places you shouldn't be, you can put it down to having memory problems and not knowing where you are. So, play the character down. You know the sort of thing: a woman in the twilight of her years who is a bit tired of a world she is soon to leave…'

'Alright, alright. Don't keep pushing the "close to death" stuff. It's already been a hard enough day in that regard. I get the point. I just thought this role might have a touch more allure to it. A bit of glamour maybe.'

'No, Maggie. Subdued is less likely to arouse suspicion…'

'Subdued, really? And you're sure you've picked the right person for that?'

'I'm positive, Maggie. Your record over the years proves your adaptability. If you can work with the CIA to infiltrate drug cartels in South America, then you can do this.'

Maggie had to admit that Joshua had a point. She had survived weeks undercover in the Amazon; surely she could manage a couple of days acting the old woman in Bruges.

'But I don't see why I need to be dressed in black. I look like a demented crow.'

'It's a good cover. You look the part, Maggie. Really you do.'

He's right, Maggs. Remember, you're a professional. You do what you have to.

She voiced a worry. 'I'll do my best with the accent, but what if he speaks Italian to me?'

'He's German. They lived in Germany, so used to speak German at home. You can say that living in America for so long that you've forgotten most of it. That will account for any lapses in the accent too. We don't think he speaks Italian, but if he does, improvise and steer it back to English. You've already ably demonstrated your language skills with that receptionist back at the hotel.'

'Don't take the pi…'

'Here, wear this.' Marijke interrupted, wrapping a black headscarf round her and tying it under her chin. It elicited another round of muttering. 'Pretend you have bad knees when you walk…'

'I do!'

'… and bend your back more,' she said. 'Do you have a stick you could use? If not, I can lend you one.'

'No, I don't have a stick!' she lied.

'A stick would make you seem more vulnerable, less open to scrutiny,' said Joshua. 'Really play on that side of things. Think of times in the past when you've had to lay the old woman scenario on thick.'

Maggie had plenty of examples of those. The old woman act had got her to the front of many a queue: discounts in shops (counting out money for small purchases in one pence and two pence pieces often resulted in sales staff getting impatient and letting her off quite large balances); free jobs around the house from tradesmen visiting to complete other jobs ('I'm having terrible trouble with my shower. When you've finished plumbing in the washing machine, would you mind awfully…?'); and even, on one occasion only, admittedly, it had got her free replacement windows in her flat, after she had heard a salesman had ripped off one of her friends. She had approached him acting very frail, pretending to fall for his slick sales patter, only to claim afterwards (falsely) that she had recorded the whole conversation and would go to the papers unless his company gave her friend her money back. The company had been so frightened that they replaced her windows for free too.

'The suitcase is part of the look,' said Marijke. She produced an old battered case and put it down on a chair, flicking the latches up and opening it. Maggie groaned again as she saw a case full of black clothes. 'Make sure you are vogue about everything.'

'Vague.'

'Vague. Pretend you have memory loss.'

'Pretend?'

'Make it more… how do you say it… announced.'

'Pronounced,' corrected Ben, 'When you want to emphasise something, make it more noticeable, it's pronounced, "pronounced".'

'Pronounced, "pronounced"? That is very confusing.'

'As I explained in London,' said Joshua, 'we will make sure you have the credentials to back up that you are who you say you are: papers, internet story, etc. You, though, are more likely to succeed if you pretend to be vague about details. Forget your name occasionally, put things down and then pretend you can't find them, wander around in a daze in the middle of the night, put your clothes on back to front, leave a pan to boil dry if he asks you to cook. That sort of thing.'

'I do all that all the time.'

'Just exaggerate it then. You're going to do a great job.'

He was backed up by encouraging noises from Bill, Ben, and Marijke who offered a pair of clumpy, black shoes for her to try on. Maggie scowled before quickly putting them in the case.

'Right, well I want to make it clear that I'm not happy, but that I'm doing this for Carlos, as much as for anyone or anything else, now. If this helps get to the bottom of whoever is going around shooting at and poisoning people then I will put up with not being a fashion icon for once.'

'That's agreed, then?' said Joshua.

'Yes, okay. Let me get changed back into my things and we can go to wherever we need to go now.'

'You won't need those things anymore,' said Joshua. 'From now on, you are Signora Colombina Concetta Neumann, "Colo" for short. Get into role and stay in it as much as you can. We'll pop back tomorrow before we go to Bruges, and you can show Marijke the full transformation after the nose-job. She can make any other adjustments. Until then, practise, practise, practise. And remember: your surname is Neumann, not Voigt. Voigt is the false name he's currently using.'

'I'll need a new handbag, I guess. Something that's more in keeping with a shy, fashion-blind, clueless old woman.'

'The one you already own is perfect!' said Marijke with a broad smile.

'Perfect for clouting elderly ex-prostitutes!'

Joshua indicated that it was time to leave and ushered them towards the door. The two friends embraced again while Joshua stood waiting, holding out Maggie's coat ready for her to put on.

'It's been lovely to see you again after all this time, Marijke,' said Maggie.

'You too, Colo. I will see you tomorrow.'

Maggie's fold up stick was still firmly at the bottom of her handbag but, on Joshua's insistence, she retrieved it and did her best to bend her back slightly as they walked down the path to their car. She spotted the unmarked car further down the road with the two agents sitting inside watching them go. It had been a frenetic day and losing Carlos was still sitting heavily on her. The agents' presence gave her some reassurance that their passage through Holland should run smoothly from here. When they got to Voigt's place, that would be a different kettle of fish again, fraught with danger, no doubt. One of their group was dead already. She was not sure she was happy with the possibility of losing more of them, especially Joshua. She had only just found him.

On the more positive side, seeing Marijke again had brought back so many memories of not only her and their friendship, but also the reasons why she had always done what she did. She reminded herself that she was a damned good agent and, as such, would have a beneficial impact on this mission. Her concerns about getting into the role of Colo were genuine, but, as with everything she had always done in the Service, she would apply herself and do the best she could.

She would take on board Joshua's and Marijke's advice about how to carry out the role. They were, after all, professionals who knew what they were talking about. Their views on how she should act the part were entirely sound, so she would listen to their advice… and then do it the way she thought it should be done. *Just like you always do, Maggs.*

'I think that's plenty for one day,' said Joshua as Ben drove them back to the city centre. 'Let's hole up at the hotel until tomorrow. We've got one more visit to make in the morning before we drive to Bruges.'

'Yes, you mentioned something about an enhancement to my nose. Are we seeing a plastic surgeon?'

'Sort of, Maggie. Nothing quite as sophisticated as a surgeon, though. Your nose needs a small adjustment, not so much on size but shape.' He handed her his phone with the picture of Voigt's mother during the phony evacuation of the old people's home in San Francisco. 'What do you notice about the picture?'

Maggie gave her glasses a quick wipe on her skirt and then

focussed on the screen.

'It's a bit blurry, but look at the face. and specifically the nose. Zoom in and you'll see.'

Maggie kept the phone perfectly still and very deliberately lowered her head slowly towards the screen.

'Not like that.' He placed his fingers on the screen and pinched out, enlarging the face.

'Oh yes. That's clever! That could be me, except the nose is all crooked. It looks like it's been broken.'

'Exactly. Just like the real Signora Neumann.'

'You mean...'

'Yep. That's what we're going to see someone about first thing tomorrow morning.'

'Can't wait. You certainly know how to treat a girl!'

*   *   *   *

Chapter 17

They were in the bar again having had confirmation from a different receptionist on the desk that an extra room was indeed available. Their Dutch escorts, a replacement pair, were pretending to relax at a nearby table. Maggie sipped her Tia Maria, her first – and only one – of the evening, she had decided just minutes before ordering another one. In response to Joshua's stern look, she had explained that it was to give her the Dutch courage she needed before she had her nose dealt with.

'That's not until the morning. You can't give that as an excuse; it won't make any difference you having a drink now. Besides, it won't hurt. We're not taking you to some back-street nose-breaker.'

'What about bruising or marks?'

'If it's done properly, the marks will be minimal. Nothing that a bit of makeup won't cover.'

'I still think I need to be worried about it… Danke, dear,' she added receiving her drink from the waiter on a platter. 'Très bien. Leave it ten minutes, then bring me another one, please... What?' she added in response to Joshua's raised eyebrows. 'This is medicinal. The youngsters call it preloading. I'm preloading with enough anaesthetic to help me cope with the potential pain you're going to subject me to tomorrow.'

She put her drink on the table and leaned to the side towards Joshua, drawing him in so that they could not be overheard.

'Something's bothering me a little. Well, a lot actually, Joshua. I know how things work in the spy world. Us workers on the ground get told things on a "need to know" basis. That's only right, to some extent. We work within certain parameters, set by those people who have the benefit of a wider perspective, if not greater wisdom. 'Twas ever thus, one might say, if one was posh. Those who really know what it's like on the ground end up being given the run-around by those who think they know better, but don't.'

'As you say... 'twas ever thus. Isn't that just life, Maggie? Most people in work have to put up with that.'

'True, but there's a lot going on in this case that I don't either understand, or I don't know about it. That's fine because you are guiding me through it, sort of. I'm used to that with the various handlers I have worked with. But they were always as honest as they could be with me. I made sure of that.'

'What's your point, Maggie? Are you saying that I'm not being honest with you? You know that protocol says I can't tell you everything. For example, I knew about your connection with Marijke, but you know that we never reveal our foreign contacts in advance. That's always been the case. Similarly, I can't reveal Voigt's current business address in Bruges. I've only been told it because I need to know it to get us there. You don't. Not yet anyway. That's why they call it, "need to know".'

Maggie was a little irate; she did not want a lesson in Service protocols from anyone. However, getting angry would serve no purpose. She needed to play this conversation carefully, and calmly, if she could. *Think before you speak, Maggs. For once.*

'I appreciate that. But you "need to know"...,' she put her two fingers either side of her head and waggled them in that way some people do to indicate the use of inverted commas. She hated other people doing that, but found now that, having started it, she felt obliged to do it every time. '… that I think I "need to know" a lot more than the current "need to know" parameters. I'm scrabbling around day to day, hour to hour, often in the dark, getting bits of information which either someone is allowing me to know because I "need to know" or I am getting to know them by accident, contrary to the "need to know" parameters. Please help me to stop doing the rabbit ears.'

'Sit on your hands.'

'Good idea.' She did as he suggested, then continued. 'Let me give you an example: Bill revealed that he is working for the Service. Now, was that by accident? Was it forced upon him because of the situation, or were either of you going to tell me anyway? Was it something I…' she withdrew her hands in anticipation of the waggle, but forced them back, '… needed to know? Was the plan to bring Bill over here undercover and hope I wouldn't question that? Just assume he was along for the ride.'

'Maggie, I…'

'He was undercover in Frampton for two years, ostensibly to protect an ex-agent. That's an enormous resource, particularly since you had no guarantees I would do what I am doing now. He wasn't put there just to protect me in anticipation that I might be asked to be called up on this case, however long you may have been staking out Voigt and his cronies. Bill's been undercover, not to protect me, but something, or someone else, connected to me.'

'Bill's situation is... er... complicated.'

'Complicated? In what way complicated?'

'I'm sorry, that's need to know.'

Maggie had always prided herself on her ability to read body language. Joshua's reaction, in that moment, gave little way. However, her instincts told her Joshua was doing his best to tow the official line. But there was something more there. *Is that embarrassment, Maggs?* Or worse... a slight jumpiness – a reaction to being found out, maybe? Whatever it was, he was not prepared to reveal anything more so far.

'Okay, I've got another example.' *Careful, Maggs. Do you want to go down this route yet?... Oh, what the heck!* 'You let Carlos, God rest his soul, take the hit back in the canteen on the ferry.'

'What do you mean?'

'When I was doing my "When Harry Met Sally" scene, trying to pick apart the sequence of events in Sukuel, you said very little. Now, we both know that you were by my side with a gun before that car came crashing through. So not only was Carlos, God rest his soul, and karate girl expecting that text and an attack of some sort, but you were, too. You have not even acknowledged that, yet you know that I'm not so stupid not to work it out. So, by the "need to know" rules,' she gave in to the urge to wave her fingers around again, '… that tells me you think I "need to know" that that text was significant, but I don't yet "need to know" what it said or who it was from. I'm right, aren't I?'

Maggie, much to her frustration, could see that Joshua had opted to take her last question to be a rhetorical one. He remained silent. *I'm right then...possibly.* She took another sip of her drink. Bill and Ben were busy arguing over the route to Bruges, seemingly too engrossed to notice a little bit of tension building across the drinks table.

She continued to probe. 'Bill was supposed to be my

longstanding protector working for the Service. He was in the restaurant then, yet he apparently did not "need to know" that my life was potentially in danger. Yet you – someone who also works for the Service – did "need to know". I'm going to stop saying that. Perhaps I don't…' and she pointedly raised her fingers either side of her head again. 'oh, bugger it... "need to know" that either, Joshua!' She looked at her great grandson before sitting back, exhausted, to await a reply.

'Finished with your bunny impressions?' She nodded. 'Could you please also stop saying "God rest his soul" when you refer to Carlos. You've only done it twice, but it's a habit I want to nip in the bud.'

She folded her arms. 'Fair enough.'

He looked around. Apparently satisfied they were out of earshot, he beckoned Maggie towards him. 'Have you got your hearing aid in, Maggie?'

'I can hear you fine, if that's what you mean.'

'Switch it off for a moment, and tell me what you notice. I'm going to start humming. Tell me if you can hear any difference.'

Maggie was too tired to argue, so did as she was asked. She turned her head a little as she listened. 'You haven't changed how loud you are humming?'

He stopped. 'No. It's the same. Could you hear it okay without your hearing aid?'

'Yes! That's amazing. What's going on, Joshua?'

'You'll understand after I've explained more, but I should say that, officially, this is something you definitely don't…' he mirrored her rabbit ears, '… "need to know" according to our bosses. However, I think you do. And I have done all along, which is why I've been deliberately dropping in a few things in the eventual hope you will be able to work out what's going on. It's getting too dangerous though, so for your sake and those around us, I think you need to kn…' he paused, a pained expression beginning to creep across his face.

'…be more fully in the picture?' Maggie offered helpfully.

'Yes, thank you. You have to understand that I'm going out on a massive limb here, Great Granny Spy.' He waited for her confirmation. 'Listen very carefully, because it's quite complicated.'

Maggie sat there wide-eyed throughout Joshua's briefing. She had heard, and indeed been involved in, many stories of double-crossing, triple-crossing, even double-triple-crossing, but nothing quite as incredible as this.

It turned out that their mission was not a straightforward case of 'infiltrate, assess and disrupt', as Joshua had described it when they first met – although that was still very much part of the plan. It was, in fact, a precursor to something far bigger. If their mission was successful – once Voigt's organisation was brought down – the expectation was there would be massive repercussions. Indeed, parts of the British establishment were a veritable 'House of Cards' waiting to be blown over. Or so he hoped.

Joshua began by fleshing out Voigt's plans and motives. 'We know that Voigt has the names of all the bureaucrats, ministers, leaders of industry who have an interest in the world's computer security systems. Some of them are his clients – *'The List'* as it's been named. These people control their organisations' security contracts. Voigt's intent, with their help from the inside, is to 'hit' their systems all in one go to cause significant damage. In a strong position to influence matters, those on the list will then blame it on illicit hackers and respond to such a breach with the appropriate high levels of outrage afterwards.'

'Let me guess,' Maggie chipped in. 'Those affected will then have to pay to get it fixed.'

'Exactly – we're talking about hundreds of millions of dollars in ransom that Voigt will demand. His insiders will take their own cut, but leave Voigt with a substantial profit.'

Joshua then went on to explain that this was not the only form of corruption. It was thought, initially, that the UK was immune to Voigt's planned security breach – hence the Service was in a good position to stop him. But Joshua now suspected there were unscrupulous government officials who wanted their part in Voigt's potential bonanza. They had been using Carlos to get what they wanted.

'I've looked into Carlos, Maggie. There are stages of his life which are sketchy: poor records of where he was or what he was doing at certain times. We do know that he was considered to be a bit of a whizz with computers when he was a teacher. It's possible that these insiders somehow tapped into all that. I'm speculating that, maybe, he decided he didn't want any involvement, but was then persuaded, using the threat of not seeing his children, to disrupt our plans to infiltrate Voigt's setup by kidnapping you.'

'He wasn't a whizz at kidnapping that was for sure. Surely they would have been better using a professional?'

'True. Maybe he wasn't in Sukuel's originally for that.

Something went wrong and the blackmailers might have panicked.'

'Twice?'

'Who knows?' Joshua said that Carlos had stood firm on providing any specific details to him, even when questioned away from Maggie. *Stubborn to the end,* she reflected. Joshua did not say as much, but Maggie guessed that the blackmailers must be suspects for having disposed of Carlos, fearing that, now he was with Maggie and with Service agents, he might talk and give them away. Working for government insiders would certainly explain why he knew about Peter.

Peter... again. His exact role was still in doubt, but Joshua maintained he had reliable information that, as he had stated when he brought Maggie back into the fold, he was Voigt's right-hand man. Joshua's theory was that he was the one who had gone out to make the contacts in the higher echelons of society and sussed out who would be willing to make a fast buck by compromising their nation's, or organisation's, safety. In other words, Peter was the compiler of *'The list'*.

That was hard to take, so she diverted her thoughts with another problem. 'Okay, what about the karate girl? Is she working for Voigt? Or is she working for these insiders too?'

'Don't know. She could be working for another country who wants to encourage Voigt's actions so that other major government systems are brought down. She's in custody, but there is the possibility that she's not talking to the right people.'

'What do you mean?'

'I mean that there is potential for corruption all over the place, Maggie. I can't discount that some of these insiders are working within the Service. I don't know, but she could be being interrogated by those people, even as we speak.'

'No, not corruption within the Service! Surely Sheldon would know that and put a stop to it?' Despite Maggie's antipathy towards her former boss, she could not see her as a turncoat. She lived and breathed the Service. Always had. Maggie knew that.

'Not if the corruption is above her pay grade.'

First her son being on the wrong side of the law, and now this. Parts of the Service corrupt? The full implications of that suddenly hit her. Her life had been built on truth and trust, even in a dirty world where those qualities were abused. But the dirty world was the bad guys. The Service was the good guys – her moral foundation. As frustrating and bureaucratic as it could sometimes be, it was still *her* Service, and the principles which Frankie had espoused when he recruited her had kept her going through some dreadful situations.

'Any corruption will be tough for Sheldon to take.'

'Which is why we're all trying to put a stop to it. That's where you come in.'

'Stop Voigt...' *and Peter!* '...and bring down the house of cards.'

'Exactly. With the help of a bit of technology in the form of a data chip.'

'Explain.'

'The data chip contains the codes which will stop Voigt.'

'Carlos mentioned something about that. He said I had it.'

'You do.'

'Where? How?'

'It was in your hearing aid.'

'My hearing aid?'

'Yes, we had it inserted at your last check-up.'

'With that nice Mr Ahmed?'

'Yes. He works for us too. Off and on.'

'Mr Ahmed?' *Ignore that, Maggs. There are other things you need to find out.* 'You said it was in my hearing aid. It's not now?'

'Not exactly, no....' There was a pause.

'Come on, you're committed now.'

'When you were in hospital, they put the whole thing as an implant into your inner ear. I was against the idea but was... overruled.'

'An implant?'

'Yes, with the data chip inside. It has two functions: it holds codes that will dovetail with Voigt's systems to stop him carrying out the cyber attacks. It only works within a certain range, which is why we have to get you physically nearby. That same data chip, because it was part of your hearing aid, is able to augment your hearing. All of that was transferred from an external function in your hearing aid to an internal function.'

Maggie harrumphed; one of many skills that she had honed in her dotage. 'And it didn't occur to you to do something about my bloody knees while you were prodding about with my body?'

'I'm sorry.'

'You were going to tell me that I'm the bionic woman when?'

'We weren't.'

'You weren't... Typical bloody Service. Don't tell me it's...'

She glared at him as, with an apologetic look, he put his fingers either side of his head.

*　　*　　*　　*

With her eyes closed, it might have looked to others around that she had just gone to sleep again. She was tired, for sure, but Joshua's revelation about her implant was so mind-blowing it had just made her want to shut down temporarily and give herself a moment to take it all in.

There were many major areas of concern that she could not get her head round, not least the incident that had started the whole thing off: the text that Carlos received. Who was it from, and what did it say that unleashed the whole chain of subsequent events? She felt that if she could get to the bottom of that one, it might answer a lot of other questions. But did she have the energy to tackle it now? *Later, Maggs. Later.*

Joshua gave her a gentle shake. 'You okay, Maggie? You suddenly zonked out.'

She took the glass of water that he held out to her. 'I will be. You certainly like to keep your great granny on her toes, don't you?' She pointed to Bill and Ben who glanced up, smiled, and then returned to their discussions. 'Are those two still bickering over the arrangements for the morning?'

'Leave them to it. They're fine. It's you I'm worried about. I don't want to push you, but is there anything you want to ask me? I'll try and answer if I can.'

Get on with the mission and watch and learn for now. 'Have I anything to ask you? Joshua dear, I have loads. But I'll leave it to just the one question for now.' It was the one that had sprung into her mind – that she had promptly pushed back – the moment he had asked her to impersonate Voigt's mother. Now she was here, and it seemed all the more real, she had to ask it. 'A mother always knows her son. A son always knows his mother. You've put out a few stories on the internet, dressed me like a Sicilian hag, and you're planning to break my nose, or some such. It's going to dupe no one, certainly not Voigt. He's an intelligent man.'

'I disagree. You can do this, Maggie. We have every confidence in you. The preparation has been done, and we believe he might be ripe for plucking. He's had nearly a lifetime away from his mother, and now that he's on the verge of making it really big, he will want to share his success with her. You really are the spitting image of her, Maggie. You saw the picture, didn't you? I've got one or two more I can show you.' He fumbled around for his phone, but she put up her hand to stop him.

Just go with it, Maggs. 'I've had enough for one day. Another time, maybe.'

'Look, don't worry about that side of things. We've got all that covered. The boss has personally made sure everything has been done to make sure you are accepted, particularly in terms of the resources needed to lay the groundwork for the back story. She's been very thorough. As I said, the physical likeness is extraordinary...' He sat forward and held both her hands. 'You're extraordinary, Maggie.' Then he lowered his eyes and cleared his throat self-consciously. 'You're the best agent the Service has ever had.'

There was a long pause as Maggie processed his words. Then she gave him a thoughtful stare before saying, 'You're just like your great granddad – you smooth bloody talker, you.'

* * * *

Chapter 18

A part of her had really intended to get a restful night, to do as she was told. She was exhausted and fully appreciative of the dangers she could put herself in if she did otherwise. Joshua had persuaded Reception to put their two rooms together, and they had an adjoining door which she agreed should be unlocked in case anything untoward happened. He, Bill, and Ben checked her room to ensure all the windows were secure and the entrance was double locked. One of the Dutch agents was posted at the end of the corridor; the other remained in the hotel lobby on the lookout for suspicious activity around there. She knew Joshua was waiting a while until she was asleep before taking to his own bed, a put-you-up in the corner of the men's room. Bill and Ben were planning on taking the double.

She knew she would not need to set an alarm to wake herself up; biological needs would prompt her. It was around three am when she felt the inevitable prodding on her bladder. Rather reluctantly, she slipped into her new clothes, topped up her spare underwear and stockings from the suitcase, grabbed some money and the documents Joshua had given her, and stuffed them into her handbag. She congratulated herself on how quietly and efficiently she was still able to conduct herself after all these years.

She had a quick look through the curtains. Calmness had fallen on Dam Square after the revelries of the previous evening. She smiled to herself at the thought of Dano and Bazza sharing their finely honed choral skills, both in the stadium during Arsenal's win, and subsequently around the streets and bars of the city. Hopefully, they were holed up somewhere safe and warm, but somehow she doubted it.

There was enough artificial light shining through from outside to see what she was doing as she tiptoed towards the door, listening out for any movement from the men's room adjacent. Joshua was right about the clearer hearing the implant had given her; it would come in handy at the bingo on a Tuesday evening at the Frampton Social Club, and it certainly came in handy now. She reached for the latch and began to carefully pull it down, but then suddenly stopped. *There was a reason you woke up in the first place, Maggs, remember? And you haven't got your teeth in, you silly old fool.*

Cursing herself, she carefully retraced her steps to go into the bathroom to do what she had originally intended to do, and also put her dentures in which had been sitting in a glass next to the sink. Her skills in stealth did not extend to preventing silent tinkles and splashes. She decided to go all-out and flush the chain too, on the premise that someone from next door might already have woken up and be suspicious had there not been a conclusion to her ablutions. *Not as slick as you thought you were, Agent Matheson.* It was a practical reminder of her limitations these days. On stakeouts years ago, she would have been disciplined enough to go for quite lengthy periods without needing to relieve herself.

She lay back on top of her bed until she was satisfied a decent amount of time had been left to try to leave again. After what seemed like hours, during which she could not be sure she had not dropped off again, she got up, and made it to the door. Poking her head out, she checked along the corridor. It was clear.

She was well aware an agent had been posted round the corner by the lifts, but she had a plan. If he was still there and awake, she would play the confused old lady on a wander around the hotel in the night, a role that would need little exaggeration and absolutely no practice. If worst came to the worst, he would return her to her room, with no harm done. However, as she peered round the corner, it was plain that some modern agents did not have the stamina of ones in her day, as this agent was fast asleep on one of those rather comfortable chairs often seen placed randomly around smart hotels. She had once overheard a couple discussing the merits of having such chairs. They had complained that they never seemed to be in places where anyone would want to sit for any length of time and were far too low for people with mobility issues to easily get in and out of. Having spent many hours hanging around hotels on various missions, Maggie had concluded they had to be part-funded by Secret Service organisations, solely for the purpose to which this agent was putting it.

As she began to creep past, she reflected that her unusual attire was hardly inconspicuous, especially with the clumpy shoes and heavy heels. Her long black skirt tucked into the back of her knickers would also, to more vigilant agents, have been a red flag – metaphorical and literal, bearing in mind the colour of her underwear – that something was amiss.

She took the stairs – backwards to reduce the chances of anyone mistaking her heels on concrete for a band of clog dancers absconding without paying their hotel bill – and sneaked out of an open fire escape door to the rear, thus avoiding the other agent in the lobby. She was surprised at how smoothly it all went, and before long she was in a taxi heading, once more, for the quiet suburbs of Amsterdam… totally unaware that she was being followed by a black V.W. Golf.

* * * *

Twenty minutes later, she was back in Marijke's house.

'Thank you, Marijke. I knew I could rely on you.'

'It is okay, Maggs. Are you sure this is the right thing for you to do?'

'Yes, especially after what Joshua has told me.'

'What did he say?'

'You don't want to know, Marijke, believe me. Suffice to say that it's as serious as anything I've dealt with before. I've decided I definitely have no choice. The whole thing stinks, so it will be safer all round if I do this alone. I couldn't bring the suitcase with me. Do you have something I can change into later?'

'Yes. I've got a bag with a spare outfit and a few other things you might need, toilets and things like that.'

'Toilets? Ah... toiletries, you mean?'

'Exactly. I see you managed to get out with those beautiful big black shoes on.'

'They were so awkward and surprisingly loud on the tiles of the hotel floor. Where are all the carpets these days? No thought for octogenarian spies trying to sneak around in the middle of the night in a pair of shoes with bricks for heels.'

'It was a good idea to pull your skirt up like that at the back. Stops you tripping over it, I guess.'

Maggie stood up and checked in the dressing mirror. 'Oh, bother. I'm always doing that. I went up for a raffle prize once at a big do in London with my knickers on display.'

'Poor Maggs.'

'And it's okay for me to borrow your car?'

'Yes, it's parked round the corner. A Fiat Cinque-cento. I hope it is alright?'

Maggie smiled, 'It happens to be one of my favourite cars. I don't need anything fancy. I owe you one, Marijke. Thank you.' She held out her hand to take the keys Marijke had picked up from the sideboard.

'I will drive,' said Marijke.

'What?'

'I will drive. I'm coming with you.'

'I can't let you. It's too dangerous. Besides, you are a civilian and not authorised to come on this mission.'

'Neither are you now, Maggs. You are – what do they call it? A robed agent.'

'Rogue. You're not an agent – rogue or otherwise, Marijke.'

'Ben was allowed on the mission. He is not an agent.'

'That's different. Ben is Bill and Joshua's responsibility. I can't be sure I can protect you if anything bad happens.'

'You do not need to. Look, Maggs.' Marijke had her hands on her hips, a sign, Maggie knew from their time together, that she meant business. 'Why did you agree to take on this job? Do not answer that; I know you. It is because you are getting old and you want some excitement in your life. I am correct, no?'

'That's part of it. I have a lot of family issues wrapped up in this too. Anyway, from what Joshua told me last night, I never had much say in the matter. They chose me.'

'But you wanted to be chosen too, yes? It is true. I can see from the sparklers in your eyes. It is the same for me. I am nearly eighty. What more do I have to live for?'

'There's Max at the Sex Club.'

Marijke laughed. 'He died two years ago. Exhaustion, I think. We all do, in the end. Let me come with you. Who knows… after the job, we might meet two handsome Belgian men in Bruges and be – how do you say – whipped off our feet!'

'We usually say "whisked off our feet", but I suppose whatever takes your fancy.' She studied her old friend thoughtfully. 'Do I have a choice?'

Marijke was already putting her coat on and grabbing Maggie's new bag, plus a small one of her own. 'No. Let's go before they realise you are missing from the hotel.'

* * * *

Maggie felt surprisingly alert. In the last couple of weeks she had discovered a real purpose again, something that had been largely absent from her life for many a year, and with it came excitement. She was fully awake, in tune with her senses now, as Marijke drove them down the motorway towards the Belgian border.

Despite some reservations, she was pleased Marijke was with her. She had operated solo many times in her career. It could be a lonely profession from that perspective. But she had always enjoyed the joint missions, ones where she had had to work with colleagues, because they played to her strengths. She had always thought of herself as a good communicator, able to support her teammates when things got tough, and the camaraderie had always been a massive part of the job satisfaction. Although, what Joshua revealed yesterday had made her now doubt some of those she worked with back then.

She had not told Marijke everything, more for her own good as much as anything else. *The dreaded 'need to know'.* And she had not shared her most recent concern that Joshua was holding something back – possibly, a lot back. Whether he was doing it for her own good, or whether it was for another reason, she did not yet know. She desperately wanted to believe it was the former and not the latter, as that led her mind to very dark places. One thing for certain was that she needed to work independently of Joshua, at least for the time being. He had said enough last night about high-level corruption to convince her that was the right decision for the benefit of everyone; for the safety of her family. *For his safety.* When questioned by Marijke how she planned to bring down an organisation like Voigt's singlehandedly, she had shrugged and told her: 'I'll know what to do when the moment arrives.' As for the wider corruption issues, they would follow on naturally. If Joshua was implicated, then so be it. If he was not, then he was best out of the way, out of danger.

Car headlamps intermittently flashed by as they came off the motorway and made their way along one of the smaller trunk roads. It was gone five now, and there was a surprising amount of traffic around, Maggie thought, for so early in the morning. Then she remembered it was Friday, a week day, and people would be on their way to their offices, factories and other work places. She was often awake at this time at home, pottering around in her kitchen, cleaning out the cupboards she had only cleaned out a couple of weeks before, or washing her net curtains for the second time that month. Anything to keep herself busy until the sun came up and she could feel connected to the world again. The nights, in particular, could feel very long.

But this was much more like it! She allowed herself a little smile of satisfaction as she glanced across at Marijke who, with her confidence behind the wheel, her brightly coloured hair, and her unconventional way of dressing, seemed so much younger than the two and half years difference that actually existed between them. Maggie looked down at the drab clothes she was in but, if truth be told, would she be wearing anything much more flattering if she was choosing from her own wardrobe?

'How do you keep yourself looking so young, Marijke?' she asked. 'You were into all sorts of substances when we were together last. They don't seem to have had any effect on you.'

'The pimps used to make us take those things. As soon as I left Amsterdam, I had much more control on my life. I refused to work for a pimp anymore. I was much more, um, classy. I was a call girl, working for an agency. It was much more easy and safer, but it did not stop me getting amused by men now and again.'

'I think you mean abused. It's different from amused. That means funny.'

Marijke's face wrinkled in disgust. 'It definitely was not funny. There were some horrible men.'

'It sounds tough.'

'It was, and it was not. I made good money as a call girl, enough to eventually give up. I came off the drugs and started a new and better life.'

'I'm pleased for you, Marijke. I've always worried about you.'

They said nothing for a few minutes, a contemplative silence which Maggie would normally have been comfortable with but, for some reason, was not today. It was finally broken by Marijke. 'Go on, ask me.'

'Ask you what?'

'I may not have seen you for many years, Maggs, but I know you better than you know yourself. I see it in your eyes. The only thing that is stopping you asking me is that you do not want to hurt me. You will not hurt me, so ask.'

Marijke had adjusted the rear view mirror so it was angled towards Maggie. She was glancing at her now every now and again while keeping a watchful eye on the road. Maggie knew she was being probed, challenged. Marijke's scrutiny took her back to the many hours they had spent together just talking, sharing feelings and experiences, enjoying one another's company, being friends. Marijke had always had an uncanny knack of working out what Maggie was thinking, often before she had done so herself. She was right: Maggie did have a nagging concern about her old friend.

'Okay, smarty pants, and I mean that literally with those flowery leggings you are wearing, I will ask a question that has been vexing me, just a little bit. Here goes... Does your role in all of this go beyond simply being asked by the Service to supply and fit my outfit? In other words, have you been told to look after me in case I went off on my own? And you're right. I do feel bad now.'

'You feel bad because you cannot fully trust me.'

'Yes. No. Oh, I don't know! I want to trust you, and I do, sort of, of course... maybe. But this mission has had more twists and turns than my underwear on a fast spin. I'm finding it difficult to trust anyone. Sorry.'

'That is good you ask me. I wanted you to. It is now out in the open. It has been a long time, and a lot has happened since we were together in Amsterdam. We have both changed. I might now have … er… exterior motifs.'

'No, you'll have to help me out there. "Exterior motifs"?'

'When you have other reasons for doing something. Exterior motifs.'

'Oh, I know. Ulterior motives! Good one.'

'I'm sorry again for my English.'

'No, don't be. So… have you got exterior motifs? Were you just employed by the Service to make me look like Al Capone's great aunt, or have they got you doing something else too?'

'It is just the Al Capone thing. I promise. It must be hard for you to believe anyone at all, at the moment. I hope you can believe me. I have no proof but that we are the oldest of friends.'

'That is more important than proof, so I will say that I do trust you. I'm pleased I asked you, though.'

Marijke took one hand off the wheel and squeezed Maggie's. 'Me too. It has helped to clean the hair.'

They came off the main road to stop for a rest and find something to eat. Maggie had not noticed they had crossed the border some miles back, and it was only because she now saw signs in both French and Flemish that she realised they were in Belgium. Marijke pulled up at a McDonald's on the edge of an industrial area on the outskirts of a small town, an area that looked exactly the same as any other industrial area in any town in any country in the world.

'I'm sorry it is not more typical Belgian,' said Marijke as they got out the car. 'I like the food here though. It's not good for you, but it does the job.'

'It's my first time.'

'What? You've never been to a McDonald's? I don't believe it!'

'Never, I'm proud to say. We don't have one in Frampton where I live, and I've never had cause to go in one anywhere else. I think it's the clown that puts me off. Scares the willies out of me.'

'Scares the what out of you?'

'The willies. Hard to explain that one. Anyway, I'm proud to say that a McDougal's has never passed my lips.'

'McDonald's. Well, now is your chance. I suggest also that you try out your Italian old lady act.'

'Really? Now?'

'Yes. The plan is still to be Voigt's mother, yes? So now is a chance. Pretend you speak no Flemish or French.'

'Pretend?'

'Are you going to use your stick?'

'Do I have to?'

'It will be better. Remember what I said about moving slowly, and bend down more than usual.'

'I'll see what I can do.'

They emerged twenty minutes later with two brown bags, full of food and drinks.

'You could have helped. Flemish is virtually the same as Dutch, isn't it?'

'I could, but you have to practise. You did okay in the end. We got some food.'

'Nothing of what we wanted though. It was embarrassing when they got one of their staff from out back, the Italian girl, to come and take the order. I didn't understand a word of what she was saying!'

'Big Mac is the same in any language.'

'But we didn't want Big Macs. You're a vegetarian for a start.'

'I'll eat the fries.'

'And what on Earth's a McFuzzy?'

'A McFlurry. It's a type of ice cream with lots of candy. I can eat that too.'

'Chips and ice cream for breakfast. Hardly appetising. And I won't manage five chicken burgers. That girl asked so many questions, none of which I understood.' Maggie looked in one of the bags. 'There must be half a dozen cups of I don't know what in here.'

'You should not have kept saying, "Si," to everything.'

'My Italian vocabulary, as I keep telling everyone, is limited. I didn't like to refuse, in case we missed out. Oh... if I can't manage this, I don't know how I'm going to pass myself off as Voigt's mother.'

'You will be fine. I thought you did "confused old lady" very well. Maybe not so much of the Marlon Brando Godfather next time though. There is a famous part in the film. What is it?' She puffed out her cheeks, furrowed her brow and nodded in a mock exaggeration of Maggie's 'Brando' likeness. 'Revenge is a dish best served cold.'

Maggie collapsed with laughter, holding her stomach. 'That's hilarious in a Dutch accent!' She returned the favour, hunching her shoulders and cocking her head to one side, before drawling, 'Big Mac is a dish best served cold.'

Eventually, they managed to stop laughing enough to get back in the car. Between mouthfuls, Maggie aired her concerns again. 'Seriously though, Marijke, I am worried. Joshua revealed something to me which cemented my decision to go it alone. He and I both knew from the start that me going in there pretending to be Voigt's mother was fraught with difficulty. I'm being set up by someone to fail. He knows it, I know it. If Voigt does not already know it, he soon will.'

'Then why do it?'

'I've got to try. '

'Is your Joshua a bad person? Are you sure, for example, that he is really your great grandson?'

'No, he's not a bad person, and yes, I do believe he is my great grandson.'

'Yet, you do not trust him.'

'I don't trust him enough to make the right decisions for himself. He reminds me of my Frankie. A bit of the, "Fools rush in where angels fear to tread". He's no fool, but I feel that he has a reckless side to him that would make him do foolish things, especially where I'm concerned. I don't know why, but I feel I need to protect him.' She paused while she thought that one through. 'On second thoughts, I do know why: he is part of my family, and I've only just found him. I've already given up one member of my family.'

'Peter.'

'Yes, Peter. I don't want Voigt or anyone else to get a whiff of Joshua's involvement. I couldn't bear to lose him.'

'It will be hard to protect him. He will work out where you are going and find you.'

'By then it will be too late. I'll already be in. That's what I hope, anyway.'

'And how are you going to contact Voigt? You said you do not know where he is.'

'No, but if I get near enough to him, something tells me he might be able to find me. Come on. We best be off.'

As they left the car park, Maggie made a point of using the wing mirror to check behind for anything that might be following. There was nothing obvious, but she did not see the black VW Golf which was parked in a side road opposite the exit to the car park. The hire car containing Joshua, Bill, and Ben had been tailing her since she had left the hotel.

Two hours later in the centre of Bruges, she still had not spotted they were on her tail. She also had not spotted the one way signs which resulted in her and Marijke ending up on a canal towpath, too narrow for anything other than pedestrians, bikes and very small Italian cars.

And far too narrow for a VW Golf.

They arrived in the main square after leaving the car 'parked' very conveniently close by. Marijke insisted that it was too small to be noticed, placed as it was between two skips in a new pedestrian area currently under construction. Maggie was highly dubious about the legality, but was very grateful for the short walk. They found a bench and sat while they got their bearings.

The Belfry dominated the square, its octagonal upper tower sitting on top of the more traditional lower tower with its four spires and perpendicular lines and arches. Even on a cloudy day, it looked impressive as it stood guard over Bruges' medieval buildings. Dots of people – the first visitors of the day – could be seen taking in the views of the city from the top. On another day in a different situation, Maggie reflected how she might have liked to have been one of those dots – assuming there was a lift to get to the top.

'Well, we made it here. Thanks for your help, Marijke.'

'No problem. But I have an important question: how do you know Voigt and his people will meet you here?'

'Don't you watch any spy films at all, Marijke? There's always a scene that's based in the main square, usually starting in a café, and usually involving a car chase which happens because the bad guys realise the good guys are there and have the micro documents on them. Either that or a third party has them. Then they get shot at and killed by the baddies, and the documents fall into the wrong hands.'

'I hope that does not happen here, Maggs. I'm not sure we are quick enough to get away from anyone in my little Fiat.'

'After what we've just managed along the canal? It was just like the Minis in the Italian Job. You know the film. Ahem…"You were only supposed to blow the bloody doors off!"' Marijke's blank look told her that, either she had not seen it, or Maggie's Michael Caine impression was as bad as her Marlon Brando. Maggie quickly moved on. 'Talking of Italian jobs, are you sure I look the part?'

'You look fine. Keep the scarf on and remember, do not make a fuss. The aim is to keep a low profit, Joshua said.'

'Profile. He said to keep a low profile.'

'I still do not understand how you are going to make contact with anyone. It all seems miss and hit to me'

'Miss and hit is as good as it gets at our age, Marijke. Say goodbye to me now in case we're being watched. I don't want you implicated. Give me a polite wave and smile, as if we've only just met and you've been showing me how to get here.'

Marijke did as she was asked and turned away. Maggie made her way over to one of the cafés on the edge of the square, and sat down at a table. Out of the corner of her eye, she saw Marijke, after some feigned hesitation, take a circuitous route round to sit at a table further back, to the right of Maggie's. It was midmorning and the tourists were already out in force, wrapped up in more layers than the ones Maggie had seen the previous day in Amsterdam. The weather had taken a turn for the worse, and rain threatened, but her table was covered over and there were outdoor heaters warming the space. She was thankful for that.

'Uno tea, with latte, per-favore.' Maggie asked a passing waiter. She casually looked round and was greeted by Marijke mouthing, 'Speak English, speak English,' her hand rubbing the side of her face in an attempt to conceal the communication. Maggie nodded. She found it hard. She had done some practice speaking in an Italian accent with Joshua – a little on the boat, on the car journeys and at the hotel last night – but it did not come easily to her. *Relax, Maggs. Go with the flow.* She would need to for what she had in mind next.

Her tea arrived and she mumbled a 'sank-you' in English, before taking a sip, followed by a few deep breaths to steel herself. *Time to get into role, Maggs.*

She then took a photo from her handbag and held it out in front of her, imagining it was her deceased German husband, Kurt, rather than what it actually was; a snapshot of her with some girlfriends on the beach at Margate in 1973. She stared at it intently for a minute or so, taking sideways glances and watching for possible interest from those around her. Seeing none, she decided to up the ante.

Sobbing quietly and with a look of deep sorrow on her face, she clutched the photo to her chest. Eventually, a quiet wailing developed – an, 'ai, ai, ai', complemented by a gentle rocking movement backwards and forwards. Every now and then, she looked up to the heavens, continuing to discretely check around her as she did so, lifted her right hand next to her head, and waved it backwards and forwards, as if chopping very small tomatoes in midair. For added effect, she muttered random Italian words that she knew, under her breath – 'Mamma-mia, spaghetti, Roma, quatro, pizza, Cornetto' – and the odd phrase in English: 'My 'usband, I miss 'im so much!'. The intensity grew as she threw in a few more gut wrenching sobs and clutched her stomach in pain.

By now, she was attracting the attention of the odd passerby. She overheard a comment from an English woman as she walked past with her partner, her voice full of concern.

'Is she alright do you think, Tim?'

'I should think so,' came the unsympathetic reply. 'Looks like she's Italian by the black garb she's wearing. Probably just found out she's got a hole in her tights or something. Either that or she's won the Euro Millions. Hard to tell with Italians. Emotional lot.'

Looks Italian, eh? Encouraged, Maggie exaggerated her movements and the volume increased. She kept the language simple as she called out, 'Ai, ai, ai! Mamma-mia. My 'usband. Non, non. Mamma-mia,' throwing in the odd disbelieving shake of the head for good effect.

Maggie ventured a look behind her at Marijke who was still in her seat. Her expression, a mixture of embarrassment and horror, made Maggie pause momentarily. *Oh well, Maggs... in for a penny...* She shrugged before continuing with renewed vigour, unaware that, actually, her efforts were having the desired impact.

Across the square, a man stood nonchalantly smoking a cigarette and occasionally checking his watch. He had been there since the very early hours and was incredibly bored. He became more interested as Maggie's performance attracted attention. Tossing his cigarette stub to the floor, he moved a few paces closer to get a better view, before stopping next to a bench to get out his phone from his back pocket and pressing a contact for a speed dial. He did not have to wait long for it to be picked up.

He spoke a few words which Maggie would have been delighted to hear before hanging up.

'She's here, Mr Voigt. Your mother's arrived.'

*   *   *   *

Chapter 19

Eventually, a tap on the shoulder from the waiter, followed by a sympathetic smile and a polite enquiry as to her wellbeing, persuaded Maggie to quieten down, and she returned to sipping her tea. As she drank, she looked up, squinting through her spectacles to check the square for any obvious signs of Voigt.

She was interrupted by Marijke who sat down at an adjoining table.

'Maggs, what are you doing? Why did you do that?'

Maggie hissed a reply. 'Marijke! I told you to stay away. You're supposed to be just watching, not getting involved. You're drawing attention to us.'

'Me? I did not shout and throw my arms everywhere!'

'It was all under control. I'm an Italian woman in mourning. Now, move away before they see us talking.'

'Maggs, that was too much. Joshua said you needed to be quiet, not noticed.'

'But that's the whole point. I do need to be noticed. Otherwise, they won't come and get me. I'll do it my way.'

'I'm sorry, Maggs, but that was not a very good performance. It was like a comic character.'

'The British couple who walked past believed I was Italian.' Marijke's steady gaze back suggested that that was not necessarily a good barometer of how realistic she had been. 'In any case…' she deliberately flicked her eyes to her left and nodded, alerting

Marijke to the green Range Rover that had pulled up in the corner of the square closest to the café, '… it worked.' A burly man got out, spoke to another man by a bench, and then they both started heading towards them.

Maggie rummaged around in her handbag, taking out a few things before eventually finding her handkerchief. She blew loudly into it, then opened her purse and put down a ten Euro note to cover the cost of the tea. Slowly, she eased herself to her feet. Once straight, she did up her coat and tightened her scarf, before grabbing her stick and picking up her holdall, making ready to leave.

'Your phone,' Marijke whispered as the men got closer. 'Joshua said you had to have it with you all the time.'

'I don't know how to use it. You have it.'

The men were just a few meters away, so she made a point of smiling at Marijke and saying loudly, 'Sank you so much, Signora. I am so grateful for your 'elp and kindness. I 'ope I see you again sometime.'

Marijke did a curt nod towards her before replying, 'I hope so too, Madame. And I hope you meet your friend.' She remained seated and pretended to be busy looking at the menu, as one of the men spoke to Maggie.

'We saw you were upset. Can we help?'

Four minutes later Maggie was sitting in the back of the Range Rover. Had she turned round as they sped away, she might have seen Marijke standing in the corner of the square trying to work out how to turn on Maggie's mobile phone so she could take a photo of the car.

She might also have seen Joshua arrive with Bill and Ben, and witness a rare sign of frustration on Joshua's part as he explained to the others that Maggie's phone had the tracker device in it.

* * * *

'Dis is very nice of you nice men to take me to Lucinda. I do not think I will find where she lives without your 'elp.'

The two men in the front of the car had acted the part of good Samaritans when they picked up Maggie, but had said nothing more after their introductions and the offer to take her to meet her friend. For Maggie's role to be credible, it was essential that Voigt believed he had found her, rather than the other way round. As a result, Maggie was sticking to one small part of the agreement with Joshua, namely to peddle the story that she was in Bruges to visit an old friend, Lucinda.

The plan was that she bump into Voigt by accident (at least from her perspective) and be surprised when she found out he was her long lost son. The carefully contrived internet stories and links had her travelling in Europe after recovering from a short bout of illness in the U.S.A. There had been a brief exchange via email between Maggie's character, Colo, and Lucinda, making arrangements to meet in Bruges which they knew had been intercepted. The Service techies were confident Voigt was already 'hooked' into her, as it were, and was keeping an eye out for her in public places, such as the Square. The hope was that it would not take long for him to find her.

It was a subtle plan, Joshua had been at pains to reiterate, and needed carrying off with precision and skill. Maggie's not-so-subtle performance in the Market Square had lacked precision, but had the desired effect of making contact quickly, which was exactly what she wanted in order to get ahead of Joshua, and so keep him out of harm's way. She was operating on good old-fashioned instinct, and had been as soon as she had left the hotel room in Amsterdam.

Uppermost again in her thoughts as they drove along was how long Voigt, when they eventually met, would be convinced that she was his mother. Was Joshua right when he had said that he was 'ripe for picking'? Maybe, and hopefully, he would be fooled for long enough for her to work out what, on a deeper level, was going on in his organisation. She was still wrestling with what that deeper level could actually be. *Corruption of some sort, Maggs, that much Joshua told you.* Joshua had given little more away, reluctant to say precisely who he suspected was involved. His reticence still bothered her.

It made her wonder whether she could still trust Joshua. *Yes, because you have to trust someone, Maggs. He is part of the family.* Family. She smiled at the thought of her and Marijke joking around outside MacDonald's doing their *Godfather* impressions. Putting her hand flat to her chest now, she lifted her chin up, and looked down her nose in what she perceived as a welcoming, yet slightly threatening, Mafioso manner.

'Hey, you're one of us, Joshua. You're family now.'

She stopped, hastily sucking back in her Brando cheeks. *Did you just say that out loud, Maggs*?

There was a slight turn of the head from the passenger seat.

Bugger! Yes you did! Quick fix it. She coughed and directed her comments more loudly towards the front. 'Yes, family... I… I missa my family now…' She patted her chest again. *Pathetic!*

She waited on tenterhooks for a reaction, but the silence

remained. Relieved, she forced Don Corleone's mob from her mind, and told herself to fully concentrate on the character she was supposed to be. *Remember, Maggs, be subdued... be subdued. Not the Godfather... not the Godfather...* She let out a sigh.

'I visited here with my 'usband many years ago. That isa why I am so sad in the market,' she said. 'Many 'appy memories, but so sad at the same time.'

Nothing again from the front. In the continued absence of conversation, she decided to get out her knitting. There was something about the repetitive click clack of the needles that she found comforting, but she could see from the slight twitches emanating from the passenger seat that the man found it anything but soothing. She had taken an instant dislike to his rather abrupt manner from the start. His attempt at politeness in the market square was forced, and she judged that his dark side was probably a lot darker than most. He was what she would call, in old fashioned parlance, a *typical hood.* He likely did what he was told, had no need to think for himself, and would not hesitate to wring the neck of an innocent bystander, providing he got paid at the end of it. His muscles had muscles, she guessed, looking at his ill-fitting suit. Muscles he no doubt put to good use on a regular basis.

She turned her attention to the other man. *Muscles'* partner was a much slighter version, but in many ways more menacing. She had noticed he had barely taken his shifty, rat like eyes off of her from the moment they had met in the square. Even now, she could see he was observing her in the rear view mirror as he drove them out of the city centre. Some would have found this intimidating. Maggie just nodded and smiled whenever she caught his eye, and went straight back to her knitting. She was not going to be intimidated.

I've met your kind before, Ratty.

She put her knitting on her lap and looked at the changing view outside of the car. The old charm of the buildings and canals in the centre had given way to a more modern outlook as they headed to the suburbs, and she guessed that they were now on the outer edges of the small city. It was clearly an affluent area, with a large variety of sprawling houses of different ages, shapes and styles hidden behind large wrought iron gates with fancy walls and fences. It shouted out wealth and power.

She tried again to engage her hosts. 'It isa very nice here. Si?'

It earned Maggie another ratty glare in the mirror. So far he had said nothing at all, having left his partner to do the very limited introductions back at the square, and she had no idea whether he was a local, English or some other nationality. Muscles had already given away his possible origins, his twang suggesting a New Zealand heritage. 'Yis,' was all he said now as he continued to stare to the front.

As the journey progressed, she noticed Ratty paying more and attention to her in his mirror. There was the occasional narrowing of the eyes, a twitch of an eyebrow, the odd slight inclination of the head. She knew the signs: something was bothering Ratty and he was checking her out.

She pulled out her compact case, looked in the mirror and nearly let out a yelp. *Your nose!* She had seen the original pictures of Signora Neumann, and they had discussed how the crooked nose was a prominent feature. She had left Amsterdam before anything could be done about it. *You are a bloody idiot, Maggie!*

She deliberately dropped her compact case – 'Whoops!' – and bent down to rummage around for it to put herself out of the line of sight. Panicking somewhat, she grabbed hold of her nose and twisted it in an attempt to alter its trajectory. She sat up again, gasping with the effort, and checked her mirror again. There was no change.

One more go. 'Oh, no! Now it'sa my kneeting needles.'

This time she pulled really hard from side to side, before coming up for air again and opening up her compact once more. She still had a perfectly straight nose, but now it was a very red, perfectly straight nose. Ratty's glances in the mirror were still as frequent, she noted, but she had underestimated the versatility of his expressions. What had previously been rather one-dimensional contempt and menace was now layered with confusion. Hurriedly, she smothered her nose with as much powder as she could – *that's right, Maggs, turn it crimson first, now point at it over and over again with a pad covered in white powder, that'll draw their attention away* – and spent the rest of the journey with the knitting right in front of her face, pretending to study the stitches.

She felt relieved when they stopped outside large silver painted gates, and Ratty leant out the window to buzz for entry. They drove through. Compared to some of the other houses she had seen on the way there, Voigt's was not as large as she had imagined it might be. The driveway was impressive, sweeping round in a semicircle to another gate, but the gardens either side showed signs of, not so much neglect, but more lack of love and attention. The lawn was quite short but, there were no flower beds to speak of, suggesting it was a functional place, maybe with a regular turnover of inhabitants. The two storey house itself, a fairly recent build she guessed, framed a decorative blue door, a bit too large and fancy for a habitation of this type. *Hardly a master crook's lair,* she thought. She wondered whether it could be temporary, rented accommodation while Voigt was based in Bruges.

Muscles opened Maggie's door and invited her out of the car towards the covered porch, indicating that he would take her holdall for her. She smiled and thanked him, self-consciously touching her nose as she got out. She had had a final check in the mirror as they arrived and decided that it looked better with a touch of red showing through. *Don't stress: you'll think of some excuse for having a warning beacon in the middle of your face.* Ratty remained in the car.

'I cannot wait to see my Lucinda. Isa she inside?'

'Yis,' came the uncertain reply again as Muscles opened the blue door.

Maggie was ushered into the hallway and was asked to wait while her escort went through another door. She felt surprisingly calm. Apart from the nose and Ratty's obvious suspicions, she was as confident as she could be in her disguise. The accent was not perfect but it would do, and she felt (worryingly!) comfortable in her widow's clothes.

But as the far door in the hallway began to open, and she heard the deep tones of a German accent filter through, she had a sudden moment of self-doubt. *What if your son Peter follows Voigt out? What will you do then?* It was a distinct possibility. She shook herself. *Stay calm. You've done this sort of thing before, Maggs.* She undid the top button on her coat, then did it up again, before adjusting her headscarf – conscious acts to force herself to focus on maintaining her composure. She reassured herself it was going to be okay. And then assured herself it was not: *It's not as if you got rid of the backup and thrown yourself into a situation where you don't know what's happening, is it?*

But actually, she realised, it was going to be okay. This was what she was here for. She was in a game, the spy game, and she had played this game hundreds of times before in her long career. It was a game where she and the other players were trying to outmanoeuvre one another, a game of second, third and fourth guesses about what your opponent would do next. A game that required stealth, cunning and determination. She was good at determination. As for the other two… well she would soon find out if she still had what it took to be a good spy.

Anyway, games had rules, she reflected as the door fully opened. She was good at following rules too, even if they were not as clear as she would ideally like them to be. She put on her best Italian Nonna welcoming smile and got ready to meet her long-lost sons: real and fake.

* * * *

Chapter 20

She had never met Voigt in person before, since her role on that mission, many years ago, had been as a remote handler. She had been in a management role – a role she never took to so never repeated, preferring to concentrate on field work from then on. At the start of this mission, Joshua had shown her a recently taken zoomed in shot of Voigt sitting in a café. The face, she had decided then, had not changed much from what she could remember of the countless images that would have been produced by the surveillance team all those years ago. But, as he came through the door, she was convinced, based purely – and illogically – on the size of the glass of beer on the table in Joshua's picture, that he should have been a lot taller than he actually was.

She was struck too by how young he looked. He had to be in his late sixties or early seventies, but he seemed at least ten years younger than that. She stooped a little lower as he approached, reminding herself she was supposed to be twenty years older than him. Something else she had not realised about him previously was how incredibly blue his eyes were. Such was the depth of colour, she wondered if they were actually real and not some fancy contact lenses. His short hair was greying at the sides only – *the rest has got to be dyed* – and he had a long fringe which he kept flicking back. There were few signs of wrinkles in his skin, despite the deep tan which just stayed on the respectable side of 'sun bed' orange.

Two other people followed him through the door – a man and a woman – but Maggie was concentrating too hard on Voigt to take in their details. He did not take his eyes off of her as he got closer, the deep blueness almost sucking her in. *Hold your nerve, Maggs.* He was now less than a couple of paces away, and she was tempted to say something. She held off. He, too, said nothing. A twinge in her back (the angle she was at did not suit her posture) made her flinch, but it gave her the opportunity to look away for a brief respite from his intense gaze. To her surprise, when she looked up again, she saw a tear. It was followed by a sniffle and then a huge smile, before he turned round to address the others in the hall.

'It is her. It's certainly her.' He turned back towards Maggie, and held out his arms, ready for an embrace. 'Mamma. It's my Mamma.'

His reaction threw her. She had hoped he would accept her, but she had not expected such a fulsome welcome. It was all she could do to stop herself saying out loud her thoughts which were: *Blimey, Maggs, this might actually work.*

Instead she said, 'Scusi. I do not understand. I ama here to see my friend, Lucinda.'

'Mamma, it's me. Your son. Little Chrissie. Christian. Don't you remember me?' He had stepped back now, but his hands stayed in contact, lightly clutching her wrists. 'Surely, you must recognise your own son?'

Recognise her own son? Now there was a question. The other man with Voigt was not Peter – he was the wrong age – so where was her real son? *Stay in the moment, Maggs, Concentrate on Voigt.*

As Voigt released his grip, Maggie deliberately raised her glasses and cocked her head forward. She moved her head round in a subtle circular motion as she took in his features. She had practised this a few times in the mirror since she had accepted the mission again, determined to channel her inner Meryl Streep. The idea was to appear first anxious, then confused, and finally disbelieving. Her private auditions had not gone well – though she was sure that if anyone had wanted a constipated looking Meryl Streep, she would have been top of the list.

'Chrissie? My Chrissie? Is thata you? Non, it cannot be!'

She kept her voice as slow and as croaky as she could; Marijke's instructions. 'Sound confused and muddled, Maggs,' she had advised. 'Make your words sound not clear too. Forty years is a long time. It's okay that your voice will have changed with age.'

'Yes, Mamma, it's me, Chrissie.' He wiped away a tear before grasping her elbows. 'I can't believe it.' He turned his head sideways so that the others could see and hear his reaction. *He's trying to convince them too.* But it was not an act; he looked genuinely overwhelmed by the situation.

Maggie wobbled before teetering backwards. Voigt tightened his grip to prevent her falling over. *Remember, Maggs, Streep, not Charlie Chaplin. And definitely not Brando or Caine.*

'Here, take a seat… she must be shocked.' This time Voigt did plainly address the others who, much to Maggie's satisfaction, were looking a little concerned for her wellbeing. *I might actually pull this off!* Frankie would be proud... and a little amazed.

She was lowered into a chair. 'Can we get you water, Mamma?'

His English was good, perfect almost, except for the odd accented word or phrase which gave away his German origins. It had a slight tremor to it too, a sign of worry, possibly. Maggie nodded, then fluttered her hand in front of her face, and puffed out her cheeks, as if trying to cool down after receiving such dramatic news. She took a quick glance up at his two accomplices. The woman had gone, but she was aware that the man was standing by the door, studying her closely. She could not make out yet whether they had been called in to deliberately watch Maggie's reaction, Voigt's reaction or both. Or maybe they just happened to be there anyway? The woman arrived with a glass of water and handed it to Voigt, who carefully passed it on to Maggie.

'There, Mamma. Sip it slowly. It will help.'

'You keep calling me "Mamma". Why do you think I'ma your Mamma? My Chrissie is ... is... I don't know where he is. It 'as been so long.' She stared at him for a few seconds. 'But maybe you do look a leetle like 'im. Oh, I am so confused!' She put her hands to her head. 'Ai, ai!' *Don't overdo it, Meryl...*

'Look.' He reached into his jacket pocket, pulled out an old crumpled picture and showed it to her. 'This is us, together. I must be about six or seven.' Maggie lifted up her glasses and studied it. It could easily have been her as a young woman. *And the boy next to her could have been Peter, Maggs.* Except that it was not. *Peter was long gone when you were that age.* She did nothing to suppress the genuine sniffle that followed.

'Here's another photo,' Voigt continued, handing a second one. This must have been taken a year or so before...'

'Before you left me, Chrissie? Is that what you wanted to say?' She grabbed his wrist. *Mournful, Maggs. Do mournful.* It was not hard. Voigt, she could see, was moved. She could imagine what it must feel like – *will feel like, even, Maggs* – for a mother and son to be reunited after such a long time. He was crouching down beside her. He put down the photos and just looked up at her. 'Oh,

Chrissie,' she said. 'My Chrissie.'

The next thing she knew, his head was in her lap, and he was sobbing. *What the hell!* She could not help herself. They sobbed together.

*   *   *   *

When they had both recovered, she was helped through to a lounge area, and invited to sit on one of the armchairs. It was a sparse room with just the two armchairs and an assortment of dining room chairs placed round a table at the far end. Voigt pulled up a chair next to her. Muscles was nowhere to be seen, but the man and woman had followed them in and pulled up chairs too to sit nearby. Voigt seemed reluctant to let go of Maggie, and he had hold of her hand again. She noticed his hands were beautifully manicured, and he was wearing a gold wedding band. Everyone seemed a bit calmer now, so she took the opportunity to study the other two in more detail. She spotted a wedding ring on the woman's left hand too. *Could she and Voigt be married?* She was a good twenty five years younger than him, yet it was possible. If that was the case, judging by the expensive clothes and jewellery, she may well have been attracted to other things besides Voigt's diminishing good looks. *That's a bit catty, Maggs. Don't make assumptions.*

'This is lovely. What fantastic news!' the woman said with a smile that clearly said: I'm not convinced by you. 'Together again, after all this time.' Maggie was mightily relieved that there was no hint of an Italian accent. *British, probably, maybe Welsh.* Whether Maggie's run of luck on that front would extend much longer in what was obviously an international organisation, she had her doubts.

The man had not said anything yet, but was clearly eyeing her up and down. *Another sceptic,* she thought. He wore a smart grey suit, likely was in his forties, had a brown briefcase with him, and sported round glasses which sat on a stubby nose below his balding head – *definitely the accountant..*

'I am forgetting my manners! Mamma, let me introduce these people to you. This is Beth, my accountant.' *Got that one wrong, Maggs.*

'I am so pleased to meet you, Signora Neumann. Should I call you Signora or maybe Granny Colo? Or Nonna perhaps?' *Sarcastic. She definitely doesn't believe in me...*

'And this,' Voigt said drawing the short fat, bald man forwards, 'is Richard, or Dick as he likes to be known. He runs my overseas operations.'

'Buongiorno, Signora. Piacere.' *Sod it! He's Italian! But Dick... Really? What kind of Italian family calls their son 'Dick'?* 'Excuse my bad Italian, Signora.' His smile, now that it had finally arrived, looked false, smarmy almost. *Thank God for that – American, not Italian! Although not a strong accent. New England maybe...* 'I would like to speak Italian much better. You could teach me, maybe?' *Not bloody likely.*

She felt she ought to say something to them, acknowledge them at least. Ignoring them would only make her less credible. 'Wella, I'ma a leetle shocked. But I'm also very 'appy to meet you all.' She tried out her best Italian Nonna smile. It was met by polite ones from Dick and Beth, and a beaming one from Voigt.

She had learnt the script about Voigt's early life the best she could in the very short time she had been given, but Maggie had always known she could rely on her back story that she had been diagnosed with dementia. The Service had alluded to it when they had posted the shots of her being evacuated from the nursing home in the States, picking a home that provided dementia care. Several of Maggie's friends lived with the illness, so she was aware of how serious it was and the effect it had on them and their families. Her 'diagnosis' was categorised as very mild – she was still purportedly able to function independently on a day-to-day basis – but she planned to take advantage of her perceived memory loss as they began to talk over tea and cake, which was already laid out on the dining room table.

She was being tested, at least by Beth and Dick. On the face of it, it all seemed very natural, but some of the questions could have been construed as traps, and she knew she had to be careful. One particular one, quite early on from Dick, raised an uncomfortable eyebrow from Voigt, but she saw him listening intently to her answer.

'You must be pleased to see your son after all this time, Mrs Neumann.'

'It is a biga surprise, but yes, I am.'

'It had to be kinda tough when you lost touch. Did you try to make contact with him again?'

'Of course! I tried and tried. Many times. But... it was too 'ard. There were too many things that stopped me. In the end, I 'ad to give up.' *Familiar story, Maggs?* 'But I never wanted to, and I never stopped loving you, Chrissie.'

She was pleased when Voigt chipped in to support her. 'You have to understand, Dick, that they were different times. The iron curtain was up and, being German, I had to decide what side of it I wanted to be on. I'm from the East, so I chose the East. Mamma, being Italian, wanted me to join her in the West, but I refused. I was young and in many ways idealistic. I saw the communist ways as being the only way. It was my fault, not Mamma's.'

'It was both,' said Maggie, sadly 'but the government made it very 'ard also.' She decided to lighten the mood. 'You have changed a lot since you were a young man. Your 'air is not the same colour and your face is...'

'Fat?' laughed Voigt.

'Non! Not fat. A leetle round, maybe.'

'I've changed in lots of other ways too, Mamma. I'm not a communist anymore. I did not like what the East German and the Russians did, in the end. I made lots of mistakes, but now...' He turned to Beth and Dick and smiled, 'Now... I'm with good people, clever people, and we have something very exciting about to happen which I want you to be part of.'

'Your son is quite the capitalist now,' said Dick, returning Voigt's smile.

'It's true, I am!'

'How did you find me?' asked Maggie. *Risky question, Maggs, as it may not tie in with what the Service set up.*

The risk paid off. 'I found out you were alive by chance. It came up on a random background check when I changed my old name – I'm sorry, Mamma, I'm called Chrissie Voigt now, not Neumann. From there, we did various searches on the internet and other complicated computer stuff. It's what I do now.'

'You always were a clever boy.'

Maggie then tried to get on the front foot by weaving in general childhood experiences into dates and locations she had learnt about

Voigt, ensuring they were sufficiently woolly to be consistent with her limited capacity for recall.

'I remember, Chrissie, your papa always liked to play with you when 'e came home from work...'

Or, 'Do you remember that time we went to the zoo in – where was it? Wetzlar?'

'Mamma, I don't think Wetzlar has a zoo.'

'Oh, no. Which town am I thinking of then?'

In response to a question from Beth: 'Was your son a troublesome boy, Signora Neumann?'

'Troublesome... Naughty, you mean? He could be sometimes. Are not all boys?'

She tackled questions about the nursing home and the fire, using the back story Joshua had given her in the car on the way to Amsterdam. 'I moved to America to look after my aunt who was very ill. It isa wonderful country. After she died, I also became quite ill, and went to a home for a while. The fire was scary, but not so bad, really. They got us all out in chairs. I was in the newspapers!'

It was easier than she had imagined and, after a short while, she found she was even starting to quite enjoy herself. At one point she excused herself to go to the bathroom, and a large fuss was made as she was shown through the hallway into a small cloakroom. When she came out and returned to the lounge, she saw that Ratty had reappeared and was deep in conversation with Voigt. She could not hear what he was saying, but he pointed to his own nose several times and at one point rocked his head forward slightly as if recreating her failed attempts at breaking her nose in the car. Voigt's response was firm and she was pleased to see that he seemed to have been sent away with a flea in his ear.

However, she decided she ought to make reference to her nose to avoid it becoming a sticking point. She sat down and, after the conversation got going again, she made a point of wriggling it occasionally, rubbing the side and wincing. It caught Beth's attention who asked after her. 'Are you okay, Signora Neumann?'

'Si. It is justa my nose.'

'What's wrong with it?'

'It 'urts now and again. I'm a leetle, 'ow do you say..., embarrassed. Now, where did I put my glasses?'

'You're wearing them,' said Dick pointedly.

'Silly me. And my scarf?'

'Your handbag, maybe?' said Beth.

Maggie opened her bag and made a show of looking for it. 'Ah, yes. There it is. Now, my 'at...'

'You don't have one,' said Dick. 'You had a headscarf instead. Remember?'

'Of course... Have you seen my scarf anywhere?' She started looking around her again. *Don't overdo it, Maggs. Just enough...*

'It is in your bag, Mamma,' said Voigt gently.

' Ah, si! Forgive me, it is because I 'ave, um, dementia.' Voigt nodded sympathetically. 'I 'ave moments... and then I am okay again. I forget where things are, and dates are very 'ard.'

'We understand,' said Voigt. 'You were telling us about your nose.'

'Yes, my nose. You see, I 'ave never liked it. I broke it when I was a leetle girla. Your father, God bless him...' and at this point she swallowed a sob and made the sign of the cross on her chest, 'always loved mya bent nose. But as I 'av got older, I 'ave found it more 'ard to breathe properly. I wanted to do something about it. I 'ad a leetle money, which my aunt left me, and so I saw someone. When was it? Last week? Maybe last month. Oh, I don't know. Anyway, it is not a lot of money. '

'So you had it straightened!' Voigt finished off. 'That makes perfect sense. We did wonder.'

'It sometimes goes a leetle red and biga. It bothers me still. I 'ave tried to cover it with makeup. Can you see the red? I 'ope not.'

There were sympathetic noises and closer examinations which developed into questions about how she broke it in the first place ('I fell off the back of a tractor when my Mamma was collecting spaghetti at the farm.' That response brought about very confused looks. Her subsequent raised eyebrow and mischievous expression, backed up by Voigt's sudden burst of laughter, seemed to only add to her credibility as an eccentric old lady).

The conversations went on with Maggie batting off questions competently, gaining more and more confidence in her new role. And so would she likely have continued, if she had not been knocked off her stride by what happened next.

'Good, you are here,' Voigt broke off from the conversation and looked up at the very tall, mature man with an angular face who came waltzing confidently into the room. Voigt grabbed the new arrival affectionately around the shoulders and placed him proudly in front of Maggie. 'This is my Mamma. Mamma, meet my best friend and business partner…This is Peter.'

*　　*　　*　　*

Chapter 21

She nodded a welcome and managed a smile, but inside her head, she had an awful lot going on, all of a sudden. *Peter? My son, Peter, at last, here in the flesh?* She knew it had been coming, but now he was actually here, well…she did not quite know what to do... or how to feel.

She had been mentally prepared to meet her son on this mission. *That's hogwash, Maggs! You barely thought about it until you saw Voigt. You've deliberately shoved it to one side, as you always do when things are emotionally difficult. Particularly where your son is concerned.* His involvement had been one of the draws for her, surely? Of course it had. Yet she had still pushed it away, and Joshua had hardly mentioned Peter, presumably because he did not want her to become too preoccupied with it. *You could have pressed him for information, Maggs. Why didn't you?* She knew the answer to that, though: it was in case her worst fears were realised, and more evidence came to light that her son was a bad person. *And you're here to prove that he's not. Is that right?* She would have to wait and see about that.

Now he was in the same room, and, somehow, she had to deal with it. As Peter and Voigt moved away to talk, she fell back on her training. An extract from a manual came to mind:

If an agent is faced with a compromising, or potentially compromising, situation that could impact on his emotions and therefore his ability to make sound decisions, it is essential he

remain focussed and calm. He should continue to observe the surroundings, and accumulate information until able to evaluate or re-evaluate his position. He should base the decision going forward on that information and not on any emotional response that could cloud judgement.

The manuals referred to '*He*', of course. Despite that, it made her feel slightly better. The regulations always provided that anchor. On top of that, she had something to do, at least, which was to observe.

She watched Peter and Voigt talking, then Voigt called Ratty over, and Peter spoke to him in hushed tones before sending him away. Voigt seemed quite animated as he and Peter spoke, but she saw Peter put a reassuring hand on his shoulder and mouth something like, 'Don't worry, we have time.' He had a quiet confidence to him, an air of authority and calmness, and she could see why they would make good business partners. Voigt's enthusiasm and energy complemented Peter's levelheadedness. *Criminals plotting together,* she tried to remind herself. They moved to the other end of the room. Whatever they were saying now was too hard to pick up. The implant, unfortunately, did not give her any superpower, that was for sure.

She slipped the manual back onto the shelf, as worrying questions came to mind. She wondered how her son had forged such a different path to her. What had happened to make Peter get involved in illegal activity? How had a son of hers gone so far off the rails? She was normally a firm believer in nurture, but surely nature had a role to play here too, didn't it? How did he turn out like this? He came from good, honest stock. Neither she nor Frankie had a bad bone between them. Perhaps he had inherited something from a distant ancestor, a rogue Matheson, if there had ever been one. From what she had seen so far, in some ways he was a bit like Frankie in the way he conducted himself. The only time Frankie ever got flustered was when she had been physically hurt or threatened. 'Mild Mannered Matheson' he was known as. His demeanour allowed solid decision-making under extreme pressure. Cool, calculating people made excellent spies. Cool, calculating people also made excellent criminals.

Nurture had to be the villain in this, then. After all, she had no idea what sort of an upbringing he had had. As her friend Shirley once said to her: 'There's no such thing as bad genes… unless they're being worn by a seventy-five year old woman, like me, with a fat arse.'

She was going round in circles, but it all led to one thing: *You let him go, Maggs. You lost control of him. You should have tried harder. It falls on you. Nature or nurture, this is your fault.*

Someone was speaking to her. 'Mamma, are you okay? You've gone quiet.' Voigt had finished his conversation and was now hunched down next to her.

'I am okay, Chrissie. Bene, grazie. I am just very tired. It must be the 'appiness of meeting you again.' *Keep it up; you have no choice.* 'Please can I lie down somewhere for a rest?' She needed a few quiet moments to think. Not long, just ten minutes away.

'Of course! I'm sorry,' said Voigt. 'There has been a lot of emotion today. We can talk more later on, over some lunch perhaps? I have some important business to attend to. Beth, could you show my mother to the bedroom across the hallway, please?'

'Goodbye, Signora,' Peter said as she was directed back through to the hall again. She had started to make her way out, but stopped at the sound of his voice. He was directly behind her. The last time she had spoken to her son was to say a tearful goodbye to him as her friend gently prised him from her grasp and reassured her that she would see her son again soon. He was only four months old. Now, decades later, as she turned round to face the lanky 'stranger', balding and in his sixties, all she could manage was a polite, 'Nice to meet you, Peter.' Close up, she took the moment to appraise him more carefully. Part of her wanted to say more, to talk to him properly, find out more about him, even touch him, hold him. Instead she smiled. A mother's smile, a warm smile, a smile to bridge a sixty year gap. A smile between a mother and a son.

But the mechanical twitch of his lips in response, a sneer almost, and the coldness of his dark brown eyes told her something different. She did not feel the connection. The one with Voigt had been stronger and that had not even been real. With Peter, there was nothing. *He's no Matheson, Maggs. No, definitely not... He can't be... can he?*

* * * *

Chapter 22

The bedroom was simple, quiet, and just what she needed. The last couple of hours had taken it out of her. It was not just the shock of meeting Peter. It was also the concentration she had needed while she was in role. Feeling a little queasy, she lay down on the bed to wait for her stomach to stop churning, and for the room to stop spinning.

It did, eventually, thanks to sleep. She woke up, initially confused and with a mild headache, but the sickness had gone, much to her relief. There was a glass of water on the bedside table, so she propped herself up on one elbow and gulped it down, before tentatively swinging her legs round ready to stand up. *Easy does it, take your time.* She followed her own advice and sat for a few minutes.

Sleep had given her only a little respite from her worries, but she felt more ready to tackle them; specifically, her concerns about Peter and the implications that had for the mission. If he was not her son, why had Joshua told her he was? It occurred to her that it could have been a careless mistake on Joshua's part, to add to his others. In fact, she very much doubted he would have a job much longer after she had given him the slip. Sheldon would be furious, and she was not one to easily forgive lapses in performance. Maggie had had many a run-in when she had had to either defend herself or a colleague against the onslaught of a Sheldon rollicking. No doubt, she would have had Joshua in her sights after he had failed to recruit Maggie first time round. Since then, Maggie had nearly been killed in Harwich, and Carlos, an important witness or suspect, had been poisoned. Both events happened on Joshua's watch. Now, by wanting to protect Joshua and going it alone, Maggie had probably done him more harm than good.

And there was Bill too, of course – an experienced agent who had also been duped by an old lady at the last minute. It did not look promising for any more of those cosy chats she used to have with him and Ben in Sukuel's. *More guilt, Maggs.*

She pulled herself together. *Right, enough of this negativity. You're here to do a job. Get it done.* There was a clock on the wall which told her it was only a little after ten thirty. It had been a long morning, lengthened by the lack of sleep and the very early start. She was conscious that time was precious and, judging by Voigt's urgency earlier on, things could be happening very soon – whatever those happening things might be. She kicked herself for taking time out to sleep, but she had not been able to help herself. At least this way she had had a decent rest and was beginning to feel more refreshed.

What next? She got up, walked over to the door and quietly pulled it open. *Do what all good spies do, Maggs... spy.*

She was relieved to see the hallway was clear, which gave her an opportunity to get her bearings again. The door opposite was the lounge she had been in earlier. Devoid of any ornaments, pictures or anything interesting which might give her an inkling of Voigt's activities, it was not worth another visit. The starkness of it had only strengthened her suspicion that the house was very much a temporary place of residence. Perhaps other rooms might present a few clues about what Voigt was up to – providing the clues were not hidden somewhere deep inside a computer. In an odd way, her ignorance of I.T. took the pressure off. How could she feel guilty if she missed something technical, if she did not have the faintest clue what it was she had missed?

Generally, she was intolerant of ignorance, seeing it as cause of many of the world's problems. But when it came to her knowledge of computers, she wore her ignorance as a badge of honour. Sure, technology was everywhere, a part of everyday life. She just saw no reason for it to become part of hers. It was the needless jargon that annoyed her most. She had heard of things such as ROM, RAM and upload, but if they jumped up and slapped her in the face – and for all she knew about them, that was entirely possible – she would feel no better acquainted with them. She was happy for computers to fall into a burgeoning category in her head which she had labelled *'stuff I just don't get, and don't want to get'*. (The list included such incomprehensible things as paying a fortune for clothes she used to buy from a jumble sale for pennies on the basis that they were now called 'pre-loved'; people on reality T.V. saying how wonderful the 'journey' had been when they had not been anywhere; and putting bananas into plastic bags when they already had a perfectly robust and hygienic purpose-built packaging system).

The house seemed quiet, although she was not naïve enough to believe that that meant it was empty. There were stairs going up which looked an interesting place to explore, and another door to her right which was slightly ajar. She opted for the flatter route. When she pushed the door, she found it led to another small corridor, off of which were three further rooms. One of them had bi-fold doors which opened out onto a conservatory with views of the garden. The room looked a lovely place to sit in the sunshine, if there had been anything to sit on. It was totally empty. The room next to it was a WC come shower room.

Opposite was definitely more interesting, when she eased the door open and peered around. Blinds against the window limited the amount of light, but it was a space which had things of potential interest in it, for once. It was a decent sized room which, judging by the neat files and reference books on shelves, and the computer, was being used as a study. Behind the enormously large desk – not much smaller than the table tennis tables Maggie used to play on in her youth – was a black swivel chair. It was nothing fancy, just functional and comfortable looking. There were two trays on the desk, clearly labelled 'in' and 'out'. The former had a few papers in it, stacked, ready for attention. She got the feeling that the occupier was fastidious, and doubted that papers would stay in either tray for long. A blank notepad in the centre, along with the paperwork, would merit further examination. The metal bin was empty, and all the owner's pens, pencils and other stationery were neatly set out in certain places on the desk for easy access. On the wall facing the chair was a huge television screen. It was switched on with the sound muted. A news programme, CBC – Canadian she guessed by the amount of snow on display – was flipping between stories as bulletins ran along the bottom and scrolled down the side. Maggie preferred the traditional news programmes which told one story at a time. She could never understand how anyone listened to a newscaster explain one story, watched the scenes from another story in a little box, while, somehow, reading about other events which zipped the screen across from all angles. All done, probably, while checking the news on a phone. She was in favour of multitasking, but only when it involved mixing one activity with drinking a cup of tea.

She sat down behind what she hoped might be the jackpot so far as finding out more about Voigt's methods and motives. She was really starting to enjoy herself now. *Just like old times!* As she studied the desk, she felt a thrill, a knot of excitement in her stomach – the 'spy factor', as she liked to call it. It had been so long, she had nearly forgotten what it was like. She was in fight or flight mode, but in control. On many occasions in the past, she had been grateful for that heightened feeling of awareness, caught in compromising situations and having to fight her way out of them. Or indeed take flight – quite literally, once, via the second floor window of an apartment in Manhattan. That case was a nasty one, linked into a branch of the Mafia, involving, guns, knives and all sorts. She did not feel that kind of directly violent threat from Voigt, but his 'hoods' looked quite handy. As did Peter, come to that.

To start with, she ignored the computers and their screens. There was no point fiddling around – she could do nothing with them – but she was excellent at rifling through paperwork, particularly with her glasses on which she was pleased she had remembered to wear before leaving the bedroom. *Bifocals – no good modern day spy should be without them.* Organised into date order, she saw that the papers were nearly all invoices and bills of lading, most of them to do with the acquisition of computer hardware. There were receipts for services: cleaning, car hire, restaurant bills, even clothing – suits and the like. Everything seemed very normal, just like a proper business, and the fact Voigt – she assumed it was his study – was keeping all of these had to mean he was either intending to pay them or, if already paid, perhaps they were to be retained as part of his records. *Bloody modern-day criminals – prepared to engage in illegal acts, but make sure it's all tax deductable.*

Maggie reached over for the notepad she had spotted. It was blank all the way through, but she was not fazed by that. Individuals engaged in criminal activity were hardly likely to write a compromising note and leave it hanging around for everyone to read on a notepad. They may, however, write a compromising note on a notepad, dispose of the note then leave the notepad around with the imprint on the next page – a classic mistake which she had come across so many times before. A thought went through her mind that things may be different these days with all the modern technology which used complicated codes and encryption. She dismissed it though as she started to examine the pad. The concentration on technology could work to her advantage here in that people might have all the protection they need for their computers – and from what she had been told about how hard it was to crack into Voigt's network, that certainly seemed to be the case – and then forget the basics with something as simple as a pen and a bit of paper.

She switched on the lamp and held up the top page to the light. Her heart skipped a beat as she could see she was in luck. Holding the page at the right angle and adjusting it slightly, she could just about make out the writing. The word 'urgent' was written large at the top in capitals. Underneath were two words:

Read this!

It was not so clear after that, but by holding it right up to the bulb, she could just, letter by letter, make out some of the words. There was a date – yesterday's – and a time: *14:00.* Her heart sunk. Whatever was on the note could well have happened by now, but she persevered, hoping it might give some clues about Voigt's plans. *Something ch....* she read. Chips, was it? Short for microchips, maybe? They seemed to be in everything these days, even inside her own head, according to Joshua. Voigt would almost certainly have need for them too for his computer things. *Computer things, Maggs! Quite the geek now, aren't you!*

What was that other word in front of it? She could make out some of the letters.

Cr_c__l ch____...

It was a bit like doing the crossword in the *Lady* but without the clues. Part of the problem, apart from the lack of definition on the page, was the quality of handwriting. Maggie's was hard to read, but this was atrocious! Still, at least it was in English, which made her wonder if the note was written by Voigt at all. Possible still; most of his staff seemed to be English speakers. She pulled the lamp closer and cursed herself for her clumsiness as it knocked a stapler which fell into the metal bin with an almighty clang. With her shoulders hunched, she froze, waiting for a response from someone, but there was none. *Keep pumping away, heart – you've coped with this sort of scare for decades. Don't let me down now.*

She continued her examination. The proximity of the light helped as she was able to hold the page up really close to the bulb where the impression was much clearer. Now she could make out the word before the 'ch....' – 'Crucial ch... ' *You're right Maggs. It is important.* So, she had a date, a time, something possibly about crucial chips or microchips. The sense of urgency was clear to see.

She joked about her inexperience, but she could have done with a little more computer expertise, really. If it was as important as she thought it was, she had no way of really making any use of it without help. And she had done a fine job of losing her only help on a canal path in the city centre.

Still, she was here now and in a position to accumulate some information. Who knew where it might lead to? The rest of the note was not as clear, but the next word after 'chips' was on the next line. It was underlined and she decided it probably said '*and*'. There was another word she could not read, followed by a full stop, then a longer sentence which had been underlined three times and had four exclamation marks after it. *The crux of the message, Maggs.* Her heart beat a little quicker. It took another five minutes or so, but she finally worked out what most of that last sentence might say. She concluded that the last word was the same as the indecipherable word in the first part and it began with 'S', only it was capitals. She was left with the following:

Crucial ch_ _ _ _ and s_ _ _ _ _. Don't come back without s_ _ _ _ _!!!!

If only she could get a closer look. Then, a flash of inspiration: the Christmas party she had been to at the beginning of December with the very posh Christmas crackers. The chairman of the Bowls Club had reported a budget surplus – a rare occurrence – so the committee authorised additional expenditure on the Christmas trimmings. Maggie's cracker had a decent measuring tape, but she owned loads of those. So she arranged a swap with Sheila who said her one at home had been a victim of her mad Yorkie called Tiger, which was eating everything at the moment, including her

Tupperware. Maggie (who took no pleasure from the fact that she had a cupboard jam-packed full of un-chewed Tupperware) was rather disappointed with the mini magnifying glass Sheila offered in exchange. (Her suggestion that Sheila keep it to forensically examine the teeth marks on her Tupperware to ensure Tiger was the guilty party, fell on deaf ears – as did most comments to her elderly friends these days, to be fair.)

She had shoved the magnifying glass in the side pocket of her handbag and forgotten all about it – until now. Amazingly, it was easy to find. She held it to the paper, moving up and down the lines on the page, alternating between the two last very similar 's' words. Feeling increasingly smug, she was able to decipher them. Smug until she worked out what both words were:

'Salami!'

And the other word was cheese, not chips. Her shoulders slumped as she read the whole thing back to herself:

'Crucial cheese and salami. Don't come back without salami !!!!'

It's an addendum to a bloody lunch order! All that for nothing! It was a big blow. Frustrated, she pushed the pad to the side and accidentally knocked the mouse. The screen at far end of the desk came to life. She stared at it, trying to make sense of what was on it.

The screen saver was set so that thumbnail sized photos danced and zigzagged their way across the screen, some popping in one corner before 'fizzing' out, others spinning or doing loop-de-loops. The screen was on a fancy extendable wall-mounted support which had been pushed flat back against the wall. A tidying function, she guessed, with an added benefit of being able to frustrate short-sighted and short-armed octogenarian spies. Detail was hard to ascertain, but the pictures mainly looked like holiday scenes: mountains, lakes, towns etc. Two pictures that regularly came into view caught her eye. They were shots of a couple who looked like they were posing for the camera in one, and embracing in the other. She cursed quietly to herself as the pictures appeared, did double flips and Salchows worthy of a gold medal skater in the Winter Olympics, before waltzing off again. She waited patiently for the couple to come round again. When they did, she could see that they were posing against a blue sky on a mountain somewhere, but facial features remained blurred. She concluded that it was probably not Voigt because the hair colouring seemed all wrong. The man in this photo looked quite a bit taller than his companion. Peter was a good six foot two or three, she would guess, having stood near him earlier. It could well be Peter, and this could be his office. Voigt had had to move his operation from Vienna at short notice. Maybe Peter had already rented this place here, and Voigt had joined him. The well set out room was consistent with the impression she had of someone with a calm and organised approach to things. The woman in the picture, she had no idea about. She needed a closer look.

What had Joshua done to make the picture bigger on his phone? Grabbed it or pinched it? How did that work? Maybe if she could touch the screen it would stop whirling around and she could enlarge the pictures. The screen was right at the back and dead centre on what she now concluded was more akin to a theatre stage than a desk, as she stretched across in vain. There was only one thing for it. *Enough prevaricating. Just get on there and get up close, Maggs.*

She hitched up her skirt before attempting to cock her leg up onto the desk, letting out a squeal as she heard something crack. She had stiffened up since her antics at Harwich when she had performed that forward roll. The sound could have come from anywhere: ankle, knee, hip, lower back. The problem was that the desk was built for giants; another reason to suspect it might be Peter's. After a few false starts she gave up on that method and decided she needed a bit of leverage. Placing her hands on the desk, she hoiked her left foot up behind her onto the swivel chair, drawing it closer to the desk. With one leg successfully up, she did a little jump, hoping to get the other foot on the chair and therefore her legs at greater parity with the desk height, from where she hoped to shuffle and crawl her way towards the screen. But she had not reckoned on the chair's wheels, and the space behind the chair into which it now gently rolled. Her arms slowly collapsed as the chair trundled backwards. She managed to grab hold of the side of the desk with her right arm, but she was left in the rather unenviable and uncomfortable position of being stretched out full length, her toes of her left foot clinging to the seat of the chair, the other leg dangling down at the wrong angle to help her stand, and her face squashed flat next to the only loose piece of paper on the desk. She could now see this was a bill from a jeweller, possibly for a ring of some sort, with something else scribbled on it. She did her best to read it as she felt her body from her chest down slowly droop into the space between the desk and chair, until it hung like a sack of potatoes suspended on a piece of elastic between two tent poles.

'Sod it!' she said out loud which turned into a quieter, 'Oh shit!' as she heard the click of the study door. She turned her head slightly, and watched as the shaft of light from the conservatory opposite crept forward to illuminate the space under her belly.

Ratty Hood's voice showed no emotion. 'Can I help you, Signora Neumann?'

Under the strain of the stretch she was now feeling across her right arm, back and legs, there were many words she would have liked to use. But she remembered she was a both a professional and, crucially, an Italian. She was quite proud of herself in the circumstances to restrict it to a subdued – but heartfelt – 'Mamma Mia!'

She tried to keep her voice steady. 'Come ina.'

Her temporary bedroom door eased open. 'I've been asked to enquire whether there is anything you would like, Signora.' It was Beth. 'Are you well rested after your earlier… ahem…exertions?' Was that a hint of sarcasm she detected in her voice? Almost certainly. *A triple dose with brass knobs on!*

When Ratty found her in that compromising position in Peter's study, Maggie had had no inclination for either fight or flight. That controlled knot of excitement she had enjoyed earlier had morphed into what felt like a hernia. Ratty had unceremoniously supported her underside while he hooked the chair closer, so that her feet got within the normal five feet two range of the top of the head, rather than the unnatural six foot distance it had felt like when she was suspended. From there she managed to drop her left foot to the floor, then slide off the desk and onto her haunches. She adopted a posture of what looked like quiet contemplation and prayer, her arms splayed over the front edge of the desk, while she got her breath back.

She did have the wherewithal to fall back on the default position of acting the senile, old lady to explain her suspicious circumstances. The realism of the performance was helped enormously by the fact that, in that moment particularly, a senile, old lady was exactly what she felt like she was.

'Oh dear. Where am I?' she had managed breathlessly.

'What are you doing in this office, Signora?' Ratty had replied.

'Oh, I wasa looking for somewhere nice to sit in the garden. I came in this room and then I saw a picture of my Chrissie on the computer. I think it isa him anyway. Perhaps it isn't. My eyes are not so good and 'e kept jumping around. I wanted to take a closer look, but then I fell. It isa a big table, no?' *The best lies to carry off are ones closest to the truth* – another Service tip she had learnt.

Yet another handy tip (self-taught, this time) was that if someone who catches you in a compromising position seems like they do not believe you, pretend to faint. Having seen extreme scepticism being added to Ratty rapidly expanding repertoire of facial expressions, this is what Maggie had done, and was the reason why she was now back in the bedroom.

'I am feeling much, much better, thank you, Beth. I would like to get up now and walk around a leetle.'

'We don't want you fainting on anyone again. Are you recovered enough?'

'Yes, really, I ama okay now. But, can I ask... where is my son?'

'Herr Voigt is attending to business. He has just phoned me to find out how you are. I told him you were asleep.'

'Oh, I would very much like to see him.'

'He suggested you have lunch here, and he will catch up with you in a couple of hours or so. He was very concerned when we told him you had seemed unwell.'

'He was always such a kind boy.'

'He said you used to make fresh pasta for him. He has bought a new pasta making machine, especially for you. Maybe a gentle, familiar activity might help you to feel better. You can prepare some pasta for him to be cooked later. Would you like to try it now?'

Don't be a mug: they're testing you. But her mouth was fractionally quicker than her brain and she could not stop herself. 'I would love to make pasta!'

Fresh pasta? Why'd you agree to that, you silly fool, Maggs? It sounded like an idea concocted by Beth and Dick to confirm she was who she said she was. Or maybe it was Ratty's? Either way, she was in big trouble. Opening a tin of spaghetti hoops for Sharon was as close as she had ever got to making pasta before.

'Oh, bugger!' Her expletive, although under her breath, was not unheard.

'I'm sorry?'

'Oh… um…O-bah-ga! It is a Sicilian word. O-bah-ga.'

'What does it mean?'

'It is 'ard to explain but… um… it means, "Let us …" 'ow do you say... "rejoice, for today we make bowlfuls of pasta!" It is not used very much these days,' she added, sounding far more sheepish than she would have liked.

'It doesn't sound very Italian.'

Help! 'No…' She frantically searched her brain and had a vague recollection of Sicily having links with various historical invaders. 'It's a very old word… Arabic I thinka,' she said with hope more than certainty, and praying that she had not fallen asleep in some edition of Q.I. and dreamt up the Sicilian connections to that part of the world.

The doubt in Beth's voice was still there, but she seemed appeased as she put up her arm to show Maggie the way out. 'Interesting. Well, O-bah-ga it is then!'

The pasta making had started well enough. Maggie had watched enough cooking programmes to know that you began the process of making fresh pasta by smothering a flat surface with flour. She decided to make this her main focus. Her audience, limited to Beth and Dick she was relieved to find out, had watched in amazement as she strutted up and down, flinging huge clumps of flour onto the marble top which ran one length of the kitchen. She milked this part for all it was worth, hurling handfuls from a height and splattering it down before extravagantly spreading it over with the palm of her hand. Every now and then she would bend down, close one eye and look along the line of the work top, checking to make sure it was evenly distributed before throwing more on. Blowing, she found, helped with the general dispersal, but not with the general mood in the kitchen. Inevitably, some of the flour ended up on the floor, quite a lot on her, and the rest over Beth and Dick.

'If we don't do this, it will sticka,' she explained. It sounded convincing, but in truth she had no idea what to do next.

Cooking had never been her strong point. Her busy lifestyle when she was in the Service, often being away from home for long periods of time, gave her the perfect excuse she needed to cover up her complete lack of skills and total disinterest in cooking. She marvelled at other people's ability to combine food groups together, and then heat them through to make something that was a different shape, temperature and texture to what they had started with. The process was a mystery to her. She had always kept her meals at home simple, happily compromising her Luddite ways and investing in a microwave as soon as they became available. Even when her hearing deteriorated, she was still always able to hear the sweet 'ping' which signified her ready meal chilli con carne or roast dinner on a plate was ready. Why bother to learn how to cook when others could do it for you? Eating good food, she could do. Watching people preparing good food on TV, yes – it was good entertainment, and gave others the opportunity to show how clever they were. Making it herself? Not in a month of Sundays! It was always a complete shambles whenever she had tried, so she had simply stopped doing it.

She liked the idea of pitching to the producers of 'Master Chef' the proposal of making its 'devil-child' version and calling it, 'Disaster Chef'. She had even worked on a variety of suitable facial expressions in the mirror, the 'gurning gallery' as she named it, imagining the presenters' reaction to the contestants' menus as they prepared their awful meals. She had gone so far as to picture herself nervously walking up to the judges and presenting her plate with the hushed tones of the voiceover in her ear.

"For her signature dish today, Maggie has made tinned pilchards, washed, strained through a sieve and then gently twice-fried. Cabbage, raisins, a quenelle of Smash, topped with melted cheese triangles and presented with a layer of beef curry pot noodle. It is dressed in a baked bean jus."

The judges would wait patiently for her to tell them what a wonderful life changing experience it had been for her getting to the grand final. She would then gather herself to listen to the judges' final words of wisdom on her dish.

"I like the traditional horizontal, rather than vertical presentation, Maggie, and it all hangs off the plate nicely," would be the bald one with the glasses' sage observation, before cutting into her food and tasting it. A pause, then, "You certainly know all about flavours and you have delivered it here today for us… in bucketfuls!"

"I agree. The whole thing works for me," would be the Australian one's comment, followed by a respectful nod. "Mate, that's incredible. I could quite happily stand here and bring the whole lot up."

In this actual kitchen nightmare, Maggie laboured away. After ten minutes of huffing and puffing and trying to ignore Dick's real life sceptical gurning, Maggie suddenly realised that the first packet of flour was empty. 'Okay,' she said, trying her best not to look terrified as she frantically made a search for the other ingredients she might need for pasta in the *'I wish I had paid more attention to Jamie Oliver's Italian Experience'* part of her brain. 'Now for the…the…'

She let out a deep sigh as Ratty came through the door into the kitchen. He studied the snowy scene with some distain before addressing Beth and Dick.

'Herr Voigt wants you at the office. He says to tell you the launch has been brought forward. The car's outside. I'll take you.'

It was by far the most she had heard him say, but it was well worth the wait to save her from her pasta debacle. 'You're to come along too,' he added grudgingly, nodding towards Maggie. She could have kissed him.

'Enough pasta?' said Dick sarcastically, grabbing his coat from the hook on the back of the door. 'Or as you Italians might say: "Basta pasta, Signora?"'

She nodded and smiled behind the cloud of flour she had started beating off of her skirt. *Couldn't agree more: bastard pasta...*

* * * *

Chapter 23

Maggie found that pretending to be asleep was an excellent way to avoid any awkward questions, although the others seemed preoccupied with other matters in any case. Both Beth and Dick had laptops open and headsets connected to their phones, liaising, she assumed, with people at Voigt's office. Every now and then, she would be aware of Beth or Dick turning to check on her and mumbling a 'She's fine' or 'Don't worry', presumably in response to an enquiry from Voigt.

She kept half an eye open in an attempt to remember the route in case she needed it later, but she found it difficult to pick out distinctive landmarks, especially in the early stages, as Ratty took them on a convoluted journey through the residential area. Eventually, she gave up knowing full well that it was a hopeless task anyway. She used to have an excellent sense of direction when she was a fulltime spy. In a world devoid of Google Maps and sat-navs, she had had to rely on good old-fashioned maps to find her way around or, in many cases, just her wits and observational skills. If the lead agent asked her to be in certain place at a certain time, she was expected to do it without question. Most missions had a time critical element to them, and wasting it getting to places was not factored in. One of her friends had commented once how unrealistic it was in a James Bond film that, during a car chase, everyone seemed to know exactly where they were going, even under extreme pressure. Maggie knew that was possibly the only realistic aspect of the whole film, the fact that as an agent, one had to come to grips with the geography of places very quickly.

Nowadays, if she could find her way out of the tinned soup section in Asda's to the tills, without asking for directions, she considered it a minor miracle.

Maggie soon found herself in another area of Bruges, this time more bland and industrial. The businesses and shops had familiar hoardings and looks, following the formulaic style of their parent companies, but interspersed amongst them were many independently run office blocks and retail units. Most had unpronounceable names in Flemish above the doors or on car park entranceways. Others had the more international brandings in English, Japanese and other languages. It was the perfect place to hide away an organisation that did not want to be conspicuous. She assumed it was similar in all of the cities Voigt had been based in.

They pulled into a car park outside of a two-storey building, and Maggie made sure she was fully alert now to take in whatever details she could. *At least remember the name of the place, Maggs*. The unassuming company signs read simply in English: 'Solutions International'. It could have been any company, dealing in any type of business. *Smoke and mirrors, Mr. Voigt. Well done.*

As Ratty parked the car, Dick and Beth were still fully preoccupied, with laptops open, both on their phones. Beth looked like she was texting or checking something, while Dick spoke to Voigt to inform them of their arrival. They looked serious and initially paid little attention to Maggie as she readied herself to get out.

She noticed Ratty's glance at the back seat and seat well, as he held the car door open.

'It's okay, younga man,' she said, leaving a floury trail behind her. 'Most of it will come off with a good scrub.'

She could not resist the opportunity to brush some more of the white stuff from her shoulder, enjoying his little cough as she went past.

'This is Herr Voigt's office,' said Beth putting her phone away and ushering her into the lobby.

'It is very nice. What is it my son does?'

'Boring things, mainly,' Dick said, joining them. 'Computers, stuff like that.'

'And you 'elp 'im, isa that right?'

Dick's answer, as she knew it would, shed no more light. 'Yeah, I help him, Signora. We both kinda do.'

'Ooh, that isa very nice.' She then decided that 'nice' had been overused and sounded far too English, so she waved her hands around a little and added a, 'Molto bene.' A grunt from Dick was all she received in response.

Inside, Maggie was struck by how sparse the security appeared to be there, at least on the face of it. There was a receptionist, who looked up as they entered, but no obvious guards. It made sense, she figured, and was consistent with the overall location which presented itself as a legitimate low-key business. On closer examination, though, as they walked through, she did notice a small room off the entranceway with a possible two-way mirror, from where she was sure general security would be monitored. Now she looked around, she spotted several cameras tracking left and right, supported, no doubt, by the behind-the-scenes observations. She suspected that were any unwanted guests to pay

Voigt a visit, backup would be quickly on hand.

She felt her stomach jump a little as she realised she was probably entering the point of no return. Back at the house had been tense, at times, but in many ways she had been in her element there, playing a part to get what she wanted. Now came the time for real action. They waited at a door until the receptionist buzzed them through. There were two further sets of doors needing a pass key which Ratty produced.

'Herr Voigt is upstairs in the boardroom with the rest of his staff,' he explained – *can't stop him chattering away now he's started* – 'We'll take the elevator.'

To call the lift, he had to put his eye to a small glass plate. It took a moment for what Maggie assumed was some sort of retina check to verify his identity, and then the doors opened. She heard a whirr above her as she got in. *More cameras – cameras everywhere in fact. Worse than Fort Knox once you get inside.*

It was not a large lift, and Maggie was forced to stand almost right under Ratty. She could feel the top of her headscarf hovering under his chin, and she was left staring at his chest. He was not overly tall, yet she felt tiny in comparison. Dick and Beth towered over her too. When had she stopped being an average height woman in her middle ages, and become an elderly woman who looked like she was walking around in a ditch all of the time? It seemed more exaggerated in such a confined space, but she did not like the effect it was having on her, the sense of inferiority. She still had her stick with her, so she made a show of using it to straighten herself up to her full height. As the doors began to open and more light came in, she caught a glimpse of herself in the mirror. She nearly groaned out loud as she saw a black attired woman with flour down her front, teetering on the tips of her toes, straining to gain some sort of parity with the man opposite. *Pathetic, Maggs! You look like a penguin trying to chin a giraffe.*

'After you, Signora Neumann.' Ratty's voice was heavily loaded and she decided his earlier suspicious tone had turned to one of downright hatred now, possibly after a dressing down by Voigt for challenging his mother's credibility. *He definitely doesn't believe me. Play it cool, and don't do anything else to wind him up, Maggs.*

Some chance. 'Grazie, Ratty Hood,' she said quietly as she came off her toes.

'Sorry?'

'That's okay, Mio Amore. I forgive you.'

She fell back into an old-woman shuffle as she followed Dick and Beth along a featureless corridor, aware of the man's ominous presence behind her. There were doors that led off, all closed, and she suspected that the rooms were empty. A thriving business hub it was not, and she was struck again by the ordinariness of it all. Judging by this section, she could be in any office block in any part of the world. Like Voigt's, or Peter's, house, it was hardly the stereotypical criminal lair, except for one thing: the security to get in, bearing in mind the lack of obvious human presence, was as impressive as she had seen anywhere. They stopped at another set of doors, thick metal ones with no handles. This double set needed both Ratty's security card and a spoken password into a microphone on the wall. She watched another camera follow them as the doors opened onto yet another corridor, this one bathed in a red light which she took to be some sort of additional security feature. It switched off before they went through, presumably to prevent an alarm going off. No doubt, Ratty would be packing something. She noted that the walls looked solid, not the paper thin and flexible partitions modern offices used these days which were easy to install and move according to need. Joshua had said originally that Voigt was based in Vienna. She could not have imagined he would have gone to the same amount of trouble there, if he already had this setup in Bruges. Perhaps he had always intended to carry out main operations from here.

She detected voices as they approached a rather grand set of sliding doors at the end of the corridor. The fact she could pick up the sounds brought into sharp focus again the implant she had in her head. She now thought that her hearing, without her aid, was not only comparable to when it was fully turned up, but possibly improved.

Ratty slid back one of the doors to reveal several members of staff, busy behind computer screens. Two conducting a conversation as they went through some paperwork were probably the source of the voices she had heard. Beyond that was another closed door which Dick headed for. 'I'll see if Herr Voigt and the others are ready for us to go through. He did say earlier that things are at a delicate stage, so it's best I go check it out.' He tapped in yet another code, before it swung open and he went through.

They hung around waiting for Dick to reappear. Maggie nodded and smiled whenever Ratty or Beth caught her eye, but she got nothing by way of empathy in return. There was a tension she detected that went beyond the simple distrust she knew they felt towards her. It had been building on the way over; another indication that Voigt and Peter's plans were possibly reaching a critical point. *Better be ready then, Maggs.*

The trouble was that here she was on the verge of breaching the walls of Voigt's organisation, yet she had no clear plan quite what she was going to do should she actually punch – or in her case hobble – her way through them. Joshua had known what to do. He had a plan. But, knowing Sheldon's intolerance for failure, he was probably on his way back to England now, along with Bill and Ben. Safe, hopefully, but probably feeling very angry and resentful towards her for going her own way. She had some work to do on repairing that relationship with her great grandson, if she ever got back home... and assuming he would want to.

Her knees and back were aching from the strain of her unnaturally bent frame, and she was tempted to take a chair. She had just decided to ease the load and was halfway down to a nearby seat, when the inner door opened again.

'It's cool. We can go straight in,' said Dick.

'Sank you, Dick. This place is so, 'ow do you say… posh, si?' She began to move forwards again, deciding the tension in the air needed alleviating with some steady chatter. She commented on the posh office seats, the posh carpet, the posh computers and the poshly decorated walls. Her cheery, 'Bye, bye, sank you for 'aving me, so nice to meet you,' to the staff was met with silence, as she crossed the floor to the door that led into Voigt's inner sanctum.

* * * *

Chapter 24

'Wait here, Signora Neumann.' Maggie was definitely starting to prefer the silent version of Ratty, as his rasping voice made what should have been a polite request sound like an order.

She was at the door which she had thought led to the room where she assumed she would see Voigt again. But, after Ratty had opened it, she could see it was, in fact, just a small chamber with another door directly in front. On his say-so, she stepped in.

'Stand still and follow the instructions that you hear. The security system has been reprogrammed to accept you, but it will need to do some final confirmatory checks first.'

'I do not understand what you justa said, but grazie.'

The door closed behind, leaving her in darkness for a split second, before a red light blinked on and started to run slowly down her body. *Bugger! It's a scan!* – and Carlos' gun was still in bits at the bottom of her bag. She had put the pieces in her 'pending pocket', an area for things that needed attention in the future. A physical representation for the part of the mind where she stored things to remember later, pocket and mind behaved in a remarkably consistent fashion in that both regularly failed to remind her that they had anything in them. Until it was too late.

She dropped the bag down, praying that the scan would not go all the way to the bottom. She sighed as the scan stopped at her knees. A soulless, automated voice asked her to look directly into the lens of the camera in front, before repeating the request several times while she looked anywhere but. She genuinely had no trouble at all playing the muddled old lady in this situation. This was how she always behaved when faced with the simplest of instructions, verbal or written, from a machine. (It was always a welcome surprise whenever her bank card was returned to her from the cash point. A real bonus if money followed it).

The camera had obviously given up. 'State your name, please.' *Don't fall for that trick, Maggs, especially not to a robot.*

'Colombina Concetta Neumann. Nice to meet you.' She smiled politely as she continued to look all around.

There was a pause as the system processed her answer, and then the inner door slowly opened. She was in yet another corridor; this just a short one leading up to what she hoped was the final door.

'Place your shoes and any loose items such as bags on the scanner to your right.'

Bag... bag! – another moment of panic – *gun... gun! Think this through, Maggs. You got lucky in the body scan.*

If Voigt discovered his sweet mother not only packed a shooter, but was cocky enough to carry it around in bits, her cover would surely be blown. There were no handy plastic bags next to this conveyor belt into which she could place prohibited items (although, if she got to this point at Stansted Airport, she very much doubted she would get away with just a smile from security, as she tried to collect it on the other side with the selection of hotel complimentary shampoos and her jar of haemorrhoid cream).

Aware there were very likely more cameras looking at her, she slung her bag over the top of her arm so it was dangling in front of her. She made a show of turning round a few times as the voice repeated its request, eventually ending up facing the way she had come in through the chamber door. She knocked on the door a few times.

'Hello? Is this where I need to go in? Hello, Chrissie. Are you there?'

Ratty's voice had overridden the robot and was trying to direct her in the right direction. 'Signora Neumann. Place your bag and shoes on the scanner. It's directly behind you... in front of you... just to your right... no, there... just there... stop turning around!' His impatience was obvious, but she continued to spin round slowly and letting out the odd plaintive cry for help.

'Where are you? Is that you, Chrissie?'

All the while, she kept her hands in the bag. Locating the gun parts, she expertly – and instinctively – put them together. *You've not lost it, Maggs. Even with the arthritis in the hands and on the move, you can still do it!* The next part was going to be trickier though. Somehow, she had to get the gun out of her bag and hide it on her person before it went through the scan.

'Is it this way?' She spun once more, and then stopped.

'Turn around. Just put your bag on the scanner, Signora Neumann. It's right there.'

'Oh, dear me. Mamma Mia, I mean. It isa so difficult. Ah, I see it now.' She stepped forward, bag still over her shoulder and the gun now tucked by the side of her skirt. 'It is this way, you said?' She pointed with the other hand towards the scanner and then, as if in a rush, deliberately stumbled over, the gun in front of her as she fell. She felt a sharp pang as her ribs felt the impact of the gun. *Is the safety catch on? Too late if it isn't.*

'Signora Neumann, are you alright?' Ratty's voice had turned from exasperation and impatience to concern. *I hope Voigt gives him a right royal kick up the backside for being such a tetchy bugger.*

She lay face down, wriggling in apparent distress as she smuggled away the gun. 'Si, una minuta.'

'We'll be right there, Signora Neumann.'

There was the sound of a door being opened too at the other end of the corridor, followed by footsteps and Voigt's voice. 'What is happening? Why is my mother on the floor?'

She was gently rolled onto her side aware that Ratty, Beth and Dick had now come through the security chamber.

'I am not happy,' said Voigt sharply. 'I know we need security, but this is my mother. Look at her now. Someone should have gone through security with her.'

'I'm sorry, Mr. Voigt,' she heard Ratty say.

'Is that you, Chrissie? Oh, I'm okay, I'm okay.' It was not hard to put any signs of discomfort in her voice. Trying to find her way through several layers to stuff a gun into her knickers while lying face down prostrate on the floor, had been an unnatural and challenging task. Her voice was strained as a result. On top of that, her ribs were starting to hurt... quite a lot.

'Signora Neumann,' Beth said. 'What happened?' Her hostility and suspicion had waned somewhat, probably, Maggie hoped, in the face of Voigt's obvious displeasure at the treatment of his mother.

'Oh, I fell over. I am so clumsy sometimes. I will be okay, grazie.'

'Can you sit up, Mamma? Is anything broken?' asked Voigt.

Bloody hope not! 'I don't think so. Yes, 'elp me sit up, please.'

'My God, Mamma! Look at the state of you,' said Voigt. 'What is all that white stuff?'

'It's flour,' said Dick. 'Signora Neumann was showing us how to make pasta,'.

'Pasta! Just like we used to do together,' said Voigt, a hint of emotion in his voice.

'Si, Bello.' Maggie puffed her cheeks in and out. 'Just like we used to make.'

They fussed over her for a few moments more before she asked them to help her to her feet. Dick picked up her bag, while Voigt and Beth supported her arms as she limped through to the far door. *All that and they didn't even bother to put the bag through the bloody scanner!*

Still, it looked like she was in. That was the main thing.

'Wella, that was a bit of a Pavlova,' she said as she was directed to a sofa in a very large room.

'I'm sorry, Mamma. We have very important work here. We cannot take any risks. The security we have is set up so that we have to check anyone who is new.'

'Even your own Mamma?'

Voigt looked abashed. It was extraordinary, Maggie thought. She was still not sure what to make of his behaviour towards her. One moment she was thinking she was fooling no one; the next, Voigt was treating her like royalty. The more extravagant her behaviour, the more he seemed to believe her. Perhaps they were all becoming convinced. She looked at Ratty's expression. *P'raps not.*

'That was wrong of us.' He looked pointedly at Ratty. 'Some of us can be a little, how do I say it in English, overzealous? Are you sure you are okay, Mamma? Shall we get you to a doctor?'

'No, I am fine. Bene, grazie. A little water would be good, perhaps.' *Or a stiff vodka.*

She exhaled sharply as she felt another twinge from her ribs. She wanted to adjust the position of the gun a little, yet any movement down there hurt at the moment. She took the glass of cold water Dick brought over to her. The gun would have to stay at the angle it was for now, but the short barrel was not in the most comfortable of positions.

Voigt sat down on the edge of the seat next to her, fussing over her as she sipped. She could see now that his office was huge. In fact, it was not a personal office by any means, more an open plan arrangement that you would find in any standard business. It was largely empty. A large oval table with twenty or so chairs around it, each space with its own terminal, was to the left. To one side of it was a mahogany desk, Voigt's she guessed judging by the fancy leather chair behind it, with a solitary computer. Another door was in the far right hand corner next to the window which ran the length of the room. The window was tinted, presumably as another security precaution. The rest of the space was filled with desks, a couple of photocopiers and filing cabinets. There were a few people dotted around looking at computer screens with scrolling lines of letters and numbers. Typical of any quiet office, the air was punctuated with hushed voices, the odd phone ringing, and the sound of a printer whirring away. It was hardly action stations, yet there was tension in the air.

A sharp, sudden pang in her ear made her wince. She tried to ignore it, but Voigt had spotted her momentary discomfort. 'What is it, Mamma?'

She shook her head dismissively and shrugged, but there was another quick stab, this time accompanied by a whistling sound. *Is that the tinnitus back, Maggs? Not tinnitus... remember, you've got a foreign object inside you.* Something – she did not know what – was happening inside her head.

'Mamma?' Voigt was looking at her intently now.

'It isa nothing, Chrissie. I'ma justa a leetle shaken, but I will be fine. I fall over a lot.'

He smiled sympathetically.

It was quite unpleasant, yet, at her advanced age, she was well used to dealing with aches and pains. The best way was to just get on, so she turned her attention to finding out what she could. 'You have a nice place, Chrissie. A lot of work. But why did you bring me here?'

'I wanted you here to share my success. This is the centre of my business, very important business, and we are about to do something very big.' He looked at his watch. 'It's nearly time. In the next minute, these computers will all be manned by my top people. Preparations are going on in the room next door, at this very moment, which will send shock waves around the world. We are going to be very rich very quickly but, most importantly, I am with you. We've been too long apart. It's taken me three years to plan all of this, and nearly as long to find you. It's right that it all comes together at the same time.'

You were right, Maggs, it is all happening now. Are you too late? Have you gone through all this for nothing? The vibrations in her head were now accompanied by a whistle. Whatever they had put inside her was definitely active. Joshua had said it was designed to stop Voigt, but her role had to be more than just to sit here like a dummy, surely?

Her gut told her to get up and do something. But what? *If you hadn't been so busy mollycoddling Joshua, he'd still be here and you'd know what the plan was.* A definite option was to destroy as many of the computers as she could. Joshua had wanted her to disrupt the organisation; well a good whack with her stick was a start. Hardly a sophisticated plan, yet good old-fashioned wonton destruction often did the job. It had certainly worked in that police station in Berlin, years ago.

She felt for the gun and eased herself forward on her chair – *coiled and ready to pounce like a panther; a very old, arthritic panther with a stick, a dodgy rib and a gun wedged fast in its underwear. Oh, Maggs...*How had she got herself into this situation?

She stopped, distracted by the opening of the door by the window and a line of staff filing in, then taking their places at the computers. *If you're going to make a move, you're going to have to make it now, Maggs.*

And she probably would have, but for an almighty sudden thrumming sound which induced a blinding pain in her right temple.

The intensity of it knocked her clean out.

*   *   *   *

Chapter 25

Maggie came round slowly, squinting in an attempt to make sense of her surroundings. Gradually, things started to come into focus, and she remembered: *Voigt's office.* The light was toned down, and she wondered if she had been out of it for so long that it was the middle of the night. She turned her head to see that there was a blind now covering the main windows, blocking out any possible daylight. It could be any time of day or night. There was a low hubbub in the room, quiet intense conversations, she sensed. An occasional bleeping sound, interrupted the busy atmosphere now and again, complemented by a celebratory 'Yes!' or equivalent in a foreign language from a mixture of young male and female voices.

Maggie felt for her rib. She had cracked a rib before and not been able to talk, the pain had been so bad. She pressed it gently; it felt easier than when she had first fallen on it. *Definitely not cracked. Good.* The thrumming and whistling in her head had stopped, leaving her with a general feeling of fuzziness, similar to when she had come round in the hospital in Frampton. There was a connection there. *Maggs, get your brain in gear... ah yes! That bloody implant!*

She was still on the sofa, lying down now and alone. At first, she felt a little hurt that Voigt had left her unattended but, judging by his reaction earlier, it was unlikely he had had a change of heart and abandoned her. No doubt someone would be along soon to check on her. Meanwhile, here was an opportunity for some horizontal spying. She would stay as still as possible, so she might remain undisturbed, while she assessed the situation. She recalled her training from years ago which said to go through a checklist of established facts. The words of her instructor had always stuck with her: 'You can't easily affect what you don't know, so concentrate on what you do know, and affect that.'

Right, you're on a sofa in the centre of Voigt's organisation. That in itself was a great achievement. *No backup.* Not such a great achievement. *Voigt is not in the line of sight at present, but safe to assume he is nearby... Criminal activity on Voigt's part is probably ongoing. Cause of unconsciousness unknown, but safe to assume it is connected to the implant in your head.*

Then she did something which she detested herself for, but could not stop doing these days when in confusing situations, particularly when she had important decisions to make. She carried out a conversation with herself. It was an entirely mental conversation, but anyone observing her would have physically seen her moving her head to each side as a new voice 'spoke' – an *anti-Maggie* on the shoulder, as it were, challenging her.

Bill had noticed her doing it once in Sukuel's when she was trying to decide between pizza and a healthier fish dish for her mains. After she had explained to him what she was doing, he had actually fallen off his seat in fits of giggles, and had had to be rescued by Ben when he returned from the washroom.

'It's even worse when I have to add a third item to my list of choices,' she had explained. 'A three-way conversation really does my neck in!'

Anti-Maggie seemed to be particularly bolshie today.

So, where is this son of yours in all this?

Peter? He is not my son.

Are you sure?

Positive. He's much too tall. Besides, his eyes are too close together. I don't trust him.

You're not supposed to trust him. He's a criminal, like Voigt.

Voigt seems too soft to be a criminal. He's not at all the man I thought he was.

You're the one who's soft. Voigt's a criminal. You're here, to stop him. Anyway, Joshua said Voigt's right hand man was your son. The man you met is called Peter. Your son's called Peter, so it's got to be him.

He may be his right hand man, but he's not my son. Anyway, I want to talk about this situation now. No known backup available. Joshua currently out of the picture.

That was your doing, Maggs. You decided to go it alone for his safety. Why you should think he needed protection, goodness knows.

Because he is my family, and my instinct is to protect my family.

Is that why you're here, Maggs? For your family? All of them? How does this help 'Son, Peter' exactly? You might have to arrest him. Arrest your own son.

I've told you, he's not my son. Anyway, I'm here because I have to do what's right.

Have you always done what's right, Maggs?

I've tried to.

Istanbul, years ago, when you gave the command to capture the target? The order from on high was to dispose of him. Your decision put your co-agent at risk. Was that the right thing to do? What about your co-agent's family who lost a father when it all

went wrong? Was it the right thing to do for them?

I don't like taking lives unnecessarily. The target got away. My co-agent didn't. It was the wrong decision, but I did my best. You shouldn't have brought that up. It's got nothing to do with now. I'm trying to put it right for all of us. All my family.

Was it the right decision to give up Peter?

That was supposed to be temporary!

You like Voigt more than you like Peter. You don't want to believe Peter is your son because he's not as likeable as Voigt.

The internal conversations did not always work, with *anti-Maggie* often delving far too deeply into her emotional baggage to see what should have been declared. She put a halt to it before she got well and truly stuck in the red channel. Which was just as well, because one of the operators nearby had noticed the continual head movement and was giving her a very strange look.

With her head – and mind – still now, she could focus on events around her. It had suddenly become very busy. Even Ratty was preoccupied on a screen. There was general activity, but no wild celebrations, nothing to say the job was done. It looked like it was work in progress, which had to be a good thing, on the one hand. On the other hand, judging by the relative calmness and continued efficiency all about her, the implant, whatever it was designed to do, had not had any sort of impact. It might still be down to her to make the difference here. She eased herself up into a sitting position.

She caught a glimpse of Voigt next to one of the computers on the far side of the office, nodding encouragement and smiling at one of his staff, obviously pleased with the way things were progressing. He must have been looking out for signs of movement from her, because he immediately caught her eye, waved and started to make his way over towards her. She could see Dick at another screen, tapping away, and Beth nearby, scrutinising the work of another operative. Work in progress maybe but, judging by the mood and a sudden flurry of activity, this was definitely moving towards something very significant. She had to find a way to stop it.

Whatever you do, do something, Maggs! However hard it is.

She reached into her knickers and with an enormous effort pulled out the gun. Letting it rest by her side, she released the safety catch.

Take out the main targets, Agent Matheson. Do the right thing, this time.

I know! Leave me be.

She clocked the whereabouts of Peter standing with his back to her at a screen to the right. Could she take out her own son? *He's not your son, Maggs...* there was still that doubt. She hesitated, her finger on the trigger. She would only need a second to raise it and fire off two shots. *Voigt first, then Peter.* Voigt was barely ten metres away. ***Do it!*** He had his hands out in front, gesturing for her to take it easy, his face full of concern.

'Mamma, you must sit down. You are not well.'

His look turned to utter bewilderment and then extreme hurt, as she raised the gun to take aim.

Just as she was about to squeeze the trigger... 'Don't do that, Agent Matheson!'

Maggie stopped. The voice behind her was very familiar.

'We don't want Mr Voigt disposed of just yet. We might still need to make use of his services.'

*   *   *   *

Chapter 26

Maggie turned around. 'Sheldon!'

She relaxed her trigger hand and lowered the gun. Voigt, frozen to the spot, his hands in the air, stared at her in disbelief. Two agents were immediately upon him, one with weapon raised as the other frisked him down. Maggie watched a dozen more of Sheldon's agents, all armed, fanning out across the office, securing the area and preventing further activity on the computers. Both exits, the one Maggie had come through and the door in the corner of the room, already had guards at them. Voigt's people were unceremoniously jerked away from their screens, some replaced by Service personnel. All were checked for weapons, then shepherded to a space in the middle and forced to the floor, their backs to each other in a circle. Agents began to cuff them while the main protagonists, Voigt, Dick and Ruth – she could not see Peter for the moment – were manhandled over towards Maggie and Sheldon.

It had taken a barely a minute for Sheldon to cease all operations and engineer a complete takeover. Maggie could not help but be impressed.

'I didn't think I would ever say this, but I'm actually pleased to see you, Tina Sheldon.'

'And I'm pleased to see you too, Maggie Matheson.' Sheldon placed a hand on her shoulder. 'No wait… is it Maggie? It's so hard to tell under that brilliant disguise!'

Maggie was too relieved to even bother thinking of a comeback.

And she barely noticed the agent who eased the gun out of her hand.

Sheldon turned to Voigt, Dick and Beth. 'Why don't the three of you sit down? You must be feeling a little shaky after what's happened.' Her voice sounded calm, but Maggie knew her well enough to detect a note of triumph in it.

'You were going to shoot me!' Voigt waved a finger angrily at Maggie as he was pushed towards the sofa. 'I saw you pointing the gun. You're not my Mamma.' He gasped as a hand was shoved into his chest and he fell back.

'Why are you so surprised?' said Beth as she and Dick were forced to join him. 'We tried to warn you.'

Voigt ignored her and awkwardly shuffled forward on his seat. 'What's the meaning of this? What's going on?'

'What's going on here, Mr Voigt, is a coup d'état,' said Sheldon. 'Your little operation has now become our little operation. We've been watching you for some time, spies everywhere. You've already met Agent Matheson, of course.'

He looked up at Maggie. 'You're an agent? A spy?'

For some reason, Maggie felt the need to apologise. 'I'm sorry, but I'm afraid so.'

'Surprise, surprise,' muttered Dick under his breath.

The look of betrayal on Voigt's face was almost too much to bear. While it cut through Maggie, it was plain from Sheldon's superior expression that she was enjoying the moment. Typical of her, she thought, but Maggie had to give her credit.

'You got here just in time,' she said to her. 'It was starting to get a little hairy.' She was met by a nod, and there was a moment when no one said anything. Voigt's head was down, as were those of

Beth and Dick. Maggie hated awkward silences. 'Like my chin,' she added, straight away wishing that she liked awkward silences. Sheldon raised an eyebrow. 'Er... hairy... like my chin... these days, anyway.' She stroked it, and inwardly cursed as she realised how stupid that must have looked, given the situation.

Sheldon's lips twitched, threatening a smile, before she said in a business-like fashion, 'You must be exhausted. Please join the others on the sofa.'

'I'm not sure Mr. Voigt will be too pleased to be sharing with me.'

'None of us will be,' said Dick.

Nevertheless, Maggie found her arm being taken by one of the agents, and she was led over to the sofa, where she was encouraged – with a gentle, but definite pull downwards – to take a seat on the end.

'There, how cosy! Now, who's this, I wonder?' said Sheldon, as her gaze was drawn to movement behind their heads.

'All secure in the other rooms, Executive S,' a voice said.

'Good news! Thank you, Peter.'

'Peter?' said Maggie.

Voigt's expression, which had only just settled into one of resignation, was forced into action again. 'Peter... you're part of this?'

He's a double agent! Maggie tried – and failed – to keep her own look of surprise off her face. She had been totally blindsided by events. But on the up side, Peter not being a criminal might make things a little more comfortable if it turned out that they were related. Did it make him any more likeable? She doubted it. The jury was still out on that one.

Without so much as a glance at Voigt or Maggie, Peter drew in close to Sheldon, and whispered something in her ear which elicited a nod of confirmation. Frustratingly, Maggie's hearing was not good enough to pick up what was said, so she was left to her own devices to fill in the gaps in her knowledge about what was happening now. It took a moment to realise she could not without help.

'I have some questions…' She began to stand, but was none too gently coerced down again by the hand of one of Sheldon's agents.

'I'm sure you have, Agent Matheson,' said Sheldon. 'Save them for now. Peter, are we ready?''

'I have primed the mainframe,' said Peter, loud enough now for them all to hear, 'and we can begin sequencing as soon as you give the command,'

'Good, then we're ready to begin.'

'Begin what?' Voigt piped up.

'You'll soon see.'

'Tell me what's going on! Peter!' Ignored, Voigt turned his frustration onto Maggie. 'You tell me, then.'

'Um...'

'You double-crossed me. You're worse than him. I thought you were my mother. But I guess mothers don't pull guns on their sons.'

'You didn't really believe I was your mother… did you?'

'Yes, I did. I didn't believe it at first when those stories started coming through. But he,' Voigt shot an accusatory glance at Peter, 'convinced me. Now I know why. You were in it together.'

Maggie's instinct was to say, 'Were we? I had no idea,' but instead, she nodded in what she hoped was a wise and knowing way. It did explain a concern she had had about whether Voigt would be accepting of her. If his best friend was influencing him, she could see how and why, despite advice to the contrary.

'My guts told me she was a fake,' Dick reiterated.

'Mine too,' said Beth.

'And mine,' Ratty muffled contribution came from the floor nearby where he was lying face-down, with his own guard watching over him.

'Particularly after that pasta debacle,' added Dick. 'Italian, my God!'

Voigt turned on Peter again. 'And you were supposed to be my best friend. We had it all set up. We were going to make a fortune! Why do it?'

'Don't answer that,' Sheldon snapped. 'All you need to know, Mr. Voigt, is that he is, and always has been, working for me.'

Maggie noticed the exchange of a brief private smile between Sheldon and Peter. *Hmm... what did that look mean?* It certainly was not one of regret from Peter, no guilt there, whatsoever, about betraying a friend. In fact, other than that connection with Sheldon, he was showing little outward emotion. *Which is the way you have to look at it, Maggs. This is business after all. Service business.* She had to admit Peter seemed to have acted with a great deal of professionalism, performing a clever counter espionage job, over a long period of time. To crack into Voigt's organisation and help Sheldon catch him in the act, was no mean feat. The Service should be proud of him. Perhaps she should be too.

There was a subtext to explore here between Sheldon and Peter. *Was that a blush from The Shafter just now when Peter brushed past her?* A coy look in his direction? *Maybe... possibly...*

definitely! She forced herself not to judge. It would not be the first romance between two Service personnel. *Me and Frankie for starters.* So what if there was a thing going on between them? They were consenting adults, and it did not adversely affect the outcome. The mission seemed to be all wrapping up nicely… and Maggie's own role, judging by the complete control her fellow agents now had in the room, seemed to be complete.

Although, she had to admit she was a little unclear as to her personal contribution, other than getting in and then falling unconscious. 'Infiltrate, assess and disrupt,' Joshua had instructed. She had certainly infiltrated the organisation. She had done little in the way of assessing – she was still a little confused and annoyed with herself for her clumsy spying attempts back at the house – and she had not got round to doing much disruption yet. But that was alright, since Sheldon and her people were here now to stop all the bad things happening. Just in the nick of time.

'Well, it looks like I'm done here.' She tried to make her tone sound officious, like Sheldon's. 'It's probably time I made a move.' *Where to Maggs? You've no idea where you are.* Regardless, she made to get up, but once again she was persuaded back down by Sheldon's agent, this time rather unceremoniously, with a firm push. She felt a jolt in her rib as she fell back, and let out a small cry of pain.

'You can't leave just yet, Agent Matheson,' said Sheldon. She called across to an operative, seated at one of the terminals. 'Is the full download complete yet?'

'No, Executive S. We won't know for sure until we have linked in with the other data chip, but indications are that Voigt's actions were 90% complete when it stopped, which is what we wanted.

The second chip will connect the remaining pathways. At that stage, we will have complete control.'

'So you've taken over our systems?' said Voigt.

'Correct, Mr. Voigt. Proximity and timing was the key. It had to be done just as you were loading your systems up ready to go. The big day! The day you launch your brilliant protection system to the world's governments and top organisations. The day you blackmail them for every penny they've got. I must commend your friend Peter, here.' She pulled him in beside her and held his arm affectionately. *Well, well! Definitely together. But they make an odd couple – he must be a foot and a half taller than her.* 'His timing was impeccable. He played you along so well. To persuade you to delay your operation until your mother arrived was a master stroke. It gave us everything we needed.'

'I do not understand,' said Voigt. 'What has this woman – don't call her my mother – got to do with it?'

'You'd really like to know? Well, it's quite a story, one I'm personally quite proud of.' *Typical Sheldon – taking all the glory!* 'We knew we could not take over your systems by just sending a bug down the line. Credit where credit is due – you do specialise in security after all, Mr. Voigt. No, we knew we needed to get much closer in than that. A link needed to be physically brought in while you were running your sequences. Once it was close enough, it would automatically set things in motion. A simple Bluetooth connection, a transmitter in a data chip, and then our systems took over. Your security has been blown wide open. Maggie has opened doors, quite literally, enabling my people to get in here without detection. How else do you think they got in so quickly? More importantly, we now have access to all your computer systems and have full control. As Maggie might say, "You've been done up like a kipper", Mr. Voigt.'

Most of the time, Maggie was fairly content to sit back and let things happen around her. Well, that was not quite true: she had always been a bit of a control freak – 'a bossy moo,' as Frankie occasionally called her. But as she had got older, she had been more open to letting people do things for her. Independence was important, yes, but actually it was nice if others helped you out now and again.

As a young agent, she had always been on top of things. She had needed to be. She would not have been able to take on complex cases without being organised. On this mission, she had let her age be an excuse for allowing things to happen for her. It was her stubbornness to protect Joshua, not her willingness to be independent, which had encouraged her to go it alone when they had been in Amsterdam. Now, as she sat trying to piece together what was going on, she realised she missed Joshua quite badly; he would have been by her side, supporting her and explaining. Explaining words like 'Bluetooth'.

'So where is this Bluetooth connection?' said Voigt.

'Inside Agent Matheson's head, of course. We were going to put it into her hearing aid, but, after some technical advice from Peter here, we realised your systems might see through that.'

'It's in my head?'

'Yes. You make a great mule, Maggie.'

'Mule? Who are you calling a bloody mule?' She continued to

harrumph and mutter, 'Blinkin' Nora, a mule? I'll give you mule!' – putting to bed any remaining illusions that she may have had Italian ancestry.

'Why not just ask Judas,' Voigt shot a disparaging glance at Peter, 'to access our systems from here?'

'Come now, Mr. Voigt, you would have spotted that too. We've had to do everything externally and bring it in when ready. It really is a massive statement about your security. You should see it as a compliment. We had the technological side done, and then arranged for the implant while Maggie was being treated in hospital.'

She gave Voigt a look which made Maggie remember why she disliked this woman so much. She had seen it on her before. It was a look which showed that she was feeling something more than just professional satisfaction at having prevented Voigt's plans. It was a look which said: 'I've got one over you – you're beaten. I'm better than you.' It was the look of a 'smug cow' – another of Frankie's expressions. Like Maggie, he hated the air of superiority some displayed when they got into management positions. Maggie sensed that Sheldon was using that position of power now, and was very much enjoying the fact that she was treading all over Voigt and his colleagues.

Sheldon continued, 'We had to think how to get Maggie into hospital so we could do the implant. Carlos wouldn't kidnap her, so we had to put plan B – the crash – into place, sharpish.'

Maggie still wanted to look like she knew what was going on, but she was finding it hard to keep up the pretence. There were still too many gaps.

'Hold on, let me be clear. It was you who asked Carlos to kidnap me?'

'Yes. The idea was to drug you, put the implant in, and blame the accident on someone else. Already involved, you'd have had had to take on the mission then.'

Maggie was taken slightly aback. *Kidnap me then drug me?* That sounded a bit drastic, even for Sheldon. Nevertheless, she was probably right: it certainly would have captured her attention.

'The text, the phone slamming down and then the crash. That was you in that text?'

'Yes. Carlos was refusing to follow orders.'

Good for Carlos! 'So there were no insiders on the technical side trying to blackmail Carlos?'

'No...' Sheldon snorted a half laugh. 'There were no insiders on the technical side trying to blackmail Carlos.'

'Why did he say there was?'

'Who knows? Scared probably.'

'Hang on... so if Carlos wouldn't kidnap me before the crash, why did you ask him to do it again after I came back from Torquay?'

'I didn't. He acted on his own, thinking that because he had you, he could somehow bribe me.' *Bribe you? For what?* But she did not have a chance to ask the question. 'He bottled that too, but it turned out well because you went back to Joshua, and the mission was back on track. That's when Carlos became a liability. We can't have anyone going round trying to bribe government officials. We had to deal with him to prevent further possible transgressions.'

Maggie's heart skipped a beat. She did not like the way this conversation had suddenly turned. She knew full well what, 'to deal with' meant. It was Service parlance for assassination or extermination. Carlos, although not totally innocent, did not deserve that. He had tried to do the right thing in the end, at least. *Could be deemed as collateral damage, I suppose? That's too kind, Maggs. She's ruthless.*

'You would have thought the threat of not being able to see our... his kids again would have been enough to make sure he did the job properly in the first place. I should have known he wouldn't do it. Still, I felt I had to give him a chance.'

Did she just say, 'our kids'? But Sheldon seemed to be tiring of the conversation. She turned away to say something to Peter before Maggie could delve deeper. Desperate to get her attention back, Maggie called across. 'So, Joshua's aware of all this?'

Sheldon turned back, happy enough, it seemed, with the opportunity to crow over this new line of enquiry from Maggie. 'Ah, the lovely Joshua. A special agent who does what he's told. No, he was pretty much in the dark, but had to go along with it.' Maggie resisted the urge to smile as she recalled her exchange with her grandson – *Need to know.* 'If I was being ultra critical, I would say he's a little too honest sometimes. His role was to persuade you to join us and to manage the Voigt case. Failed on both counts. We nearly lost you after you went all sniffy on us, but you made the right decision to rejoin us. I always knew you would.'

'I make my own decisions, thank you very much.'

'True... within certain parameters. You're a good spy, Maggie, although you were a bit careless nosing around in Peter's study. He had to cover for you. Good job he's so very thorough.' She ran her hand along Peter's shoulder, and turned her attention back to Voigt. 'You've been lapse with your security updates, Mr. Voigt. Good news for us, not for you. Our plan seems to have worked well. Maggie got us in.'

Maggie was determined not to let her train of thought be diverted. 'Back to the crash and the kidnapping, Sheldon. I don't understand why you resorted to trying those? Wasn't there another way to get the implant in me? You could have just asked, for example.'

'And what would you have said? You know how you are with technology, Maggie. Not your bag at all. This was a heavily computer biased mission.'

'That's true. E.T. has never been my strong point.'

'Precisely! You do love a bit of drama, don't you, Maggie?'

'A bit of drama? I could have been killed!'

'Nonsense. It was all carefully calculated. We wouldn't want our prize asset compromised. Our driver's very good. Joshua wasn't happy about the kidnapping or the crash. He just wanted to recruit you straight. That was why he was at the restaurant. If I had asked you directly, you would have said no, just to wind me up. I know you well... and how awkward you can be.' Maggie had to concede she had a point there. 'Neither was Joshua happy when he found out we had installed the chip inside your head. He's so protective of you. I don't know why.' *Hope you never know why either. That's our secret, not yours*. 'The car was a bit over the top, but it did the job after Carlos got all stroppy. You were always a sucker for the spy stuff: action, intrigue, that sort of thing. I'm sure you were also interested when Joshua told you that your son, Peter, was working here. Admit it, Maggie. You had to find out about him.'

'Son? Peter?' spluttered Voigt.

'And then there was Mr. Voigt – would he believe you were his mother, would he not? But he fell for it hook, line and sinker. It was essential he accepted you from the word go, Maggie. A little doubt in your own mind though worked a treat, got you thinking, questioning things, kept you involved, got you doing all the things good spies do. We had to keep you on board with a bit of spy magic, or else you would have thought it was too easy and seen through it. But Mr. Voigt was always going to accept you; we had Peter making sure that would happen.'

Peter, the son, was the bait. You were the fish, Maggs. Sheldon's expression about Voigt being done up like a kipper doesn't just apply to him.

But did it really matter? The job was done, so let Sheldon have her day in the sun. It was not the first time an agent would have been thrown into a situation to perform a role, unaware that they were a pawn. And the means justified the end, didn't it? The spy world was a tough business and, although she had been played along, who was she to question the outcome? Voigt's plans had been well and truly scuppered, and the world would be a safer place as a result. Presumably, now they would be able to deal with the high-level corruption Joshua referred to.

'So the implant in me has done its bit? It's stopped Mr. Voigt.'

'Yes, thank you, Maggie. It cracked open the security here. It literally opened doors for our agents to get in.'

It explained the noises and discomfort in her head. By her physically getting inside, the data chip had overridden all the security Voigt had, enabling Sheldon to follow her in and catch him in the act. It was clever, although Maggie was not yet ready to admit that to Sheldon.

'You used me, Sheldon. That was a cruel thing to tell me my son was involved. Peter's not my son, is he?''

Sheldon shrugged. 'What do you think? It got you here, didn't it?'

Maggie noticed a smirk from Peter. *No, then.* Having it confirmed made her suddenly aware of how Voigt must feel, thinking he was going to be reunited with a loved one and being let down. *Don't shed any tears, Maggs. You're a tough agent; this sort of thing comes with the job.*

'Are we ready for that second phase, yet?' Maggie's thoughts were interrupted by Sheldon calling across to one of her agents.

'Yes, Executive S.'

'Okay, good. Peter... You have the other data chip ready?'

'He's got a data chip too?' said Maggie.

'Yes, Maggie,' said Sheldon. 'Do try to keep up. This is the one Carlos had been working on, and was supposed to deliver to us along with you. It was in his phone. He nearly lost it in the restaurant when he smashed the thing on the table. Such a temper sometimes! Fortunately, we retrieved it.'

'What does it do?' asked Voigt.

'It connects up all of your data and systems to our own, a triangulation between it, the chip in Maggie's head and your computers.'

Peter stepped forward to the operative's screen. He passed something to him, something too small for Maggie to see. The agent took it and carefully placed it into a small cartridge which he then inserted into the side of the computer.

'Run triangulation programme,' Peter instructed into the computer's microphone. He looked towards Maggie and grinned. It was not a friendly expression. 'Password: Operation moneybags.'

Voigt found his voice again. 'Triangulation programme. What is that?'

Peter walked up to Voigt and bent down next to him. 'That, my dear Chrissie, is well and truly the end of a beautiful friendship. Now Agent Matheson's implant has laid bare your security, the programme on that chip I started running will allow us to control the accounts that your clients are currently arranging payments into.'

'It's quite simple really,' added Sheldon gleefully. 'Carlos, for all his faults, was quite the innovator. He designed both chips: Maggie's and this one. That chip Peter has just put in is the final piece of the jigsaw.'

'I don't believe it!' said Voigt. He fell forward with his head in his hands.

Maggie could see from his reaction that for Voigt, the penny had dropped. Unfortunately for her, as she had feared might happen, she had been bamboozled by all the jargon being thrown about. Far from dropping, the penny was not even poised above the slot machine. It was still firmly in her purse waiting to be changed from a five pound note by the spotty youth in the arcade's cashier booth. There was also a lengthy queue.

Look like you know what's going on, Maggs. She nodded confidently, an action which she hoped would convince anyone who was looking at her that this was all part of the Service's plan, a plan she was fully conversant with, a plan she was integral to. It was a hard look to carry off when she did not actually have a clue.

Sheldon's eyes seemed to light up, and the whole room was quiet as they waited for the agent to tap away and check more numbers and figures on the screen. Sheldon then let out an unexpected squeal of triumph when she received the nod from Peter.

'And so the money starts to roll in.' Sheldon rubbed her hands.

'Thanks so much for your help, Mr. Voigt. And to you too, Maggie, for enabling all of this.' Sheldon's irritating leer was just like the one Maggie remembered when she had told Maggie over twenty-one years ago that her services were no longer needed.

Maggie looked at Voigt, a beaten man, then back at Sheldon who just held her gaze. Maggie slapped the heel of her hand to her forehead as the penny came careening through the machine and bounced on the floor. 'You have to be kidding me... you're doing what Voigt was doing? When you said that you were taking it over, you're not simply preventing his operation. You're actually taking it all for yourself. "Operation moneybags," he said. All of this so that you can make a few quid?'

'Oh, we're making a lot more than a few quid, Maggs. With my high-level contacts and their access around the whole world, we can go much wider than Mr. Voigt can with his little dabble into foreign security systems. I must say that we are grateful for his sterling work on providing the platform. He was hoping to have one or two rogue governments, plus a few corporations under his influence. We will have virtually the whole planet under our control. They'll pay billions to stop us bringing their networks to their knees.' She went over to Peter, who was leaning over one of the screens, and gave his backside a gentle squeeze. He stood up, turned and chuckled. Maggie might have gagged at the sloppy kiss they exchanged had she not been concentrating on dealing with the turmoil in her head.

'You stupid, old woman, Maggs,' she said under her breath. This was the corruption Joshua was talking about, the house of cards he was hoping would come tumbling down. Maggie could see few signs of collapse as Sheldon's agents went about their business.

She suddenly felt sick to the stomach. If Tina Sheldon was involved, then this was big. Her notoriety for ruthlessness, attention to detail and undoubted political influence meant that they were all going to be in a lot of trouble.

You've been well and truly shafted by Sheldon the Shafter, Maggs.... We all have.

In the confusion, Maggie had not noticed her gun being confiscated from her. *That was sloppy, Maggs. Very sloppy.* One of Sheldon's agents stood nearby, hands loosely by his side, his own gun a tempting whisker away in its holster. She had some decisions to take, but first, to relieve some frustration, she indulged in some chuntering under her breath.

'Bloody Sheldon. I should have guessed. Never could stand the woman. How could I be so stupid? What was I thinking?' *Still, Sheldon? Really? In it for the cash?* It was hard to accept.

She had known Sheldon for a long time, worked under her, and would never have had her clocked as someone who would set up something like this. A royalist, she epitomised the establishment: loyal to the flag, loyal to the government. For all her faults, she was not someone who would go against the Service or do anything to jeopardise the security of her country. So, was it just for the money? Or was it a power thing? Maybe it was for love, judging by the way she and Peter were carrying on together.

Maggie eased forward and looked past Voigt along on the sofa. Beth was still there with Dick on the other side, both seemingly locked in their own thoughts. Beth was shaking, out of fear,

Maggie suspected. Dick caught her eye and scowled, so she shifted her attention back to Voigt next to her. His eyes were open, firmly fixed to a spot on the floor in front. He seemed beaten, devastated. *Not surprised. He's lost everything.* However, that did not excuse his criminality.

She folded her arms. 'You'll get no bloody sympathy from me.'

'I haven't asked for any.'

'You're as bad as Sheldon is. You were happy to blackmail innocent governments and big companies.

'It was business. I was doing them a favour by highlighting flaws in their security. Besides, governments aren't innocent. You can see that from your boss's actions.'

'She's nothing to do with me, nor with my government.' She paused thoughtfully, before adding, 'Not most of it anyway.'

'Hah!'

He sunk into silence again, so Maggie checked on what was happening around her. If she blotted out Voigt's people sitting uncomfortably on the floor in the centre and the odd agent with a gun, it resembled any other busy office she had come across, very similar to the scene that had met her when she arrived less than an hour earlier, only with Voigt's operatives being replaced by Sheldon's black clad own. Peter and Sheldon moved between them, his role more proactive of the two. Occasionally, he would intervene, taking control before handing the computer back to its operator. Sheldon was strutting around like a peacock, her eyes roaming, not engaging in any of the specifics. She was the evil queen, expecting her minions to create and maintain her power and wealth. Maggie gritted her teeth before giving in and releasing an audible and satisfying, 'Sanctimonious Witch!'

'I have to agree,' said Voigt.

Maggie looked at him levelly before speaking softly. 'Did you really think I was your mother?'

'Yes.'

'Really really? I thought I made a terrible Italian. Sorry that I got your hopes up.'

'You don't sound like you mean that.'

'I do, kind of... More than kind of.' She knew what it was like to lose a child. The bond between a mother and son is a close one. *Close enough for you to want to take on this mission and find your child again.* It had not worked out, so yes: she could definitely sympathise with Voigt. 'I have to admit that you did look upset when you found out. But you have to understand that you were the target. I had to do it.'

He smiled ironically. 'Don't tell me…you were just doing your job.'

'I was. I'm an agent. Or at least I used to be.'

'We all used to be something. I used to be a director of a security firm who was going to make millions on the back of persuading governments they needed to enhance their security systems.'

'That's a very positive spin to put on it, Mr. Voigt.'

'In the long term, I was doing them a favour. If I could get in, anyone could. Anyway, now I'm just the director of a security firm who has been fooled by an old lady into allowing her boss to take over his security company. You've ruined me.'

'Wasn't just me. Don't forget your best friend Peter played a large part in all this. Having it away with my boss too! Who would have thought it? Physically shafting Shafter Sheldon.'

'What?'

'Sorry – private joke. Not an easy one to say either, especially with these cheap NHS teeth. Anyway, I could argue you deserve what's happened here. You're a criminal, Mr. Voigt, and I haven't forgotten your past demeanours. You used to be an unscrupulous computer expert working for the East Germans, bent on destroying the UK government. People got killed at that time. Remember that before you are too critical of me.'

'That was never my intention to kill. I cannot speak for the East German government, of course, but my role was purely passive. I am not a man of violence.'

'Maybe not. Don't tell me… you were just doing your job.'

It drew a half-smile, before he continued on. 'You hurt me, though. I thought my mother had really come back to me. You and Peter have really hurt me…'

'You think me and Peter hurt you? You're not the only one who has been hurt. I found out three weeks ago that my son, who I gave up at a very young age, was alive and well, and working for a major criminal.'

'Your son? I didn't really understand what Sheldon meant. It's Peter who is your son? Mein Gott.' It was the first lapse into his German tongue that Maggie had heard. 'How? He never said anything.'

'Well, he wouldn't, would he? We're spies, remember? That was the point. It was you who was supposed to be my son.' There was a pause. She filled it by fiddling with her fingers, distracted, sad almost. 'I thought he was my son, but he isn't.'

'You are a difficult lady to understand.'

'Peter's definitely no Matheson. He's too bloody ugly for a start... and he's got appalling taste in women!'

Voigt snorted a laugh.

'I don't know whether to be sad that I haven't found my son or happy that that bastard isn't my son.'

Voigt became serious again. 'All this while, he pretended to be my best friend, and then he does this to me.' His voice was full of bitterness. 'We were so close to achieving something special. Why did he go against me?'

'Greed, I guess. Sheldon has offered him more. Not just a few quid either, by the way they are carrying on together. Although…' She stopped mid-sentence. Something she had seen at the house was suddenly bothering her. What was it?

Her train of thought was interrupted. 'He would have got plenty with us,' Voigt said. 'People can be too greedy.'

'As bad as they are, you too have been stopped from carrying out an evil act…'

'It was not an evil act. It was business.'

Maggie looked across at Sheldon and Peter who had come together again. They were laughing and joking, milking every moment. She suddenly felt angry at the injustice of it all. She took it out on Voigt. 'Hardly business! You're basically a blackmailer, Mr. Voigt.' Voigt tried to interject, but she shut him down with a raised finger and a glare. 'Don't you dare argue with me.' Voigt turned away from her, like an errant schoolboy admonished by his teacher. A misbehaving son, told off by his mother. 'And don't you turn your back on me. I haven't finished yet.'

Looking surprised, Voigt turned back towards her, and sat up a little straighter. Maggie's frustration poured out of her. 'If you weren't up to no good, I wouldn't be here in the first place. Being a committed agent, keen to do her best for queen and country, I come here in good faith. But I've been well and truly messed around. I joined this mission thinking that my long lost son, Peter, is wrapped up in some bad stuff, only to find out that he's on the side of the good guys. Then I learn that Peter's on the side of the bad guys after all, and working for my former boss who I always assumed was one of the good guys. She patently isn't. Now, you could argue that Peter shouldn't be a concern for me as the bad guy turned good guy turned bad guy isn't my son anyway, but it sort of messes with my brain. On top of all that, I also learn that I'm a bloody mule, with a computer chip stuffed somewhere in her head, which those bleedin' tosspots over there are using to tack into your computers in order to steal all your ill-gotten gains.'

'Hack. Computer experts say, "hack" rather than, "tack".'

'Tack, hack, sack. It's all the bloody same to me. To top it all, I think I've ruined my relationship with two of my best friends and my great grandson.' Satisfied, Maggie took a deep breath and tried to calm down a little. Voigt, looking relieved, sat back out of her direct line of vision.

'How are they doing it?' Maggie asked after a short while.

'They're into our systems now and probably running the same sequences as we would have done. Your implant and Peter's data chip are diverting each customer's…'

'You call them "customers" I would call them "helpless victims"…'

'… each customer's payment details into their own bank accounts. Offshore, probably. I very much doubt we can do anything to stop it now.'

She sighed, fighting the feeling of loss that was threatening to take over. She could not prevent her shoulders from slumping as she too leant back into the sofa. She was running out of options.

She felt a tap of a hand on hers. Dick was leaning right across Beth and Voigt. His voice was full of bitterness and sarcasm as he said, 'Never mind, Nona. When this is all over, perhaps you could open up your own freakin' pasta restaurant.'

*   *   *   *

Chapter 27

The body language in the room had changed. Even Maggie, with her ignorance of all things computer related, could see that things were coming to a head. She tried getting up again, but a twitch of the gun from the guard kept her firmly in her seat.

Beth had been more or less silent throughout. She spoke now, rather nervously. 'Do you think they will kill us?'

'Not yet. They still need us,' said Voigt. 'They will want to make sure it all works first. Then they will probably kill us.'

'My God! Really?' Beth's fear and anger erupted, and it was all directed at Voigt. 'This is your entire fault! We did warn you that you ran the risk of being conned. As soon as Peter mentioned to you that he had found evidence over the net that your mother was alive, both Dick and I told you she was probably bogus.'

Dick chipped in. 'She's right. If you hadn't let her in we wouldn't be in this goddam mess.'

'You didn't have the disadvantage of wanting to believe it though, like I did. In any case, she was very realistic.' Maggie was beginning to feel quite sorry for Voigt, in spite of his immoral intentions.

'Was I really realistic?'

'Yes. My Mamma was just like you. Dramatic...'

Maggie allowed herself a metaphorical pat on the back.

'Forgetful...'

'Well, that was an act, of course...'

'Overweight…'

'Careful...'

'…wouldn't stop talking…'

'I'll wallop you in a minute…'

'Confused all the time. A bit annoying…'

'Bloody cheek! I'm hardly ever confused. And as for annoying…

'Stubborn…'

She huffed and folded her arms. 'I'm not stubborn at all.'

Voigt shook his head, and then sat forward to look across at Beth and Dick. 'I don't think it's fair to blame me. I've had a lot to do. You were both happy when I was doing all the running around and making all the contacts, providing the technical advice.'

They began to argue across Maggie, until they were distracted by a fracas at the far end of the room. One of Voigt's men was hauled to his feet and placed at one of the computer screens. Peter was holding a gun to his head and saying something in his ear. Whatever Peter wanted, the threat of the gun worked, and the man began tapping away on the keyboard. Peter's ruthlessness shocked her. *He's definitely, definitely not my son...*

Satisfied, Peter returned the hapless man to his place, and began his parading up and down again. Maggie looked on for a while and then suddenly slapped her thighs.

'Right, I've had enough of this. I just can't let this happen,' she said. 'It was bad enough you lot trying to blackmail a few organisations but this, what Sheldon is doing here, is even worse.'

This was corruption on an almost unthinkable scale. She understood enough to realise that the implications for world security could be horrendous. She recalled again Josh's comment about the mission being a potential 'House of Cards'. If it was so important, there was no way he would allow her to be on her own, was there? Not totally. Somehow he would be there for her... *Somehow...* but he would also expect her to help herself. Any agent would expect the same. If it was the House of Cards Joshua thought it was, the onus was on her to blow it down. She took a deep breath.

'It's time I provided a little wind.'

'What?' said Dick.

'Sorry, just thinking aloud.'

Maggie checked to see whether the agent who had been put on guard duty was in earshot. He had a hand on his holstered gun and was surveying the area, taking occasional looks in their direction. She lowered her voice just a little, but carried on the conversation as if nothing had changed. She had been in the game long enough to know that alterations in behaviour were likely to draw more attention, so she kept her voice level as she said, 'I get it now. I think I know what's going on.'

'What are you going on about now, you mad woman?' said Dick.

'Joshua, he's a clever little bugger. At least, I hope he is.'

'Who the heck is Joshua?'

'A very naughty lad, but I'm hoping he's going to be our saviour. Fooling you lot was only part of the plan. There's more to this, I'm sure. Much more. There has to be. He knew Sheldon would make a move. Now that she has, it's all going to come tumbling down around her.'

'I don't understand,' said Voigt.

'You weren't meant to. I'm afraid you have been used here in more than one way. Your operation needed to be stopped, but it's also being used to uncover a much wider problem.' She looked around her, biting her lip thoughtfully. 'Although, I am just wondering when the cavalry are going to arrive. Joshua's cutting this a bit fine.' *Still... delay, Maggs. Delay.*

'Cavalry?'

You'd better believe it, Maggs. 'Right, if you lot want to stay alive, you need to help me out.'

'Why should we?' asked Dick grumpily. 'You've hardly inspired us with confidence. And even if by some miracle we do what you ask and we get out of this, what's to stop us being arrested later?'

The negative attitude he struck irritated her. She summoned a special stare, the kind she reserved for shop assistants who had 'happy to help' plastered all over their uniforms, but whose faces and lack of action showed the opposite. 'Nothing. Dead or arrested. You decide.'

Voigt said, 'We have no choice. I don't want to take my chances with Sheldon. I'm in.'

'Me too,' said Beth nervously glancing at the guard who seemed very twitchy all of a sudden. 'I don't trust this lot.'

'You're both mad to go along with this crazy old woman.'

Maggie kept her eyes fixed on him. 'Dick.'

'Yeah? What do you want?'

'It was a comment rather than a summons,' said Maggie.

There was a moment while Dick looked like he was trying to work out what she meant. Then he rolled his eyes. 'I get it. Bloody English and their infamous sense of humour.' He looked at Beth and Voigt before settling his gaze back onto her. 'You mean I'm being an ass 'ole.'

She nodded and raised her eyebrows. 'Technically, arse... hole, but yes.'

He sighed. 'Okay… I guess I'm in too.'

'Good decision. I'm very pleased. Now, tell me about this data chip Sheldon's been going on about. I know years ago they used to smuggle data on microfiches and the like, back and forth over the Iron Curtain. Nowadays though, what would the equivalent look like?'

'It depends. Could be a memory stick…' said Dick.

'A memory what?'

'Like a little cassette. They come in all shapes and sizes. Quite small, an inch or so long. That's what Peter probably inserted into the computer.'

'Or it could be hidden in something else,' said Beth.

'Like the implant in my head. The other one Sheldon said was in Carlos' phone. Can they be easily altered? Copied or corrupted maybe?'

'If you know what you're doing, it's quite straightforward,' said Dick. 'However, I would expect the data to be protected. Encrypted maybe. That would make it hard to access.'

'Easier to swap them round then? The one in Carlos' phone, I mean.'

'Yeah,' said Dick.

'Look. I've a feeling it's going to kick off in here shortly. I need to know for sure whose side you're on. Are you definitely, definitely with me?' She smiled at their nods of confirmation. 'Good.'

Time for a bit of disruption, Maggs. She took a deep breath and shouted at the top of her voice: 'Oi, Sheldon.'

The whole room, surprised at the outburst, came to an abrupt stop. 'Yes, you… Shafter Sheldon. Come on over. I think I've worked this out.'

All eyes were on Sheldon as she sauntered slowly across towards them, her own eyes fixed firmly on Maggie. She waved a hand around the room. 'Carry on,' she instructed. 'There's nothing to see here, other than an old and bitter woman.'

'Don't be so harsh on yourself, Sheldon!' Maggie enjoyed her former boss's grimace at the putdown. 'Help me up,' she said to Voigt. He held her elbow, but they were stopped again by the guard.

'No, let the old codger stand,' said Sheldon. She waited until Maggie was upright, and then went up close to her face so that they stood toe to toe. Sheldon was not a tall woman herself, no more than an inch more than Maggie, but she presented an intimidating figure as she spat out, 'Well?'

The guard stepped back and raised his weapon, covering Maggie and the others who remained on the sofa.

Maggie lowered her voice. 'I said, I think I've worked this out, dear Tina. That data chip – the one that's helping you take all the dosh, not the one in my head – the one that your man fed into that machine just now.'

'It's called a computer, Maggie.' She sighed. 'What about it?'

'It was in that phone Carlos smashed. That's what you said. Smashing it though wasn't part of the plan, was it? He was supposed to be handing it over to one of your lot, intact. But he lost it.'

'And we found it. I told you that.'

Maggie was grasping at straws, but what other choice did she have? She felt, instinctively, that the second chip was the key. There had to have been an exchange somewhere. That chip was not the chip Sheldon thought it was. *Please let me be right*! She played through in her mind a snippet of a conversation between Carlos and Joshua she had heard when the ferry was docking and she was getting ready. Admittedly, they were on the other side of the door and they had moved away, but her implant had come good here because she had heard them distinctly:

Joshua: 'So you're telling me you've still got some of the parts from the phone?'

Carlos: 'Yes, look, they're here.'

Carlos still had the chip on the boat. The chip had to have been handed over to Joshua and he had done something with it. When, where and how, she had no idea, but it was a good theory to work on. Besides, she had nothing else to go with.

Don't reveal everything you know, Maggs. Keep them guessing. Delay, disrupt their thinking so they lose their focus. Joshua and Bill are on their way.

'You've messed up, Sheldon,' she said with as much confidence as she could muster.

'Have I? You sure? Look around you and you'll see that I quite obviously haven't. Listen, Maggie.' She went up close and playfully did up Maggie's top button on her coat, straightening her lapels, and smiling her most condescending smile yet. 'You used to be a good agent, and you've been very handy again here. We couldn't have got through Voigt's security without you. We're going to be so rich! That's thanks to you and that little device in your head. Plus the other *not lost* data chip.' She tapped her finger twice on Maggie's chest as she said the words 'not lost'. 'I think it's time to give the order to delete our junk mail.' She pointed individually to Maggie, Voigt, Dick and Beth. 'That's you four, in case you missed the computer related analogy.'

Maggie did miss the computer analogy, of course, but she had thrown away enough junk mail that came through her own letter box to understand what she meant. She ignored the threat and she ignored Beth's tiny squeal of terror. *Keep going. Wind Sheldon up. Wait for the mistake.* 'Who was Carlos supposed to pass the data chip on to?'

'Why should I tell you that? You're not in control here, Maggie. In case you haven't noticed, I am.'

'If you're so much in control and you're planning to dispose of us anyway, it won't matter if you tell me.'

'Or I could just ignore your silly questions and wipe out both you, and all of that old data inside of you. That's another computer analogy before you ask,' she added sarcastically.

'You think you've got this wrapped up, but you haven't. Joshua has got this under control, not you. He's on to you.'

'Joshua? What do you think he can do about it? Even if he is on to me, he's already obsolete hardware. That's…'

'I get the smart computer references, Shafter. I might not fully understand them, but I see what you're up to. Trying to act the Bond villain. Is that your white cat he's holding?' Maggie nodded at one of the guards and smiled as Sheldon involuntarily followed her eyes, before fixing her gaze back onto Maggie.

'Your knight in shining armour isn't coming, Maggie. All of your little friends are being gathered up as we speak, including the little old Dutch hussy.

'You're wrong. You're being set up, Sheldon. Joshua's coming for you.'

'No, Maggie. You won't be seeing him again. Believe me.'

Maggie had to admit to being thrown; she hated the feeling of desperation that was creeping in. She had been convinced Joshua had a plan. He had seemed so confident! But where was he? Maybe she had got this all wrong.

'You're bluffing, Sheldon.'

'Am I?'

She's trying to fool you into thinking he's dead. Ignore her. That was too horrible a thought to contemplate. *One last try.* 'So it was the karate kid?' she said rather too desperately for her liking.

Sheldon had turned away to check on progress, but looked back irritably. 'What?'

'It was the karate kid. Carlos was supposed to hand the chip over to the karate girl in the restaurant.' *Unlikely, but worth a punt. Anything to unsettle her.*

Sheldon looked far from unsettled. 'You don't really believe that, do you, Maggs…?' She tutted and shook her head.

'Don't call me Maggs.'

'I don't know who the girl is, Maggs. Probably works for the Russians. They're everywhere these days, so I wouldn't be surprised if they got wind of Mr. Voigt's operation. Probably quite happy for him to go ahead and disrupt The West's I.T. infrastructure, as much as possible. The girl tried to shoot you, didn't she? Think about it. Why would she do that if she was working for me? We needed you. Back then, at least.'

'If the data chip is not lost, who got it from Carlos to hand it over to Peter?'

'Oh, Maggs, you really haven't thought this through properly, have you? Who's been there all this time, in the background? Someone shadowing you, looking after you, acting as your guardian angel, ensuring that you did not fall foul to any major cock-ups. Someone we could rely on.'

'Who?'

'Carlos wasn't supposed to hand it over to anyone at the restaurant. He was supposed to bring it directly to Peter after he kidnapped you. But Carlos, being Carlos, panicked and smashed the phone. Of course, we had someone there to make sure the data chip was not lost.'

'Joshua?'

'No. Rather sickeningly, he really is a goody-goody. I tried to turn him, but he's just too full of principles.'

Maggie's stomach lurched. *There was only one other viable possibility.* 'Not Bill?'

'Who?'

'Bill. Agent Lewis.'

'Bravo, Agent Lewis!' Sheldon looked confused momentarily. 'Is he called Bill then? That's strange. I thought it was Nigel. Anyway, amongst the chaos, he had the foresight to retrieve the chip.'

There's a straw there, Maggs. Quick, clutch it! 'Ah, wait a minute. I get it. Bill thought he was working for you as part of the Service. You told him to collect the chip, but he had no idea how you would use it.'

'Good Lord, no! A lot of this was his idea. Like most of us, he's motivated by money.'

Maggie's voice had suddenly lost all of its conviction. Even to herself she sounded remote, as if she was suddenly at the darkest end of a deep cave calling out. *You were wrong about what Carlos said on the boat. And you were wrong about Bill. He was working with Sheldon all that time.* 'Bill, not Bill?'

'Don't be angry with him, Maggs. Remember what he did for you near the ferry in Harwich? He took a bullet for you. And that's a phrase you don't hear too often there… Come to think of it, perhaps you do,' she added with a guffaw. 'It is Essex.'

'No, surely not...'

'Don't act so surprised. He's been with the Service for a long time. The pension isn't bad, but nothing on the scale of what I and my associates can offer to him. He's done a great job, fooling everyone, even that fiancé of his. Apparently the young man didn't even know he was in the Service to start with. He's that good a liar.'

'I don't believe you.'

'You can ask him if you like. Peter went into the city centre earlier to collect the chip from him. Agent Lewis had a couple of other things to attend to first, including keeping Joshua off the scent, and sorting out that little whore of a friend of yours. He should be back here any moment to share the success of our little endeavours.'

Maggie suddenly felt as if she was carrying the full weight of eight decades of living on her back. She could not stop her shoulders drooping under the strain. Annoyingly, Sheldon spotted it. 'Oh, Maggs, don't despair.'

Sheldon swivelled around as her phone rang, and spoke into the mouthpiece, making no attempt to keep out the triumphant tone. 'Ah, perfect timing. Let him in.' She rang off and then watched as Maggie sat back down on the sofa, rejoining Voigt and the other two. She bowed her head, almost resigned to her fate now. She heard footsteps approach, and winced as she heard Bill greet Sheldon.

Taking a few deep breaths, she started to make a mental list of all the insults she wanted to hurl at him.

*   *   *   *

Chapter 28

'Everything has been secured, I assume, Agent Lewis?'

There was a small chuckle. 'Yes. It's all sorted. The tart won't be giving us anymore trouble. The lad neither. I've had people on them.'

'The lad? Did he mean Joshua? How could he refer to Marijke as a tart and what exactly had he done to them? Maggie did not recognise this person who had come waltzing in talking like an East End gangster.

Right up until he had spoken, she had hoped Sheldon had got it wrong. It would not be the Bill she knew walking through the door; it would be another man. But his voice confirmed her worst fears. When she eventually looked at him, she saw him through different eyes. He was shifty, ominous looking. In some ways, the confidence with which he spoke reminded her of the agent that had tackled the drunks in the hotel bar in Amsterdam, but in other ways not. If he came across them now, she felt he was more likely to smash them in their faces and ask questions later... if he could be bothered with the questions. He was no longer Bill the owner of a nail bar. He was not even Bill the Secret Service agent. He was Bill the villain. The way Sheldon and Peter talked to him confirmed that.

'As you can see, things here are going as we planned,' said Peter. 'The chip is working a treat.'

'I told you it would.'

'Yes, you did,' said Sheldon. 'I'm a bit sad we had to lose Joshua. He was a good agent.'

'So be it. He had his chance. Like you, I tried to persuade him to come over to us, but he wasn't having it. The hooker won't be missed.'

'There's plenty more where she came from,' laughed Peter.

Maggie cringed when Bill joined in. 'That's true!... The deal still stands? Darren and I get what we agreed?'

'Of course!' said Sheldon. 'I stay loyal to my people, if they stay loyal to me. You've been with us all the way, right from the point of suggesting we use Carlos. At least that hopeless ex of mine was good at something... programming.'

Ex? Carlos? So it was their kids she was stopping him seeing. The poor man.

'Carlos knew what he was doing on the technical side, even if he was bloody useless at getting his hands dirty,' said Peter.

'I agree. He had to go. What did he look like when you slipped him that poison?' said Sheldon.

What? This was getting worse by the second. Bill was responsible for Carlos' death too?

'He didn't look well. A bit on the peaky side, I would say, but it was quick.'

'I wouldn't have wanted him to suffer. For the children's sake.'

Liar! Callous old bitch! How could she? How could he?

'What will you do with Agent Matheson?'

'She, like all of them here, knows too much. Now we know it's working, well... I don't need to spell it out, do I?' There was a sharp intake from Dick and Beth. Voigt remained silent.

'No, you don't.'

There was a few moments pause. *Control, Maggs. You're angry, but don't let it take over. Stay in control.* 'You know,' Bill continued, 'it's a bit of a shame to have to end her life.' *A bit of a shame! Forget the control – get up and thump him. You've got nothing to lose now.* Then she saw him check his watch, lingering a little longer than necessary. What was he doing? She waited a moment as his eyes stayed focussed on the watch. It looked like he was counting.

Sheldon, engrossed in her own triumphant world, had not noticed the time check. 'You're not getting all sentimental on me, are you? She's passed her prime and we agreed this.'

'Still…' Bill definitely was counting by the seconds. Maggie could see it from the slight movements of his lips.

'A woman of her age... killing her at this stage of her life. So young looking too – she doesn't look a day over ninety-nine.'

Sheldon had started to move away, her interest in the conversation waning as she went to supervise the final stages of the file transfers. But she stopped and turned back. 'I'm sorry,' she said. 'What did you say?'

Maggie's anger dissipated in an instant. She had heard Bill fine.

'I said that she doesn't look a day over ninety-nine. Agent Matheson: she doesn't look a day over ninety-nine.'

He spoke to Sheldon, but he was looking at Maggie with the same cheeky grin he had given her at Sukuel when he had invited her to his and Ben's wedding and used that exact same phrase. *You're a smooth one, you are, young Bill.* The villain was gone; the Secret Service agent was back. The nail bar owner, she decided, could make a full appearance when they were out of this mess.

'What are you talking about? What's that got to do with

anything?'

Sheldon had her back to the activity behind her and had not noticed the sudden consternation of her operatives.

Maggie had. 'I don't know much about computers, but I'm sure they're not supposed to do that, are they, Tina?' Maggie pointed to Voigt's large boardroom table which had suddenly become a hive of activity.

Sheldon did an about-face, a comical movement, Maggie thought, for a woman of her relative squat size and wide stature. She would have enjoyed her look of horror too, if she had been able to see it, a reaction to the sudden panic that had filled the room. All the terminals suddenly started to bleep frantically, which her team responded to by tapping furiously on their keyboards. The data on the screens, which had been showing the accounts of various governments and major companies transferring large amounts of money into Sheldon's own offshore bank accounts, was now just a mass of random numbers and letters jumping around from side to side. Three of the terminals caught fire and smoke was starting to fill parts of the room, adding to the building sense of mayhem. Maggie could see Peter and some of the other senior members of Sheldon's staff trying to wrest back control, barking out orders and appealing for calm. People had started to shout across at each other as more terminals caught fire. Others ran around looking for fire extinguishers. Sheldon herself was standing stock still, her head moving around as she tried to take in the scene before her.

Maggie leant forward and grabbed hold of her stick which was on the floor. Like Sheldon, the guards nearby were also distracted and had moved forward to get a better take on what was happening.

'Help me up, will you?' Maggie whispered to Voigt. 'Quickly!

Ooh, bloody arthritis. That's it. I'm up!'

Voigt, Dick and Beth joined her, crouched, ready to move.

'This way,' said Voigt encouraging Maggie to go to left, away from danger. 'Follow us, Maggie. We can get out the way we came in, back through the security chamber. That way must be open for Sheldon to have got in.' He turned away with Dick and Beth as they headed for the various doors which she had struggled through earlier.

Maggie stayed where she was. Voigt turned back. 'Maggie! Quickly!'

'You go on. Check it out and let me know if it's viable. I need to see what Bill is up to.'

Sheldon, meanwhile, had recovered her composure somewhat, and had begun issuing orders of her own. There was an almighty bang as one of the terminals exploded throwing back its hapless operator. Others rushed to her aid, only to be distracted by another explosion from the other side of the room. Maggie scanned around for Bill and found him to her left, sitting at Voigt's desk studying the unmanned computer.

'What are you doing?' she called over.

'Computer stuff. Shaking this up a bit more.' He started to click and press keys, then looked up and pointed frantically.

Maggie furrowed her eyebrows. 'What?' she mouthed.

He gave up on the hand signals. 'Maggie,' he shouted. 'Check right!'

'Yours or mine?' she shouted back but realised, too late, what he meant as she felt a gun digging into her side. One of the guards had obviously remembered what his job was and tracked back.

'Don't move a muscle, old lady,' he spat into her ear.

Maggie's reacted by stamping her stick down so that it landed with some considerable force onto his little toe. His yell of pain was drowned out by the cacophony all around, but was, in any case, short-lived. Maggie followed it up with, first, an elbow (originally used to good effect on a shopping expedition to Piccadilly Circus in 1959, and maintained in prime sharp order for the new year sales) into the edge of his bottom rib, and then, as he doubled over, a whack with the base of her fist to the back of his neck. That blow sent him to the floor, closely followed by Maggie who tumbled down on top of him with the follow through.

She rolled off the guard onto all fours – not the most delicate and ladylike of positions, but a good starting point, she decided, from which to attempt to get up again. She would have struggled again without Voigt's reassuring hands which grabbed under her armpits and hauled her up.

'You came back for me. Thanks,' she said.

'I couldn't leave you here battling this lot on your own,' said Voigt. 'Besides,' he added with a lopsided smile, 'we couldn't get out that way; the security door's fuse has blown. I've left Dick and Beth figuring how to open it up. The other way out is blocked too.'

Bill joined them. 'We'll find a way through, somehow. Sheldon has a lot of guns and people here. We need to get out while they're all distracted.'

'You've planned this all along, haven't you?' Maggie said. 'You and Joshua. You've planned all this. You've been letting Sheldon think she was double-crossing just about everybody, while all the time you set this all up. I bloody knew it! Where is he? Are he and *The hooker,'* she mimed his gangster voice, 'safe?'

'They should be. I split up with them and Ben at the square. I had other things to attend to.' Bill was looking round with some urgency now. 'I don't have time to explain everything now... Ouch! Why did you hit me?' He rubbed his shoulder.

'That was for putting me through all this. Now let's get out of here.'

The bleeping had stopped, to be replaced by the hiss of fire extinguishers being used to douse the flames which had been threatening to spread. Smoke billowing across the room, increased the sense of panic. Some of Voigt's staff had already noticed the lack of scrutiny and were taking the opportunity to leave via the now open door in the far corner by the window. Maggie could see Beth and Dick making their way over in that direction too. They stopped, but Bill waved them on as he led Maggie by the arm towards them with Voigt close behind.

'What did you do to my computers?' asked Voigt.

Over his shoulder Bill explained, 'I told Sheldon that, after the crash, I had found the data chip Carlos was supposed to pass on to Peter. I replaced it with the big bad boy of a file corrupter Peter put into the main computer. Works beautifully, synching with Maggie's implant. ...Use your headscarf, Maggie, to cover your face and protect yourself from the smoke.'

They were close to the door now.

'Didn't Sheldon and Peter check the data chip you gave them?' said Maggie.

'Why should they? They trusted me. If they had any doubts as to my loyalty I had proved it to them already by poisoning Carlos.'

Maggie stopped abruptly. 'So Sheldon was right? You did kill him.'

'Bloody hell, Maggie,' Bill said. 'He's not dead. Classic spy trick

– slow the heart rate down so you think he's dead. The Dutch agents and medics sorted him out.'

'Another lie! I'll tell you what,' said Maggie angrily as Bill pointed her back towards the exit, urging her to move. 'If you keep on with much more of this bleeding malarkey, I'm going to put you over my knee and…'

'Shoot him?' Peter suddenly appeared through the smoke. 'You're going to put this weasel over your knee and shoot him? Let me save you the trouble.'

A lot of things Maggie did these days seemed to be much slower. Either that or everyone else in the world was getting a lot quicker. Maggie had known for some years which way round it was, of course, but, as Peter fired his gun, it did not stop her from trying to save Bill. Her hands went up and she dived full length, throwing herself between Peter and Bill, just as the bullet was unleashed. At least that was what she imagined she was going to do. In effect, she got no further than raising an arm slightly and cricking her neck as she moved forward.

Voigt was the first to react after Peter fired, staggering under Bill's weight as he fell back into his arms. The sound of the gunshot silenced the room, and everybody suddenly froze. Three of Sheldon's guards quickly blocked any chance of escape as Voigt lowered Bill to the floor. Ignoring the pains in her knees and hips, Maggie knelt down and put her head next to Bill's. For the first time since Frankie lay dying, she closed her eyes and prayed.

*   *   *   *

Chapter 29

Maggie became aware from the shouts of commands and responses of Sheldon's staff that they were gaining a measure of control again. The smoke had subsided and she could hear from the protestations that Voigt's people were being brought back in. Her focus, though, was on Bill. She could now see, much to her relief, his chest moving up and down. His eyes were shut, but he was, thankfully, alive. She pulled up his shirt to check the wound. The shot was to his lower left hand side, an encouraging sign since, judging by the entry point, it was unlikely to have hit any internal organs. There was, however, a lot of blood, and she knew that if they did not stem the flow he would be in danger. She whipped off her head scarf, folded it over to cover the wound, and then pushed hard against it. Voigt offered to take over which left her free to stroke Bill's forehead and reassure him. She tried to keep her voice calm as she spoke, but she was not feeling it.

'You're going to be alright, Bill. Just hang in there.' He grunted in response. 'That's twice you've been shot in just a few days. What's wrong with you? Are you trying to collect bullets or something?'

Maggie became aware of Sheldon standing over her. She could not see her expression, yet could feel the anger and hatred towards Bill. She was not feeling optimistic about her next request, but she looked up and asked it anyway. 'He needs medical treatment, Tina, urgently. Please!' she said.

'Why would we want to facilitate that?' It was Peter who spoke. He had held his position, gun poised by his side. 'I could've killed him outright if I wanted to, but the bastard deserves to die slowly. However, if you want me to finish him off…' He raised his gun.

'Stop, you idiot!' said Sheldon. 'I don't want him dead yet.' Maggie noticed a flicker of hurt register on Peter's face. 'We've got important things to sort out.' She swept her hand around the room. 'He's put something into Voigt's computer system which has caused all this devastation. We need to find out what it is. Did you check the chip before you put it in?'

'Of course I did.' *You liar*, thought Maggie. *You're not even brave enough to admit your own mistakes.* 'Some sort of glitch has got in somehow.'

Sheldon did not sound convinced either. 'Do you take me for a fool? All this bloody effort to get in here and you think I'm going to accept we've been done by a simple glitch? It's obvious what's happened. It's got to be the chip this scumbag gave you. He's switched the one Carlos was supposed to deliver. I can't believe you would be that naïve to accept it from him without checking it.' *A lover's tiff – interesting...*

'You never expressed any concerns about him to me!' Peter bit back. 'He's been planning this with us for ages, done everything we asked of him. If you had any doubts about him, you should have said. Remember, you were the one who recruited him onto our side. Maybe you should have been more circumspect?'

Maggie could not resist a quick glance up to see how Sheldon reacted to that. Mounting fury was not a good enough description; Sheldon had already reached the summit and was ready to plant the flagpole... in Peter's head.

Peter must have realised that too as he struck a more conciliatory tone. 'Look, don't worry. It's all retrievable. We just need to set up elsewhere, reset the system and go again. We've got Voigt. Her implant,' he nodded at Maggie, 'will still work which will facilitate access to the customers' systems. We just repeat the procedures. Even if we don't complete a full run, we can still threaten a lot more damage with the access and knowledge we have. Build on what's already been achieved.'

'And how long will that take to do? It's taken years of planning to get us to this point.'

Peter turned his gun towards Voigt. 'Depends how much he cooperates, but I'm sure he can be persuaded to help. We can do it within a day or two. I have a site in mind.'

'A day or two? That's too long. My sponsors won't wait that long.'

Sponsors? What did she mean by that? There was a low grunt from Bill as Voigt, his hands covered in Bill's blood, applied pressure. His recent efforts would do his case no harm when this was all over. *If we survive, Maggs.*

Peter continued, 'They'll have to. A day won't make a big difference. They'll see it's already successful as we've taken some of the victims' money already.' He held his hand out to her, but she refused to take it.

'I agree that we need to get away from here. And soon. But we can't leave a trace, otherwise the authorities will be on to us.' She raised her voice. 'Attention, agents. Prepare for code sixty-four. I repeat. Code sixty-four. On my command.'

'You can't!' shouted Maggie. 'You can't do that.'

'We can, Maggie,' said Sheldon. 'We definitely can.'

Despite her preoccupation with Bill (and a long-standing inherent aversion to some of the finer procedural points of Service operations) she knew full well what code sixty-four meant. Code sixty-four was the rare procedure used to clean out safe houses and sensitive sites which the Service had come in contact with. All evidence of the inhabitants' occupation and signs of Service involvement had to be eradicated when the code was initiated. Maggie had always been taught that it did not just apply to inanimate objects; in extreme cases it applied to animate ones too. She had never had to carry out a code sixty-four before, but she had heard rumours of the 'extreme' situations where it had been done. *Collateral damage.* The spy game had never really been a game, she reflected now; it was far too serious for that.

Nearly all of Voigt's staff, plus Ratty, Beth and Dick, had been rounded up again and returned to their sitting positions in the centre of the room. They may not have understood the meaning of Sheldon's command, but she could see from the steely looks on the faces of Sheldon's people that they had.

There was a soft tap on her knee. 'Maggie… Maggie.' Bill's voice was barely a whisper. 'Come close.'

She leant in towards his mouth. His eyes were half closed and he spoke softly. 'My pants. Check my pants.'

'Which part?' she whispered back.

'What do you mean which part? The pants part of course!'

'What am I looking for?

'There's a gun in there.'

Maggie glanced up at Peter who was still talking with Sheldon. They had been joined by the guard she had laid out earlier.

'Oh, right. How can I get it out? They're watching us.'

'Maggie… You're a spy. Just do your thing.'

'My thing? Okay...' It took just a moment to come up with something that could be construed as 'her thing'. She just hoped her thing was 'his thing' and, more importantly, 'Voigt's thing' too; she was going to need his help. She kept her cheek next to Bill's and whispered, 'Play dead, Bill.'

His breathing gradually slowed, a few deep gasps, and then he was still. Tentatively, she placed two fingers on his neck to check his pulse. She waited a few moments before shaking her head and announcing loudly: 'You've killed him.' She sat back onto her heels, and immediately regretted it. As did her hamstrings, which reminded her, in no uncertain terms, that, as much as they knew they ought to try to get along with her calves, there was a good reason why she kept them apart these days. It was not hard to show pain. She let her eyes settle onto Peter who stared dully back. Softly, she repeated, 'You killed him.'

'So? What do you want me to do about it?' Peter sneered. 'He deserved it. We offered him the world and he snubbed us.' He shrugged. *How could you ever have begun to believe, Maggs, that this man was related to you?*

'This is all very touching, but we do have to get on, with or without him,' said Sheldon. 'The sooner we close up here and get out, the better.' She turned to the guard. 'Have we got the transport ready?'

'We've four cars available for the initial exodus, Executive S. We can evacuate key personnel straight away. More transport is on its way.'

Maggie began to sob, quietly.

'Make sure it's here immediately.'

'Yes, Executive S.'

The guard stepped away to make some calls. Maggie, between sobs meanwhile, was busy surreptitiously gesturing towards Voigt. It was not an easy mime to carry out using just her eyes and fingers, but it was intended to say, *'There's a gun in Bill's underpants. When I distract them, slip your hand under the scarf we have been using to stem the blood flow, reach into his pants, extract the gun and shoot one of them.'* At first, understandably, he looked very confused. She put her fingers into a gun shape in front of her, tapped her head to indicate the scarf, and pointed towards her own knickers area, before looking pointedly at Bill's trousers. The conversation continued around them.

'There's no sign of involvement from the local authorities?' Sheldon asked Peter.

'Not yet. We have personnel posted on the two key routes into the industrial estate. Everything is quiet, but we need to act soon. The site I have in mind is outside Antwerp. It has powerful enough servers to continue our work. The present occupants will need to be dealt with, of course.'

Maggie continued the sobbing and the gestures.

'What's stopping us then? Let's get cleared up here now.'

This is it... Maggie glanced at Bill, then back at Voigt who nodded what she hoped was some sort of understanding of her plan.

'Bill, Bill, Bill!' She waved her arms about, Italian Nonna style – just as she had on the square – and shouted as loudly as she could, repeating his name over and over.

'That's enough, Maggie! Sheldon tried to make her voice heard over Maggie's din. 'We know what you're trying to do here. This is a delaying tactic.'

Maggie had some momentum now, and not even Peter standing over waving a gun in her face was going to stop her. *We're well past the 'infiltrate and assess' stage,* she told herself. *All out now for the 'disrupt' part... but do it properly this time, Maggs. It could be your last chance.*

The next part was out of her control and all down to Voigt. She watched his hand worm its way underneath her scarf into Bill's underpants. There was an unbearable moment, during which she prayed she was the only one to notice Bill's left eyebrow raise, very slightly, in surprise. Then it was all action as Voigt produced Bill's gun. He cocked it and fired once, catching one of the guards nearby, who staggered back and fell to the floor. At the same time, Maggie carried out the only option available to her from her disadvantaged position on the floor, which was to punch Peter, with as much force as she could generate, upwards into the testicles. He collapsed, groaning loudly.

'That's for being such a vile human being,' she said. *Whether you're my son or not.*

Sheldon seemed momentarily frozen, but she soon ducked for cover as another shot was fired in the far corner where the security chamber was, and glass shattered. Being so low down, Maggie could see very little, but she was hoping it was some much needed assistance, Joshua maybe? *At last, the bloody cavalry!* It resulted in a flurry of activity as some of Sheldon's agents returned fire.

Grunting, Bill sat up onto his elbow. 'You need to get to safety, Maggie. Quick, behind those desks.'

'I'm not leaving you here,' she said. 'Come on, we'll do this together.' She twisted around looking for the best safe route. 'Hang on, has Sheldon escaped?' she asked Voigt who was fighting with the catch on the gun. She realised she was wrong about Sheldon escaping just at the same time as she realised why Voigt was so keen to get his weapon working. Sheldon's hand had appeared from behind a filing cabinet with a gun pointed directly at him. A bullet, whistling across the office, forced gun, and Sheldon, to retreat. It was backed up by Joshua's concerned voice.

'Maggie! Maggie! Are you okay?'

There was no time to answer as Sheldon, briefly breaking cover, scampered low across the floor towards her, gun still in hand. For the second time in only a few days, Maggie felt the hard point of steel against her temple.

'Now, Maggie, I suggest you use that big mouth of yours to tell Joshua to stop firing at me and my agents. I've got plenty of bullets left in the gun: one for you, one for this not-dead traitor on the floor that you seem so fond of, plus several for luck.'

Maggie did not hesitate. *I'm not losing Bill.*

'Stop!' she shouted. 'Joshua, stop!' There were a couple more shots from other parts of the room followed by silence. 'Sheldon's threatening Bill,' she shouted again. 'You need to stop.'

'And you, Voigt,' Sheldon hissed behind her. 'Throw the gun down... That's it. Good.' Then louder, 'Out, Joshua... right where I can see you.'

Joshua emerged from behind a desk, his gun in two hands, raised directly in front of his eyes, pointing at Sheldon. 'It's over, Sheldon,' he called across in response. 'We've got backup.'

'Not that I can see.' Maggie could hear the doubt as she hissed, 'Right, Maggie, on your feet. I need you as protection.'

Maggie had fallen slightly to one side, her legs curled up, her arm supporting her weight. 'You are joking, aren't you? I'm going to need a winch from here.'

'You have a point,' said Sheldon who, kneeling, was not in the easiest of positions either. It was going to take some manoeuvring to coordinate things so they were up at the same time. It made a mockery, Maggie thought, of the action films where people in similar situations were instantaneously up and ready to make their escape, the baddy edging out with their captive in front of them, arms firmly placed round their necks with the gun in their backs.

'Take me instead,' said Bill.

'You're a dead duck,' said Sheldon. 'She's more valuable. On your feet, Maggie.'

'Hang on,' Maggie said. 'I'll bum shuffle over to there and use that chair for purchase.'

'Okay, but remember...' Sheldon flicked the gun towards Bill. '... I can shoot that weasel just as easily as I can shoot you.'

With Sheldon crawling low behind her, Maggie puffed and panted her way over to the chair, placing her hands either side to slide and bounce and wriggle her bottom closer. Once there, she turned over onto her hands and knees and reached up to the top of the chair, using it to pull herself up onto one leg and then the other, before standing upright. Sheldon followed her up without the chair as a prop, but, with a low grunt of pain, much to Maggie's satisfaction.

'Time you retired too, isn't it, Sheldon?'

'Make no mistake.' Maggie winced as Sheldon thrust her gun into her ribs. 'I will quite happily pull this trigger.'

Joshua was advancing ever closer, his own weapon not wavering at all from its target. 'But you won't will you, Sheldon?' he said.

'What's the point? You're finished and you know it.'

'Joshua's right.' Maggie nodded towards Peter's prostrate form. He had his hands clutched to his groin and was whimpering softly. 'Surrender now and we'll get your boyfriend a bucket of ice.'

Using Maggie as a shield, Sheldon bundled her a few paces to their left towards Peter. A kick on his leg from Sheldon elicited a loud groan. 'Get up! Peter, get up!'

'Must be painful,' said Maggie. 'I got him right in the how's your fathers. He won't be using them with his young lover for a while.'

'What?'

'You know: the blond one.'

'What blond one?'

One of Peter's eyes opened. With the rest of his face still twisted and contorted with pain, his one eye made an impressive appeal for clemency. It was not enough, as Maggie began to lower the executioner's mask. 'The lady he goes hiking with in the mountains.'

'Mountains? Hiking?'

'Yes. Hiking not your bag, Tina? Well, Madeleine looked like she enjoys it.'

There was a distressed squeal from the floor. Sheldon shot Peter a glance before rounding on Maggie. 'You're bluffing!' she snapped. Maggie winced in response to another hard poke in the ribs. 'There is no Madeleine.'

'Oh, there very much is a Madeleine. I saw her – them – on the slideshow. Looked like an amazing holiday judging by the scenery. Ratty will back me up.'

'Who the hell is Ratty?'

'Works for Mr Voigt. He would have seen it when he got me

down from the desk.'

'Where...?'

'Austria, I reckon. Switzerland, maybe. Beautiful. Have you been?'

'No! The slideshow. Where?'

'In Peter's office.'

'I don't believe you. Wait... Enough of this... I... We've got to...' She was obviously desperate to extricate herself from the conversation, yet was unable to do so. Maggie had been in many similar conversations before, both inside the Service and outside. It had proved an effective method to wear suspects down... and sell raffle tickets.

Maggie let her flounder for a moment, before putting her out of her misery. 'Anyway, I saw this picture on the computer. It took me a while to confirm who it was until I got close enough to work out that it had to be Peter here. Lanky you see. Didn't recognise the girl, but I could see from the way they were kissing that they had obviously met before. When I saw that you and Peter were an item, it made me wonder who she was. Couldn't make out her face clearly, because he had his own face all over it in one of the shots, but I know it wasn't you. She was taller... Thinner too,' she added rather cattily.

Sheldon's silence spoke volumes. *Got you!* 'I also got a rather close look at a jewellery receipt in his tray. Had a note attached to it with kisses addressed to Madeleine saying that she could use it to get her ring resized for free, if she took it into the jewellers in Geneva. The price of it had been scribbled over, but diamond engagement rings are expensive, aren't they?'

Peter had finally let go of his testicles and managed to roll onto his back. Painfully, he began to sit up. His mouth was open and he looked ready, Maggie guessed, to begin his defence. He did not get the chance. Sheldon stepped in so she was standing between his feet, swung back her leg and aimed a very firm kick. Maggie winced as she heard the squelch. She had to admire Sheldon's coolness. Within a split second, she was back behind her, and the gun, once more, in her back.

Sheldon's voice barely wavered. 'So, Joshua, we are at an impasse. You're pointing your gun at me, I'm pointing my gun at Maggie, and...' at this stage she paused... 'They're all pointing their guns at you.'

Maggie counted six of her agents, as they stepped out of their cover positions with their weapons, as Sheldon rightly said, all trained on Joshua. 'Take him down,' said Sheldon.

Maggie heard the guns click in readiness. How had she got Joshua into this position? *This was the whole point of you going it alone, Maggs!* Desperately, she looked around. Bill and Voigt were still stranded, Voigt's people, including Beth and Dick, were covered and in no position to help. It was all down to her to save the situation, and, importantly, to save her great grandson. She had been forced to give up on her son all those years ago. She would be damned if she was going to give up on another family member now.

In her prime, she would have struggled to turn and take out Sheldon before she was shot in the back. At the age of eighty, well, she had no chance. Not that it was going to stop her trying. But before she could even move, a familiar voice with a strong Dutch accent appeared to her left.

'Hello boys!'

Maggie watched six set of eyes flick over, and then widen, as Marijke, stripped down to her underwear and soaked through, sashayed into view, waving provocatively at them. 'Do you like what you see?' she simpered. It was indeed a sight.

Maggie had come across innovative diversionary techniques before in the Service, but this beat them all. Her friend was a beautiful woman. She was when she was young and, as she approached the start of her ninth decade, she was still. However, on this occasion, with sodden bra and knickers, her stockings ragged and torn, and red streaks from her dyed hair running over her shoulders and bust, she looked more like an extra after a gruelling day on a Benny Hill Show reunion shoot. Vertical lines from her eyeliner ran down her cheeks, adding to the comedic – and startling – effect. Through it all, though, it was obvious that Marijke, not put off her performance by the heavy rain there must have been outside, was having the best time ever.

'You are all so cheeky,' she said with a flutter of her fingers. For added effect, she put her hands on her knees, bent forward slightly, and blew a kiss in the manner of Marilyn Monroe. Maggie commented later that squeezing her left breast at this stage was possibly a little over the top – 'You were just showboating, Marijke'– but she could not deny that it had its desired outcome; Sheldon's men were definitely diverted.

Maggie took the risk that Sheldon was diverted too. Frankie used to tease her about the size of her head which never fitted any of the hats she tried on and, consequently, never bought. It held her in good stead now as she whipped it back into Sheldon's face. As Sheldon staggered back, her face bloodied, Maggie grabbed the gun from her hand.

'You definitely have not lost it, Great Granny Spy,' Joshua said. 'Keep that pointed at her.' Bill was on his feet now to reclaim the weapon which Voigt had been forced to discard. He and Joshua slowly moved their guns from side to side, covering Sheldon's men. Most still had their weapons raised, but two or three were struggling to concentrate, their eyes darting towards Marijke who had her back to them now and was slowly undoing the clasps to her bra. Joshua intervened just as she started to twirl it around her head.

'And in case any of you think you can still win this little battle, my colleague is behind you now with a machine gun pointing at your backs.'

'Hello!' she heard Ben say, a little too cheerily, Maggie thought, for the still somewhat tense and perilous situation. (She did not have the heart to tell him later that the gun was pointing about six feet above their heads. He had been far too excited about his role in the coup).

She need not have worried. There was a loud crash followed by a sudden burst of activity, as thirty heavily armed Belgian police officers stormed the place.

*   *   *   *

Chapter 30

Unlike Sheldon's arrival earlier, this time it did genuinely seem like it was over.

Maggie watched, once again impressed, as Joshua directed the operation, ensuring that both Sheldon and Voigt's people were dealt with appropriately. Sheldon was led away complaining loudly about her mistreatment as a high ranking official in the British Secret Service. Maggie was aware that some of the expletives accompanying her complaints were directed towards her. She ignored them, and her; she had had more than enough of the sound of Sheldon's voice.

She took the opportunity to catch up with Marijke, who explained that it had taken them a while to find where Maggie was. When Bill separated from the group at the square, Joshua had led Marijke and Ben on a fruitless trail trying to locate Voigt's house. Bill, having met Peter, confirmed Voigt's plans were in progress earlier than anticipated, and went on ahead. It was then that the rest of them dashed across the city and mounted the rescue bid.

Her explanation filled in a few holes, but Maggie was still keen to speak to Joshua to find out what his exact role had been in all of this. She found him and thought she had his attention, but he broke off just as Voigt was about to be escorted away in handcuffs by the Belgian police.

'A quick word with the prisoner before you go,' Joshua said to the police officer. 'Thank you... Mr. Voigt, you must remember that the original operation here was aimed at stopping you. The fact that more serious misdemeanours have been uncovered does not detract from what you were planning to do.'

Marijke had followed Maggie over and was in earshot. 'Two rights don't make a wrong.'

'Yes, well. You see her point, Mr. Voigt. Yours was fraud on a large scale, and the authorities won't be impressed. However, Maggie tells me you were helpful towards the end. That has to count in your favour.'

'And I can say, with my hand on heart, that my staff was not fully aware of what we were trying to do. We had planned it that way to minimise it being leaked out.'

'You can tell the courts that. I daresay that if you fully cooperate and testify against Sheldon, that won't do you any harm either. You're not a violent man at least, Mr. Voigt, unlike Sheldon and her opos who had no qualms about such things.'

Voigt nodded. 'One thing, before I go please, Agent Harley. Where is my real mother?'

Joshua dropped his eyes before lifting them and replying. 'With all honesty, we don't know. Maybe you will have time still to find out.'

'Can I say something here?' Maggie interrupted.

'As long as it does not prejudice the case, Maggie,' said Joshua.

'Sod that, Joshua. I want to speak to you in private about *prejudice* and *the case* in the context of the way I was treated by the Service. For now, I'll say whatever I damn well please.' *No change there, Maggs.* 'Mr. Voigt, I just wanted to reiterate how sorry I am for helping to build up your hopes about seeing your mother. Despite being a bit on the greedy side, I think that deep down you are probably a good man. I meant it when I said that I can sympathise with someone who thinks they have found someone they loved, only to lose them again. It's very disappointing.'

'Yes, it is. But can I say, it was very nice having you as my mother, even if it was for only a short time.'

'Really?'

'Yes. You are a remarkable lady, Maggie Matheson. You must make a wonderful mother. I would have liked you to be mine.'

Maggie felt a lump begin to rise in her throat. 'Cheeky bugger! I'm only ten years older than you.' But she softened the rebuke with a smile.

Joshua was about to move away, but Maggie tugged him back. 'I need a word with you too, young man. Excuse us, Mr. Voigt. I wish you luck, by the way. Perhaps I could visit you if you go to prison?'

'Only if you bring me fresh pasta.'

She laughed. 'My speciality!' Then she grabbed Joshua firmly by the elbow and bundled him away. 'If you can spare your great granny a minute. Right… where to start? First of all, why did you tell me Peter was my son when he isn't?'

'That was all Sheldon's idea to get you hooked. I had to go along with it. I'm sorry, Maggie. I wanted to be up front with you on that, but I just couldn't. I had to go along with her lie, as painful as I know it must have been for you.'

A flicker of anger, but it was not directed at Joshua. It was directed at Sheldon for raising her hopes, and at Peter, she realised with some surprise, for not being her son. At that moment, a stretcher went past with a police escort. Peter was curled up in the foetal position on it, his eyes shut tight, apparently unaware of his surroundings. She was pleased really; she had a lot she could say to him, but none of it was good.

She put her mind back on Joshua. 'Hmmm... Okay, I'll have to accept your explanation, I suppose. For now… Next question: why didn't you tell me you and Bill were working on this together?'

'As you well know, Maggie, that was strictly...' He mimicked the rabbit ears and smiled, but she was too peeved to return it. He coughed and struck a serious tone. 'We will have an official debrief, as per Service protocol in due course, Agent Matheson. There are obvious reasons why you could not know all the parameters of the mission guidance, suffice to say that Agent Lewis and I acted as we did in the national interest... with your safety in mind too, of course.'

If she had had the energy at this point, Maggie might have performed the double whammy – a harrumph, and a bristle.

'For now, though, I'm sure your primary concern, as the consummate professional, is to ensure the evidence is secured. You will be pleased to know that you don't need to worry on that count. Apart from testimonies from all those involved, we have digital evidence from the data chip that Agent Lewis swapped into Voigt's computer. The whole episode was recorded via Voigt's own security cameras, and we can trace Sheldon's other contacts, right up to the British Home Secretary, from the digital map which has sequenced all the events onto the external server it connected up to when Agent Lewis intervened.'

'I'm buggered if I have a clue what you just said, Agent Harley, and as for official briefings as per Service protocol… you can stuff that right up your ar...'

'Language, Maggie!' Bill was waiting patiently nearby, supported by one of the ambulance crew. 'Don't take it all out on Joshua. We're both equally to blame. Look, Joshua, just get her home. I'm sure you can do the debrief from there.'

Joshua nodded, and then was whisked away to deal with a call.

Maggie watched him go and then turned to Bill. 'Are you going to be okay?' she asked him. Her concern helped dissipate the frustration she was feeling. Besides, she was far too tired to stay angry for long.

'The medics tell me that I got lucky... again. I'm off to the hospital since I've lost quite a bit of blood. No permanent damage, fortunately. You and Voigt saved my life with your quick actions.'

'Shall I come with you to the hospital?'

'No, it's fine. Ben's coming. We'll meet you back in Frampton.'

'If you're sure...' Deep down, Maggie was pleased. Exhaustion began to overwhelm her and she slumped back onto the same sofa she had been on earlier with Voigt.

'Bye, Maggie,' Bill said. 'Take me away, Ben.'

She waved a tired wave and closed her eyes, vaguely aware of Ben's protests as they left.

'You do know, Bill... I mean Nigel... that I'm not called Ben.'

'I know that, Ben.'

'Well, call me Ben... I mean, call me Darren. It is my name after all. I'm not Ben.'

'I know, Ben...'

'Darren...'

'Sorry... Darren...'

*   *   *   *

Chapter 31

It was Sunday afternoon, Maggie's favourite time to eat, and a perfect time to all get together. Sukie had promised to make a fuss of them, but was first keen to get Maggie up to date with events at Sukuel's.

'We've arranged some counselling for Dave, Maggie. The doctor's said that it's not Torrez or nothing like that.'

'Tourettes, love,' said Samuel. 'Call it by its right bloody name, for God's sake. Fernando Torrez is a footballer. Played for Liverpool and Chelsea.'

'Whatever. Tourettes, Torrez, Tories, Dave hasn't got it. Apparently, he's just a foulmouthed, attention seeking git, who can't keep his gob closed. Excuse my language. What am I like?' She laid out the cutlery and serviettes as she explained, 'We had to take drastic action, Maggie. We got too many complaints in the end. Hopefully, the counselling will sort him out. In the meantime, he's been advised not to say any words beginning with f, b, c or sh. They might be a trigger for the swearing coz they start with the same letter as words like fu…'

'Yes, I get the idea,' said Maggie.

'The alphabet ban has caused all of us a few problems, admittedly, because he's taken it a bit too literally. French fries, bacon, calamari and shellfish are no longer on the menu. Still, you do what you have to do to support your staff, don't you?'

'The alternative,' said Sam, winking at Maggie, 'is to give in to his natural needs, go the whole hog and serve nothing else but shitake mushrooms.'

The serving hatch opened, and Bella started to bring over their orders. In the background, Maggie could just make out Dave's plaintive cries in response to things not quite going his way in the kitchen. She had kept the implant, enjoying the clarity it had given her. Apart from the enhanced hearing, she wanted to see whether she could operate the vacuum cleaner and the toaster from the comfort of her armchair. She had been informed that it did not work quite like that.

The conversation stopped as she heard a crash from the kitchen. There was a long pause. Maggie imagined that Dave was working his way through the alphabet to come up with an acceptable expletive that met Sukie's stringent rules. It took a good fifteen seconds before she eventually heard, 'Oh… no… goodness gracious… silly me… what an absolute bloody… shit – can't say bloody. What an incompetent so-and-so. I've only gone and dropped the nuisance pan.' There was another loud clatter. 'Fu... Flip... Fu...king thing. Sorry! Bugger, sorry! Sorry everyone! Shit! This is so hard!' She had a good view of the hatch and watched as Dave's hand popped out to back up the verbal apology with a quick wave, before disappearing again into the kitchen.

'Your hardnosed policy is clearly working, Sukie,' Maggie said.

'Little sod. He's trying at least. I'll go and give Bella a hand to bring over your orders. Come on, Sam. You can't stand there all day chatting.'

'My name is Samuel and…' His voice tailed off as he headed towards the kitchen to help clear up whatever mess had been left by Dave.

As Bella came over and served the rest of their meals, Maggie looked round the table at the relaxed scene. She smiled in satisfaction, enjoying Bill and Ben sharing a quiet moment. She was delighted the boys had cleared the air. Their relationship had been under a lot of strain and had withstood a lot. It was a testament to their love for each other that they were still so solidly together. Ben, in particular, impressed her. He had suffered many surprises, she reflected now, and had lived with many lies, but still he was committed. Their relationship was clearly flourishing.

'Shuffle along a bit towards Marijke, Granny,' said Joshua.

'Great Granny, actually,' she smiled back. 'Anyway, why do I have to move?'

She felt a tap on the shoulder and looked up to see Carlos standing there, grinning down at her.

'Surprise!' he said, arms outstretched, a grin stretched across his face.

'Flippin' Ada! What are you doing here, Carlos? I thought you were staying in Amsterdam.'

'Joshua told me you were having a small celebration. I didn't want to miss out. Anyway, I needed to be in the UK to talk to the police. Apparently, they have some questions about attempted kidnapping, possession of an illegal weapon, and conspiracy to carry out extortion of government bodies.'

Maggie glared at her great grandson. 'Joshua?'

'Formalities. The new Home Secretary will sort it, but we have to go through the motions.'

'I'll speak up for you, Carlos,' said Maggie. 'You're far too nice to be a real kidnapper. You were really crap at it; you know that, don't you?'

Carlos nodded as he took a sip of the red wine Bella had placed in front of him. Bill tore off a slice of pizza and put it on a plate. 'Pass that along to Maggie, will you, Marijke?'

As Maggie chomped on her own pizza, she realised she should be feeling very happy. The mission had given her the excitement in her life that she had craved, and it had also helped her appreciate what she had already got; a good life, reasonable health and, most importantly, fantastic friends. *Plus a great grandson, Maggs.* Joshua had made promises, when she and they were ready, for her to meet up with that side of her family. She had a granddaughter to get to know.

Lots to enjoy and look forward to... but still, there was a gap. There always had been. *Peter...* She had got tantalising close to filling it, and it was tough to learn that the Peter she had met was not her son. That punch she had given him was not just a means to get out of trouble. There was a lot of anger in her punch, and she knew it.

Marijke picked up on her sullen look. 'What's up, Maggie? You've suddenly got a face like a dry weekend.'

'Wet weekend, Marijke. I don't know what's wrong. I'm still trying to get my head around all this.'

'Is it Peter?'

'If I'm being honest, yes. I was so close to seeing my son again. I know I should feel good about what's happened since, but somehow I feel... guilty... no... angry... yes, that's it, angry with myself. No... angry with that Peter for not being my Peter. Oh, I don't know.'

'That is hard, I agree. But you know, I think you're feeling angry with yourself for giving up Peter when you should feel angry with the job and the situation which stopped you from being with your son. All of that guiltiness and angriness you are putting onto yourself.'

'That sounds a bit like displacement theory,' said Sukie who had reappeared, and was leaning across Carlos to put down some garlic bread. 'Dave told me his counsellor had said he might have displaced anger, and it manifests itself with swearing. I think that's rubbish: the only thing he's been displaced from is the school for good manners.'

'She's right you know, Maggie,' said Carlos. 'You're blaming yourself for actions outside of your control.' Maggie was so shocked at all their frankness that she did not even notice Carlos first smile smugly then dab away at the pizza sauce which was dribbling down her chin.

'Blinkin' heck! Is everyone here suddenly a bloody expert on Maggs psychiatry?' she exclaimed.

There was a sudden resounding, 'Yes' from everyone around the table who had all stopped their conversations to turn their attention onto Maggie. She sat back, surprised.

'You know we all love you, Maggie,' said Sukie.

'She's right, you know,' said Bill. He reached across, clasped hold of her hand, and looked at her earnestly. 'And you've got absolutely nothing to be guilty about. You're an outstanding agent, a brilliant friend and, most of all, a fantastic mother.'

'Some mother I proved to be! I should never have allowed them to convince me my son was better off where he was.'

'On the contrary. You did what you felt was right. You always have, Maggie.' Bill dropped his eyes and took a deep breath. 'Even when you hid me all those years ago. You did it for me, for my safety. What's more, you were prepared to let me go... for my future happiness and security.'

Maggie blinked a few times. She looked across at Joshua who just nodded and smiled. She glanced at Ben who, by the look on his face, had apparently given up looking surprised all the time and decided resignation was a more positive way forward, presumably because it put less stress on the eyebrows.

'Joshua did the groundwork into our connection. He and I wanted to tell you a long time before this, but the mission had started. We just couldn't. If Sheldon got a sniff, it would have compromised everything.'

Maggie wanted to say something, but, rarely for her, nothing came out.

'I can tell you now that we're all here. I changed my name to Nigel Lewis just before Joshua's mother was born. I was young, confused about my sexuality and needed a new life. Part of me regrets leaving his grandmother like that, but another part doesn't. I wouldn't have met Ben otherwise.' He gave Ben a shy smile before lifting his head up and addressing the table. 'So, everyone...I have to tell you that my adopted name is Peter Saunders, but I was born Peter Matheson...' He grabbed both Maggie's hands and squeezed them tightly. '... proud son – very proud son – of Maggie and Frankie Matheson.'

She wanted to use the right words; words that had gone through her mind in the last few weeks in anticipation of the moment when she would come face to face with her child, for good or ill, words she had not been able to use.

What she meant to say was something like:

'Peter, my long lost son. At last we meet again, after all these

years. It's incredible to see you.'

What she actually said was: 'Bill… you bloody bugger.'

* * * *

Epilogue

The young girl crouching in the bushes outside the restaurant was not at all happy. The quality through the headphones from the microphone she was holding up to the window was very poor. Ranting from the kitchen made it very difficult for her to hear any details of the group's conversations, and the additional noise distortion coming from the other side of the window made matters worse. Betty's flatulence, followed up by numerous *Pardon me's* as she ate a chunk of lemon meringue pie, would take some explaining to her Russian bosses.

The girl frowned in consternation as she realised, too, that she had failed to get any sort of reading whatsoever from Maggie's implant.

She sighed, switched off her equipment, and headed for the train station. Being a spy was not always as glamorous as she had hoped it would be.

On the positive side, her fact-finding trip to see Mister Ahmed, Maggie's hearing specialist, had been productive, despite his reticence to reveal any information about specific customers. After a thorough examination, he had told her that her hearing was in great working order, exceptional even.

She should expect, he had said, to have perfect hearing... well into old age.

Acknowledgements

With many thanks to the people who have read draft copies of Maggie and given me encouragement to go on writing about her.

Special thanks go to my daughter Abbey, for her continued support and regular feedback. Also, to my mum for proofreading, and – to be perfectly clear – for not being the source or the inspiration behind any of the material in this book. She is not a spy; even if she was, I would not be able to tell you.

Other books by Ian Hornett

'The Quarton Trilogy'

Quarton: The Bridge
Quarton: The Coding
Quarton: The Payback

Available on Amazon in paperback and as an e-book

Sci-fi to die for...

And in the pipeline...

Two sci-fi books for younger readers, and – you never know – a Maggie follow up.

About the Author

I wrote the first draft of Maggie Matheson before I finished book 2 in my sci-fi Quarton Trilogy. I was getting a little stuck, and wanted a complete change. Maggie Matheson was not an 8 foot tall humanoid from another planet who ends up being reincarnated multiple times on Earth, so, suffice to say, she provided me with the change I craved. I loved writing about her. She is feisty, has a wicked sense of humour which keeps her on an even keel, and, most of all, is full of life. These are things I aspire to as I approach my seventh decade. I used to be a police cadet, a customs officer, and a teacher, but I am unlikely to be called back into any of those professions at the age of 81, as Maggie was to hers. I only hope that, like Maggie, I still have the wherewithal and determination to do exactly as I please.

Do tell me what you think of this book. I would love to hear from you on any of my social media links. Or why not leave a review on Amazon or Goodreads?

Follow Ian on:

Website www.ianhornett.com

Facebook @ianmichaelhornett

Twitter @Iancolufan

Instagram @ianhornett

Printed in Great Britain
by Amazon